THE DEAD CELEB

THE

DEAD

A Lucy Freers Mystery

CELEB

✴ *Lindsay Maracotta* ✴

WILLIAM MORROW AND COMPANY, INC. ✴ New York

Library of Congress Cataloging-in-Publication Data

Maracotta, Lindsay.
    The dead celeb : a Lucy Freers mystery / Lindsay Maracotta.
        p.   cm.
    ISBN 0-688-14499-3
    1. Title.
PS3563.A6225D35   1997
813'.54—DC21   97-12386
                                                              CIP

Printed in the United States of America

First Edition

1   2   3   4   5   6   7   8   9   10

BOOK DESIGN BY LEAH S. CARLSON

Acknowledgments

For help above and beyond, lavish thanks to Detective David Simon, Detective Bess Shelton, Sara Jane Boyers, Graciela Sandoval, the gang at the Beverly Hills Library, and always to Peter Dorsett Graves.

THE DEAD CELEB

P a r t

1

ONE

My husband, Kit, the suddenly famous movie producer, wanted to murder his latest director.

The director was the vastly more famous Jeremy Lord, and the movie that had thrown them so infelicitously together was a winsome family flick called *A Merry Christmas to All;* it was being shot in a sun-scorched little town in the wilds of northern New Mexico, the biggest thing to happen in the territory since, two decades before, a third-grade teacher with bipolar disorder had stripped down to her Maidenform and skipped through the school halls belting "Puff, The Magic Dragon." The primary location was a sprawling tin-roofed ranch house. At the moment, Kit was pacing in a spare room that had been commandeered to store props, wrapped up in a tirade about how he'd love to wring Jeremy Lord's celebrated neck.

"He's destroying this movie!" he fumed. "He's completely out of control. The studio knows it. The stars know it. It's an unmitigated disaster!"

"Don't you think you're overreacting?" I cut in.

He glanced at me, startled, as if he'd forgotten I was in the room. I had just arrived on the set from L.A.—a harrowing journey, heavy turbulence the entire way, then landing in a thunderstorm in Albuquerque, during which I tried to keep the words *wind sheer* from flashing like a motel sign in my mind. I'd been met at the gate by a Fu Manchu-bearded production assistant hoisting a placard with my name, Lucy Freers, except Lucy was spelled Loosy, as in Loosy-Goosy. He then treated me to a breakneck drive through the Sangre de Cristos in an Isuzu Trooper, a vehicle I happened to know had a reputation for flipping, especially when maneuvering hairpin turns at Watkins Glen–worthy speeds.

When I'd finally tracked down Kit, I had expected a little sympathy for my ordeal. A "poor baby, what an awful trip" would have been nice. A cradling hug even better. Instead, after allowing me a perfunctory peck on the lips, he'd launched immediately into this death-to-the-director spiel.

I dropped onto the only chair available, a he-man artifact made of elk antlers that looked far more suitable for impalement than for cozy lounging. I propped the battered canvas duffel that served as my overnight bag beside me. "I can't believe it's all that bad," I went on. "Jeremy's a top director. Every one of his movies has been a hit."

"Yeah, sure, his action movies," Kit said. "That's exactly what he is, an action director. Violence is his thing. This is supposed to be a feel-good family picture—kids and elves and happy-ever-after. Nobody's head gets shot off. Nobody's car gets blown to smithereens. But that asshole's got the elves acting as if they're packing AK-47's under their little tunics."

I could believe this. Jeremy Lord was not exactly Frank Capra: When *Premiere* ran its cover story on him, it was captioned "The Maestro of Gore." It was hard to imagine him truly relating to a script about the family of a folksy backwoods sheriff that stumbles on a local branch of Santa's workshop.

"Just take a look at these props, for God's sake!" Kit raged on. "These are the toys he's got the goddamned elves making. They're supposed to be cute and cuddly, right? Stuff kids might actually want to play with?" He snatched up a stuffed rabbit with filed-to-a-point buck teeth. "Does this look cuddly to you?"

"It looks more like it craves red meat," I admitted. "So why did the studio pick him?"

Kit flung the carnivorous bunny back onto the floor. "*He* picked *us*. He's got some sudden bug about losing touch with his kids, so naturally he thinks that if he directs a nice little family film, it'll somehow magically make up for seven or eight years of neglect. And no studio in the world is going to say no to a director whose last three pictures grossed over half a billion bucks." He emitted a hollow laugh. "It's a nightmare."

"For God's sake, Kit, it's only a movie," I said.

It was as if I'd said to Dr. Salk, "For God's sake, Jonas, it's only a vaccine." Kit's blue eyes widened with astonished indignation. "I've got a hell of a lot riding on this project," he declared rather stuffily.

"Okay, fine. I'm sure it's been the seventh circle of hell. But what about me?" My voice ascended to the squeaky Alvin the Chipmunk pitch it always acquires when I'm upset. "I've just had the scariest plane ride of my life. It was so choppy when we landed, the guy behind me actually started reciting an Our Father. Then I had the pleasure of two and a half hours in a jeep driven by a Generation Xer with a death wish to get up to this place in the middle of nowhere, and another half hour just to find you. And when I finally do, you act like you don't even remember why I'm here!"

This outburst finally caught Kit's attention. He blinked contritely, then came over and appropriated the duffel bag's seat. "Of course I remember why you're here," he murmured and wrapped his arms around me.

I snuggled into his embrace. The reason I had braved turbulence and wind sheer to come to a movie set in The Town That Time Forgot was, plainly and simply, to have sex with my husband—the idea being for us to start a second child while we were both still young enough not to need walkers. And according to the somewhat complicated ovulation prediction kit I'd been prescribed, the next few days were prime baby-making time.

"I brought that nightie you like," I said in my throatiest voice. "The clingy satin one—"

Before he could respond, a prop man in Farmer Gray–ish bib overalls loped into the room. He hovered uncertainly a moment, scratching his temple; then he scooped up a pair of marionettes slumped against a wall.

Kit jerked away from me as if jolted by an electric shock. "What are you doing with those?"

"Jeremy wants 'em for a shot," the prop man said.

"He can't have them. The things are terrifying. Kids will take one look and run screaming out of the theaters!"

The puppets *were* terrifying—huge heads with pinprick eyes and garishly painted stick bodies. We all stared at them a moment, as if actually expecting them to spring to life and lunge after us with sharpened hatchets.

The prop man gave an I-only-do-what-I'm-told shrug. "Jeremy wants 'em," he repeated and trundled on out.

"This is exactly what I mean!" Kit hissed. "I'm sorry, honey, I've got to get to the set." He set off briskly after the retreating prop man, leaving me little alternative but to scramble along behind.

Being on a movie set always makes me feel as if I've been suddenly beamed into a parallel world, one that, on the surface, is identical to our own, but on closer examination makes me realize I'm not in Kansas anymore. After clattering down a steep set of stairs, we hit a knotty pine–paneled rumpus room that had the same existing-in-the-sixth-dimension feel to it. The dun-colored corduroy chairs and sofas, for instance, though authentically frayed, looked a bit too stylishly constructed for the setup; the clutter of "ordinary" stuff on the shelves was as artfully arranged as a Dutch Old Master still life; and every surface was almost preternaturally dust-free. There were also more obvious tip-offs that this was not quite reality: For one thing, the opulently decorated Christmas tree shimmering in a corner, though it was only the middle of October; for another, the half-dozen or so Little People dressed in rather rakish moss-green tunics, lounging with bored, I'm-dying-for-a-Winston expressions at various checkpoints around the room.

A jungle of cameras, cables, booms, and boxes had completely overgrown one end of the basement. In the center of this luxuriance presided the director, Jeremy Lord, his hatchet face, with its shock of rusty-brown hair, familiar to me from dozens of *People* and *Buzz* magazine spreads. He was dressed, as was his trademark, completely in black: black shirt, black jeans, black suede Hush Puppies with matching ebony-colored socks. The Grim Reaper would have looked riotous compared to him.

I examined him with interest. We had something in common: Five years before, we'd both been nominated for Academy Awards; Jeremy, of course, for Best Director, myself for Best Animated Short—the difference being that he had waltzed away with an Oscar, while I lost to a stop-action film about a socially conscious toaster.

But it appeared I'd have no opportunity to explore this bond between us. At our approach, Jeremy narrowed his eyes, the way a particularly pissed-off bull might greet an approaching picador. "Problem?" he said coldly.

Kit, as was *his* trademark, opted for the diplomatic approach. "No big deal," he said smoothly. "I just wanted to remind you that the studio had definitely said to lose the puppets."

The Director in Black pulled himself up to his full six-foot five-inch height. "I don't give a monkey's fart what the studio says. This is a Jeremy Lord movie, and it's going to be done my way."

The elves, sensing a drag-out fight, immediately perked up: Everyone else sort of melted away, like the townspeople in *High Noon* when Gary Cooper moseys out into the square to face down the gunslingers. I had the sinking sensation that this could go on for a long time. What I'd do, I decided, was check into the inn where Kit was quartered and try to get some work done. I'd brought along a storyboard for the latest adventure of Amerinda, the flying blue hedgehog, the heroine of a segment of the kids' TV show *Excellent Science* that I animate. Each of Amerinda's exploits was supposed to illustrate a major scientific principle, and at the moment I was stuck on a catchy scenario for magnetism.

I swept the crowd for my Fu Manchu'd jeep driver, but he was not among the milling throng of electricians, gaffers, and harried-looking ADs. A tall girl sporting the telltale headset of a production assistant hovered nearby. I tapped her on the arm.

"Excuse me," I said. "I'm Kit Freers's wife. Could you tell him, when he's finished butting heads with Jeremy, that I've gone back to the hotel?"

She swiveled to face me. The first thing I registered was Hair—a furious meringue that ran a gamut of Crayola shades from chrome yellow to burnt sienna. Then Lips, a startling pair of overblown crimson lips that seemed artificially pinned onto the rather tiny face, Mrs. Potato Head–style.

Then finally Clothes: a lavender spandex tee, stretch white denim miniskirt, white ankle boots—a nifty outfit for, say, cheering the Dallas Cowboys, but somewhat problematic for the step-'n'-fetchit chores of a PA. An oblong crystal pendant dangled from around her neck, the kind of New Age tchotchke that was supposed to ward off everything from leprosy to the common cold.

"You're Lucy, aren't you?" the Lips pronounced. "I'm Cheryl Wade. I've met you before."

Of course we'd met before. Everyone in L.A. had met Cheryl Wade. It's hardly top secret that Hollywood runs on connections, and that the best connection of all is to have a relative in the biz, preferably a star; and in the Celebrity Relation Sweepstakes, Cheryl had drawn the jackpot—she was the baby sister of the movie star Alison Wade, currently the world's most bankable actress. And with no other claim to fame than being a Celebrity Relation, Cheryl managed to get around to an impressive degree. In fact, she was everywhere: Attend the People's Choice Awards, and there you'd find Cheryl on the arm of some aging Brat Packer; show up at a premiere on the Paramount lot, and it's Cheryl again, at the end of the buffet line, batting bronze-shadowed eyelids at George Clooney; pop in for a late-night supper at Granita, and the-e-ere's Cheryl! chowing down wild striped bass at Andre Agassi's table.

In fact, I'd even seen her just several hours before. "You were on the plane from L.A. this morning, weren't you?" I asked.

"Oh my God, yeah!" she gasped. "Wasn't it scary as shit? I've had three psychics tell me they saw a plane crash in my reading, so I don't know about you, but I was just about peeing in my pants."

"Oh, I wasn't worried," I said. "All *my* psychics tell me I'm going to go down at sea."

She gaped blankly at me for a moment, then broke into a rather excessive giggle. "That's funny. You do those cartoons, don't you?"

I stiffened. My animated films had pulled in a gratifying share of awards and acclaim, including the glorious Oscar nomination, but Cheryl made it sound like I was the brains behind *Beavis and Butt-head*.

Before I could set her straight, she was already burbling on. "Boy, am I glad you're here. I mean, at least you talk to me. Everybody else treats me like I'm lower than mud."

"You're a PA," I pointed out. "That sort of goes with the job description."

"Yeah, well, it sucks. I'd quit, except I'm really broke, and those creeps at Lexus said if I missed one more payment they were going to take back my car. I can't help it if I'm lousy with money—I'm a Capricorn with Virgo rising." She reached into the snug back pocket of her miniskirt, dug out a grape lollipop, and began to peel off the waxed-paper bonnet. "I tried to borrow from my sister, Alison. I mean, she got fifteen million bucks for her last movie, so what's the big deal? But she said she was sick and tired of always bailing me out, and why didn't I get up off my bony behind and work for a change? And I said fine, but I'm not gonna flip burgers at McDonald's or anything. So she told Jeremy to get me something to do."

This confused me for a moment; then I remembered that Cheryl had yet another enviable celebrity connection. "Your sister and Jeremy were married for a while, weren't they?"

"Yeah, a couple years ago. She was his third wife."

A marriage, I recalled from E! Channel reportage, that had lasted some three or four months, terminating in the kind of bloody Hollywood divorce in which both parties issue frequent how-I-suffered-from-that-monster statements to Liz Smith. It would appear that they had now kissed and made up—at least enough for Jeremy to be throwing jobs to his supremely ditzy former sister-in-law.

"You know, I thought it would be fun to work on a movie," Cheryl pouted, "but all I do is run everybody else's lousy errands. Like, Jeremy just had his two kids here for the weekend, the ones from his first wife, that cross-eyed girl, Judie. Naturally I was the one who had to baby-sit them the entire time and then schlep them all the way back to L.A. Which is how come I was on that plane that almost crashed." She shuddered, contemplating her narrow escape from death. Then she inserted the lollipop like a pacifier into her Mick Jagger-ish mouth. "My nutritionist says I have to give up sugar," she mumbled through the candy. "She says it's interfering with my body's ability to process trace minerals. But I'm in AA, I haven't had a drop to drink for over a month, so I need the substitution."

My overnight bag was beginning to feel like it was loaded with concrete blocks; I shifted it to my other shoulder, combing my mind for an excuse to get away from Cheryl Wade before being treated to insights from her acupuncturist, masseuse, and, possibly, feng shui master. My salvation arrived in the form of a second assistant director striding toward us. His eyes were glittering, power-mad with the prospect of getting to boss around a PA.

"I've been looking for you everywhere!" he barked to Cheryl. "You're supposed to bring Jeremy his Diet Snapple every ninety minutes, and you're exactly twenty-six minutes late. Also, the last one you brought was in the can, not in a glass like he wants it." He thrust a brown-filmed Coca-Cola glass into her multiringed hand. "And don't forget to wash it this time," he added over his shoulder as he swaggered away.

Cheryl held the glass with the tips of her fingers, as if it were emitting plutonium. "I hate that creep," she declared.

"Who, that second AD?"

"No, Jeremy. I hate his guts. And don't think I'm gonna wash his lousy glass for him. Considering all the places *he's* put his mouth, he's not going to know the difference." She swiveled abruptly on her majorette's boot heel and headed to the stairs.

Several yards away, Jeremy Lord was in mid-rant, proclaiming that it was his, Jeremy Lord's, name that put butts in seats, not Kit's, not the frigging studio's, it was a Jeremy Lord movie that audiences paid good money to see, and Kit was replying in a voice that was starting to sound like Peter Finch's after he went bonkers in *Network* that yes, when audiences wanted decapitation, Jeremy Lord was the name that packed them in, all right, if they wanted to see gobs of brain matter spattered on refrigerator doors, absolutely, it was Jeremy Lord all the

way, but they were dealing with something just a bit goddamned different here. . . .

I stood listening to them wrangle, feeling abandoned among the
purposeful ebb and flow of the movie's worker bees. And I was hit by
the sudden, chilling certainty that I never should have come.

TWO

Last Fourth of July, our life turned upside down.

Or more specifically, the third of July, which was the day Kit's last movie, *Willigher,* opened in A Theater Near You. *Willigher* starred Jim Carrey as a ghost who suffered from a persecution complex; it was crammed with edge-of-your-seat special effects, and featured cameos by everyone from Arnold Schwarzenegger to Babe the Pig. GHOST PIC BURIES BOX OFFICE RECORDS screamed *Variety* the following Monday: Kit had produced a megablockbuster.

In the course of the roller-coaster ride that's a Hollywood career, Kit had been both up and down, but he'd never soared to such a height as this before. Our phones jangled constantly. Everyone in Hollywood, as well as a hefty part of the movie-producing populations of London, Rome, and Sydney, wanted to take a meeting with him. The *L.A. Times* Calendar section included him in a list of "The Fifty Hottest Faces in Hollywood." And somewhere in the heady whirl of power breakfasts, lengthy lunches, and summits in the office suites of studio heads, he contracted what I had begun to think of as The Hollywood Mogul Virus.

I'd seen others succumb to The Virus before. It is always transmitted by staggering success; its *modus operandi* is to take perfectly down-to-earth people and compel them to spend like mini-rajahs, pursue the appearance of having been frozen at the age of thirty-two, and, more often than not, dump all former friends and acquaintances who are not similarly infected.

With Kit, the symptoms were small, but worryingly apparent. I had detected the first about a month after the movie's premiere: On a

Monday morning at dawn's early light, I awoke to find Kit already up and outfitted in a new boysenberry-colored sweat suit and Adidas cross-trainers. "My bodybuilder's here," he announced.

"Wha . . ." I muttered. I hauled myself out of bed, staggered to the window, and, with astonishment, peered down at an enormous van idling outside our gate, the logo BENDER'S BODIES writ large in purple italics on its side. The bodybuilder proved to be an ex-Navy SEAL who answered to the single name of Bender, and who arrived with military punctuality four mornings a week at six forty-five sharp. The van, filled with weights and pulleys and other instruments of torture, swallowed Kit up, then spat him out precisely fifty-five minutes later, wobbly-legged and gasping for air.

Virus Symptom Number Two was the hundred-and-twenty-dollar-plus-tip haircut, engineered to disguise the balding spot on the crown of Kit's thatchy blond head. The stylist also sported a single sobriquet—Sylvester—and he too made house calls. At Sylvester's decree, it was out with the Head and Shoulders and in with a horse shampoo—that's right, folks, a product called Tail and Mane, that had to be specially ordered from a vet in Billings, Montana, because (according to Sylvester) it contained an extra-protein formula guaranteed to beef up those thinning mid-life human hair follicles.

It was also *adios* to Dr. Felkner, Kit's long-time dentist with his cheery posters of Mrs. Molar and Mr. Tooth Decay framed in Plexiglas on the waiting room walls, and hello to a snazzy Beverly Drive tooth care specialist-to-the-stars. For an entire week, Kit tottered into bed with little translucent trays fitted on his teeth which bleached them to such a dazzling whiteness I almost expected him to attract moths at night. And at the same time, despite the fact that he already drove a spanking new BMW, he sprang for a slightly used metallic red Stingray "just for fun," making us a three-car family, complete with a rather hilarious eleven-grand-a-year insurance premium.

The most disturbing symptom of all was the new social life. Pre-Virus, Kit's idea of a perfect evening had been to rent three or four videos and watch them all in a marathon session with a freshly popped bowl of Newman's Own. But in the weeks before he'd left for location,

we'd been out almost every night, a gala round of dinners in the trendi-
est cafés of Santa Monica and Venice, shouting industry gossip above
the din with "name" actors, studio VPs, and fellow big-wheel producers.
Suddenly there seemed to be little time for hanging out with old pals—
people who, tragically, had no recent megablockbusters under their
belts.

All of which was why I was so eager to get started on a second
child. A new baby in the house, I reasoned, would have to drag Kit's
attention back to the really important things in life. Three A.M. feed-
ings, dinosaur mobiles, tiny waving hands and feet . . . what better
antidote could there be for The Hollywood Mogul Virus?

*

At just after midnight, Kit was holed up in the bathroom of his suite in
the Chipotili Inn, burnishing his whiter-than-white teeth with a sonar-
powered brush. We'd had dinner—a long dinner at a rustic roadhouse,
wagon wheels on the walls and local patrons gawking at us "movie
people." We'd killed two bottles of an '89 Saint-Julien, which Kit had
topped off with a double Rèmy before finally declaring himself relaxed.
Too relaxed, I'd worried, as I watched him lurch back up to the room.

I unpacked my nightgown—a slithery peach satin number, very
Veronica Lake—then undressed and slipped it on. I pulled back the
rather scratchy Navajo-print bedspread and arranged myself Odalisque-
like under the sheet.

When we'd conceived our daughter Chloe, it had been a snap.
One night I simply stopped taking the pill, and wham! three weeks to
the day later, the home pregnancy test shimmered up a winning cobalt
blue. But we'd both been in our late twenties then; ten years down
the line, things were somewhat more complicated. Now there was the
monthly visit to a jovial fertility specialist named Dr. Kelshok, who
possessed a disturbingly unlimited repertoire of Fallopian tube jokes.
There was the Clomid I popped down each morning with my half glass
of Loóza apricot nectar, and which, I had the horrible suspicion, was
making my feet grow larger. And there was that ovulation prediction
kit that dictated when we were required to Do It.

"Hurry up," I called to Kit. "I'm feeling particularly fertile tonight."

"Here I come," he called back and sauntered naked into the bedroom. Lately, he'd taken to spending a lot of time parading around sans attire, the better, no doubt, to show off his newly Navy SEAL–buffed body. I had to admit he did look pretty damned hot. I wasn't immune to enjoying some of the side effects of The Virus.

He gave an exaggerated wolf whistle at my clingy lingerie, then clambered onto the bed and stretched out beside me. We lay somewhat awkwardly a few moments, haunch to haunch, as if waiting for some official signal to begin. Why, I wondered, was sex-on-a-schedule so intrinsically unsexy? My most passionate desire at the moment seemed to be to catch the last of Letterman, then burrow in for a lengthy snooze.

"How about Thaddeus Thor if it's a boy?" Kit said.

I smiled. It was an ice-breaking game we played—picking the most outlandish name for our yet-to-be-conceived baby.

"Hepzibah for a girl," I countered. "Hepzibah Pansy Freers."

We both giggled. Giggling led to nuzzling, nuzzling to kissing, then Kit began a rather tentative breast fondling. Things were just starting to get really interesting when the phone rang.

Kit froze, one hand still clamped on my left breast.

"Don't answer it," I said hoarsely.

He hesitated another second. "If someone's calling this late, it must be really important." He lunged for the receiver, barked into it, "Kit Freers." A pause, then he passed it stiffly to me. "It's for you."

Chloe! was my first thought. She was on a sleepover at her best friend's house. Thoughts of kidnappers, conflagrations, bone-crushing falls skidded immediately through my mind. My stomach gave a lurch; I could barely whisper "Yes?" into the phone.

"Lucy? It's Cheryl. I need to see you."

Cheryl? Then I remembered—the hair, the lips, the lollipop. "For God's sake, it's late," I snapped. "This is not a good time to talk!"

"I'm going out of my mind," she yelled shrilly. "You've got to come here."

"Come where?"

"My room. It's number three-oh-eight, right down the hall from you guys."

This gave me momentary pause. The relatively posh Chipotili Inn had been commandeered for the "above-the-line" members of the production: stars, cameraman, director, and producers; the "below-the-line" crew were supposed to be bivouacked in a local Motel 6. But of course, I realized, none of the other below-the-liners were blood relations of a movie star the magnitude of Alison Wade.

"Can't this wait till morning?" I said.

"No, it can't!" Her voice rose to a high-octane point of hysteria. "I told you, I'm going totally out of my mind!"

"Okay, calm down. I'll be right there." I hung up and turned to Kit, who was propped on one elbow, directing a "What the hell?" squint at me. "It was Cheryl Wade," I told him. "I think she's been hitting a bottle. I'd better go cool her out before she creates a scene."

"Christ, I knew that bird-brained chick would be trouble the minute she walked onto the set," he groaned. "She's useless as a PA. Every time I turn around she's tripping on a wire or making goo-goo eyes at one of the goddamned grips!"

"I won't be long." I got up and wriggled my feet into the nearest pair of shoes, which happened to be a pair of Kit's high-top Keds; then I pulled a long nylon raincoat, also Kit's, on over my nightie.

"Don't lose the mood," I said.

He grinned wanly back.

I hurried down the hall, the too-big sneakers flip-flopping with each step, wondering how I'd explain my get-up if I ran into anyone from the production. Fortunately, the corridor was movie people–free. I found Room 308 and rapped loudly.

"Who is it?" Cheryl's voice hissed.

"It's me, Lucy," I hissed back.

She cracked the door and peered out, as if to assure herself that it wasn't, say, some extraterrestrial, cleverly assuming my voice. So assured, she increased the aperture just wide enough for me to sidle in.

Hers was a single room, but identical in its designer Southwest decor to our own suite—same Hopi rainbow-god doing backbends on the curtains; same ersatz Navajo rug; even the same Georgia O'Keeffe print of a depressed-looking steer's skull mounted on the terra cotta–washed walls. Cheryl, by contrast, looked like Vegas on a Saturday Night: She was wrapped in a shimmery pink sheath cut for maximum cleavage, ears, wrists, and neck jangling with enough gold jewelry to have made King Tut seem underaccessorized. The New Age healing crystal dangled amid the wealth of chains and nestled cozily between her breasts.

"What the hell's going on, Cheryl?" I demanded. "Have you been drinking?"

"No, I haven't been drinking!" she declared indignantly. "I told you, I was in AA."

There was music in the room, I suddenly realized—Hootie and the Blowfish chirping quietly from the bedside clock radio. It lent an odd sitcom ambience to the scene. "Then what's the big problem?"

"Look in there." She aimed a thumb at the bathroom door.

"Why?" I asked warily.

She jabbed the thumb in her mouth, à la the grape lollipop, and gave a helpless little shake of her head.

"Oh, for God's sake!" I steamed angrily across the room. It was probably just one of those little scorpions that make a habit of creeping up from the plumbing in this part of the world. For bug-squashing duty, she might easily have called the night desk clerk, instead of horning in on my domestic tryst. Furiously, I shoved open the door.

Jeremy Lord was crouched rather dejectedly on the john.

"Oh, God, I'm sorry!" I blurted. "I had no idea you were in here. I really should have knocked first—"

I broke off abruptly as I realized I was apologizing to a corpse.

THREE

That he was truly stone-cold dead, I had no doubt. I'd recently had some experience in encountering the newly deceased; I recognized only too well the gruesomely unnatural splaying of the arms and legs, the almost comical dirty-old-man leer of the rigid face.

Previously, whenever I'd happened upon a fresh corpse, my reaction had been predictable: a moment of feet-glued-to-the-floor panic, followed by the all-encompassing urge for a swift getaway. But now I was amazed at how utterly cool and collected I felt—possibly because I was used to seeing Jeremy Lord dead. As was most of the civilized world. It had been his custom to play a cameo in each of his pictures—always a character who, early in the film, meets a particularly garish end—so that the only thing that seemed strange at the moment was not to see blood trickling from a corner of his mouth or spurting Old Faithful–like from multiple bullet holes in his torso.

But there was no blood anywhere—nor for that matter any other obvious sign of mayhem. I took a step forward to better examine the body, calmly taking inventory of all sensory stimuli.

Sight: Jeremy Lord had gone to meet his maker wearing a black silk shirt, an outmodishly punk narrow black leather tie, black linen jacket, and boxer shorts. These last, I was astonished to note, were not black, but bright green and festooned with jolly little Santa Clauses. The idea that Jeremy wore novelty underwear was so disconcerting that for a moment it overshadowed the fact that he wasn't wearing pants. But such was the case; his legs were naked, two long pasty lengths, furred with rusty hair, culminating in a pair of droopy black socks in the manner of a bygone cheapo blue movie. The additional fact that the boxers were yanked up to his waist and that the toilet lid was down indicated he was not actually making use of the facilities when he checked out.

Sound: Hootie and company, still burbling on, but almost drowned out by the whirr of a recessed ventilating fan.

Smell: the ventilator had wiped out all but a faint perfume of soap and a raspberryish shampoo, mingled with a whiff of something else—a slight, rather acrid odor that I could almost, but not quite, identify.

Hercule Poirot Freers.

"So is he, like, dead?"

Cheryl's voice directly in my ear made me leap four inches, and my heart started thumping wildly.

"Yeah, he's dead," I finally managed. "What happened to him?"

"How am I supposed to know?"

"You might have an inkling. This *is* your hotel room."

Her prodigious lips opened and closed several times, like some rare species of aquarium fish. "Well, I don't." She shot a peripheral glance at the body from the corner of her glitter-painted eyes. "We've got to get him out of here!"

"What do you mean?"

"We've gotta get him back to his own room. It's on the top floor. If we both take his arms and legs, we can carry him up." To my amazement, she grabbed his bare calves, then instantly dropped them. The body, which appeared to be in the first stage of rigor mortis, tilted rather loonily against the neighboring vanity. "He's like ice!" Cheryl whimpered.

"Are you crazy?" I snapped. "We can't move him. In the first place, it's highly against the law—we could get in very serious trouble. And in the second place, don't you think someone might notice? I mean, two women carting a dead director around a hotel in the dead of the night—it just might attract a little attention!"

Cheryl combed her fingers through the varicolored cyclone of her hair. "I've *got* to get him out of here. If my sister Alison finds out he was in my room, she'll have a shit fit! She'll never believe there was nothing happening between us. She thinks I'm a slut. But she's the one to talk, boy. Before she made it, she'd have screwed a doorknob if she thought it would get her through another door."

"So you weren't going to have sex with Jeremy?" I asked.

"Are you joking? I told you, I couldn't stand him."

"Then don't you think it's going to look a little funny that he's not wearing any pants?"

For the first time, she seemed to actually register the Jolly Old St. Nick underwear. "Oh, my God, where are they?" she squealed.

"Offhand, I'd say those were his on the tub." Tossed over the side of the bathtub was a pair of rather ripe-looking Calvin Klein jeans in a shade of black that definitely said Jeremy. "It looks to me," I added, "like *he* was planning on getting naked."

She snatched up the jeans. "We've got to put them back on him."

"Don't be ridiculous. I told you we can't touch him. Anyway, look how stiff he is. You'd never even get them over his knees." The body, in fact, seemed to be getting stiffer even as we spoke. "How long ago did he . . . you know . . . ?"

She shrugged. "About an hour ago, I guess. Let's get out of here, it's giving me the creeps." She tossed the jeans back over the tub and bolted into the bedroom.

I followed her out. The clock radio now issued a Toni Braxton get-up-and-boogy number; given the fact that Jeremy's boogying days were definitely over, it hardly seemed an appropriate selection. I clicked it off. "I'm just a bit confused here," I said. "A man you can't stand somehow ends up not only in your room, but with his pants off, not to mention dead."

"I didn't ask him to come," Cheryl wailed. "He just kind of followed me back from this restaurant where a bunch of us were having dinner."

"Followed you?" I had the image of Jeremy trotting on all fours like a stray cocker spaniel.

Cheryl gave another of her helpless-little-me shrugs. "He said he wanted to talk about Alison, he felt bad the way the divorce had gotten so nasty and stuff, so how about a nightcap? Okay, I thought, a nightcap, no big deal. So he got a Corona out of the mini-bar, and I had a

Diet Pepsi, and we sat around for a while talking, yak, yak, yak. Mostly about himself. He was the biggest egomaniac the world's ever known."

I mentally agreed, recalling his recent little tirade at Kit—how he'd seemed to always refer to himself in the third person, like Louis Quatorze or Nixon. "So then what happened?"

"Then he goes into the john. Which figures, after a couple of beers, right? So then I hear the toilet flush, and I hear him drop the lid down, but he still doesn't come out. And after a couple of minutes I hear this kind of moan. So you know what I thought?"

"What?" I asked gingerly.

"I thought he was, you know . . . whacking off."

I raised my brows, rather primly.

"Well, Alison said that one of the things she couldn't stand about him was that he was horny all the time. At first she thought she was the one driving him mad with passion, but then she found out *any*thing did, young, old, in between. He was a total nymphomaniac."

The correct word, if referring to a man, was, I happened to know, satyromaniac, but this hardly seemed the time to be a stickler for correct English. I nodded encouragingly for her to go on.

She bit her lower lip. "So that's what I thought he was doing. Except then he *still* didn't come out. So after about ten minutes, I opened the door, and that's when I saw him sitting there looking so weird. And when he didn't move or anything, I thought, Holy God, he's dropped dead!"

"Why didn't you call the police?" I said. "Why did you call me?"

"You solved those murders. So I figured you were like used to this kind of thing. You'd know what to do."

Recently, I had returned home one rainy afternoon to find my ex-starlet neighbor floating naked and dead in my swimming pool; and partly to clear my name and Kit's, I had taken it on myself to find out who had bashed in her gorgeous skull. I wondered if this would be my reputation from here on: Got an inconvenient body on your hands? A corpse cluttering up your living room, a stiff hogging the john? No problem—just call Lucy Freers.

Rather peevishly, I said, "What you have to do is notify the police.

Immediately. It's already going to look suspicious that you waited this long."

Cheryl emitted a tortured little whimper.

"Okay, I'll do it." With exasperation, I picked up the phone, got an outside line, and hit 911, then explained to the rather incredulous operator that yes, the person in question was definitely past resuscitation, and no, it was not my room at the Chipotili, I was merely an uninvolved third party who, at 12:24 A.M., just happened to be loitering on the scene.

Cheryl, meanwhile, made a raid of the mini-bar. So much for those Twelve Step vows, I thought, replacing the receiver, but she pulled out an oversized Swiss chocolate bar and began greedily ripping off the wrapper. Reluctantly, I picked up the phone again to call Kit. As if by telepathy, he suddenly appeared in the room. For *his* impromptu journey down the hall, he had selected a riotously colored ski sweater, baggy brown workout pants, and a pair of moss-green Hush Puppies. The three of us were practically a textbook of fashion don'ts.

"The door wasn't locked," he said. "What's going on?"

"There's been an accident," I told him.

"Oh, Christ, what has she done?" He shot a withering look at Cheryl, who was busy cramming candy into her mouth.

"I didn't do anything," she wailed. Her lips were smeared with dark chocolate, giving her the look of an old-time minstrel singer in negative.

"It's Jeremy," I said quickly. I gave a little jerk of my head toward the bathroom. "He's in there, and he's sort of . . . dead."

With an athletic prowess I hadn't known he possessed, Kit bounded to the bathroom. "Oh my God!" he wheezed. He repeated this several more times, clutching the door for support. "I don't believe it! This is the worst thing that could possibly have happened to me!"

"It's a hell of a lot worse for Jeremy!" I pointed out acerbically. "Besides, this afternoon you were ready to kill him yourself."

Kit's face turned the color of Downy Flakes. "Holy God, everyone heard us arguing. You don't think I'll be suspected of knocking him off, do you?"

"Let's not get carried away. Who said anybody knocked him off? It could be some kind of drug OD, or even natural causes."

He gazed at me dubiously. The idea that a thirty-eight-year-old man who, just hours before, had been robustly throwing his ego around a movie set, striking terror in the hearts of all and sundry, could suddenly expire of natural causes did seem uniquely absurd.

We continued for a moment to eyeball the corpse. "He stole those boxer shorts from wardrobe," Kit said abruptly.

"Well, that would explain the little Santas, then," I said, in a thank-God-we-got-*that*-cleared-up voice.

"I need a drink." Kit backed out and made a dive for the mini-bar.

For some reason, I felt compelled to stay put. The more I stared at the dead face, the more it seemed that the wide-open eyes were staring with an expression I could only interpret as horror—as if death had come not only as a surprise, but in a form so hideous it could hardly be imagined. And then suddenly, I could no longer stand to look at it.

I whirled and raced out to join Kit. "See if there's any Absolut," I said.

*

Within fifteen minutes, the room had filled up with so many people, it had the almost festive air of a cocktail party. Most of the invitees were in uniform—Dust Bowl brown marking officers of the county sheriff's department, pale blue delineating fire department paramedics. The manager of the inn, a guy who bore a startling resemblance to Snidely Whiplash, darted frantically in and out, evidently convinced his inn-managing days were numbered. The three of us, Kit, Cheryl, and myself, maintained a close, personal relationship with the mini-bar.

One thing I had learned in my previous adventures with law enforcement was that cops produce other cops, in the manner of, say, mating gerbils or rabbits. This law apparently held true, even in the back hills of New Mexico. Over the course of an hour, sirens kept screaming up until it seemed as if the county's entire sheriff's department was squeezing into the room, like circus clowns in a Volkswagen.

The *squawk* and *urlp* of their walkie-talkies, the way they seemed to be able to simultaneously rush about and mill around . . . it all brought back memories.

After what seemed an eternity, word issued from the paramedics that—preautopsy, at least—it appeared the victim had indeed died of natural causes. This news had a rather party-pooping effect on the boys in brown. Here was possibly the most famous corpse ever to pop up in the entire history of the state of New Mexico, and no evidence of foul play: You could almost hear the collective gnashing of cop teeth.

"So you were the one who discovered the body." A gum-chewing young cop with a furry auburn mustache had been assigned to take my statement. We perched with awkward intimacy on the edge of the bed, our knees ribaldly touching.

"No, Miss Wade found him," I said. "It was such a shock, she didn't know quite what to do, so she called me."

I was expecting the same squinty-eyed distrust with which the LAPD would have greeted my every word. But Young Sergeant Hallock merely nodded, then shook out a fresh stick of Juicy Fruit and hospitably extended the pack to me. "No thanks," I said. "I don't chew."

He folded the stick efficiently in two and adhered it to the substantial wad already in his mouth. "When you got to this room, was there anything that seemed strange or out of the ordinary?"

"Besides a corpse in the john?" I asked breezily. Sergeant Hallock now eyed me rather more thoughtfully. I had killed two tiny bottles of vodka from the mini-bar; on top of all that Saint-Julien at dinner, it was starting to have an effect. With an effort, I adopted a tone of schoolmarmish sobriety. "Nothing seemed unusual to me. Cheryl— Miss Wade—was obviously very upset. She asked me to take a look in the bathroom. I did, and saw Mr. Lord, and it appeared quite obvious that he was dead. Other than that, there was nothing unusual in the bathroom either." For a moment I thought of mentioning the odor— the faintly pungent smell mingling with the raspberry shampoo that I couldn't quite identify, but it seemed too unformulated in my mind to go into.

"Did you touch anything or remove anything from the scene?"

"Absolutely not," I said haughtily. I saw no need to mention Cheryl's panicked attempt to relocate the body.

Snap, pop! went the Juicy Fruit. "The deceased was a good friend of Miss Wade's?"

"He was her former brother-in-law. He used to be married to Alison Wade, who's Cheryl's sister."

"Alison Wade, like the movie star? Hey, I just saw her, she was on HBO the other night. So this is her sister, huh?" He cast a glance at Cheryl, her status as a Celebrity Relation evidently affording her new respect. Then he put two and two together: "So that means she was carrying on with her brother-in-law. Is that right?"

"Not that I know of," I answered demurely.

"The deceased is in a partial state of undress. You know of any other reason he'd be removing his pants?"

"Maybe he was planning on taking a quick shower."

Any self-respecting member of the Los Angeles Police Department would have treated this inane suggestion with the contempt it deserved, but Sergeant Hallock scribbled it in his notepad without blinking an eye. He seemed at a loss for further questions. We sat silently a moment, him chewing, me glancing uncomfortably around the room. My eye fell on the dejected O'Keeffe cow skull; it was beginning to feel like a kindred spirit.

Cheryl, however, in a corner, flanked by two hunky young officers, appeared to have acquired a second and perkier wind. She was pulling flirty faces and tossing her coiffure, while the cops sneaked glances down her décolletage.

I stood up. "I think we've covered everything," I said firmly. "I'm really exhausted and I'd like to get back to bed now. If you need more, you can reach me in the morning."

The sergeant seemed to have no objection. I moved toward the door.

The ill tidings had evidently begun to spread among other members of the movie company—a delegation had appeared in the doorway, led by Melissa Sorrentino, the actress who played the film's villainess. Her witchy face with its tiny peering eyes was composed in a rather hammy expression of tragic concern. Spying me, she cut a decisive swath through the herd and tenderly grasped both my hands in hers. "Oh, Lucy, we just heard about Kit!" she proclaimed in a quivering contralto. "How utterly devastating for you! If there's anything, my dear, anything at all I can do—"

Kit loomed suddenly behind me. Melissa let out an *eek!*, a natural reaction to the appearance of a ghost.

"It wasn't me, it was Jeremy," Kit said gloomily.

"Jeremy's dead?" she squawked.

"How the hell did it happen?" The usually haughty cinematographer, now clad endearingly in peppermint-striped pajamas, pushed his way forward.

"It's not clear yet," Kit said. "Some sort of heart attack, I guess."

"My God!" Melissa now looked genuinely aghast. It was one thing to hear that Kit had bitten the dust: The show could easily go on without a producer or two. But a director dropping dead was serious. "What's going to happen to the movie?" she demanded.

"We shut down. At least temporarily, till the studio hires another director. Assuming, that is, the studio wants to go on with it and not just pull the plug."

A wave of terror undulated through the movie crowd. With impeccable timing, the paramedics chose the same moment to parade through with Jeremy's bagged-up body on a gurney. We all watched solemnly as it glided by; then the majority of the movie contingent fled to their rooms to go rouse their agents back in Brentwood from REM sleep.

Kit and I shuffled wordlessly back to our own suite. Peeled off our motley outerwear. Slid into bed, yanked the blankets to our chins. Neither of us, we intuitively knew, had the least interest in resuming where we'd left off. Little Thaddeus Thor or Hepzibah Pansy would just have to wait.

FOUR

"It was definitely natural causes." Kit's voice on the phone sounded hoarse, as if he'd been talking nonstop for hours. "The county medical examiner released the autopsy report today. Apparently his heart just stopped."

"What do you mean?" I said. "Like somebody just turned off the switch?"

"Basically. They figure it was some kind of congenital weakness. And Jeremy was a high liver. Work hard, party hard." Kit gave a mirthless chuckle. "His idea of moderation was sex with only one woman at a time and not mixing tequila with the Scotch. In fact, according to the autopsy, his blood alcohol level was off the charts."

"Cheryl said he'd only had a couple of Coronas. Either she was lying, or he was already shit-faced when he came to her room."

"He was certainly shit-faced when he checked out. Anyway, all this hearty partying was eventually too much of a strain for his weak heart. So it said 'Good night, Gracie.'"

I clutched the receiver, letting this news sink in a moment. It was six days after the macabre pseudo–cocktail party in Cheryl Wade's room. Kit had remained in New Mexico to supervise the production shutdown, while I, wanting to get as far and as fast away as soon as possible, had caught a Southwestern shuttle home the following morning. I was currently in my own bedroom, getting ready for a memorial party for Jeremy at Spago; I'd been in the process of blow-drying my heavy, maple syrup–colored hair out of its natural fright-wig state when Kit had called. There had been a fire on the unattended set, nothing serious, just another cock-up in a thoroughly cocked-up production, but by the time it had been put out it had become too late for him to make the plane to L.A.

"I don't know," I said now. "Natural causes just doesn't sound right."

"Why not?" Kit asked guardedly.

"There was something about the expression on Jeremy's face. His eyes . . . they looked so . . . horrified."

"Yeah, well if my heart suddenly decided to stop ticking, I'd look pretty damned horrified myself. Don't go blowing this up into something it's not."

He was right, I told myself: It *was* possible for someone of my acquaintance to die without it necessarily being murder one.

"Has there been anything more in the news?" Kit went on.

"No, all quiet on the media front."

For the first couple of days, there had been the predictable over-heated coverage. "Hollywood shocker!" screamed the local news teasers, followed by much wallowing in the more prurient details of the life of the dead director. Jeremy Lord, it appeared, had been the kind of guy who'd have found the lifestyle in Sodom and Gomorrah a tad too conservative, someone who'd left no vice untouched: He'd been a compulsive gambler, customarily blowing thousands in a single night at Caesar's; a former cocaine and amphetamine abuser turned two-fisted drinker; even, by some accounts, a shopaholic, having had in possession some eighty-odd pairs of black zip-fly jeans. Not to mention an indefatigable womanizer. This last attribute came in for exceptional play, the more sensational reports making it sound as if every starlet, model, and waitress on two coasts had tumbled at one time or another in and out of his bed. Plus, he had been a gold-star client of every madam in town, a tidbit that, when uncovered, was good for another peppering of tabloid salvos. And, astonishingly, he'd still had enough stamina to fit in three marriages.

The ex-wives had also been treated to a goodly share of media attention. Remarkably, all three, post-Jeremy, had gone on to fame, fortune, or both. The first, Judie, invariably referred to as Jeremy's "childhood sweetheart," was now wife of the gazillionaire housing magnate Morton Levritz. The second, Caitlin, who'd been nanny to Judie and Jeremy's kids before becoming Mrs. Lord II, was now a "celebrity diet guru" who hauled in millions hawking herbal products in late-night infomercials. And the third, of course, was Alison Wade, glamour girl and box-office heavyweight.

But with no late-breaking evidence of foul play to keep the story alive, it had quickly sputtered and died. "This memorial thing tonight will probably trigger some more coverage," I added to Kit.

"You're probably right. It'll be star-studded, and where there are stars, there are *Live at Five* reporters."

"I feel kind of peculiar about going alone. The only real connection I had to Jeremy was nearly trampling on his corpse."

"You've *got* to go. If neither of us is there, it will look too peculiar."

As well as suspicious, he didn't need to add.

Our conversation had been accompanied by a grating symphony of hammering, sawing, and pneumatic drilling outside my window. We were putting a new addition on our house—our wonderful house, a rambling Connecticut-in-the-Pacific-Palisades mock farmhouse on a eucalyptus-shaded lane; there'd be more room for the new baby, and also I'd be able to set up a studio at home instead of commuting to the rented space in Culver City I now worked in. Now the cacophony abruptly stopped.

"It sounds like the builders have just knocked off for the day," I said.

"I was thinking," Kit said. "As long as we're doing it, we should extend out a couple of hundred feet more and add a gym. Maybe even a sauna."

"How about a billiards room as well?"

From the silence on his end, I had the awful feeling he was actually considering it. "As far as I'm concerned," I added quickly, "this house is already embarrassingly big. The last time I was back in Minnesota, I actually heard one of my stepsisters telling someone I lived in a mansion."

"In that part of the world, anything with an indoor toilet is a mansion."

"Very funny."

"Look," he said, "like it or not, I'm involved in a business where appearances count. I think we're living pretty modestly, considering our position."

I felt a twinge of alarm. But I had no wish to start a long-distance squabble. "It's almost five," I said abruptly. "If I don't want to be late for Jeremy's thing, I'd better finish getting ready."

"I want to know everybody who was there," Kit said, with a touch of envy. We exchanged rather curt "love you's" and hung up.

What do you wear to a memorial shindig for a reprobate director at a famous power restaurant? I stood for a moment in front of my closet, pondering the question. I have a passion for old things; my favorite pastime is nosing about in thrift shops, estate sales, swap meets, anywhere I can add to my collections of Fiestaware and Depression glass, antique toys and games, and the vintage clothes that make up the bulk of my wardrobe. Now, I picked out a sleeveless sheath from the Kennedy era in a slubby orange sherbet–hued shantung; given that early sixties fashion was currently back in style, it could have just come off the rack at Neiman Marcus. A sleazier number would be more appropriate to celebrate Jeremy, I mused, doing up the zipper, something in the black-leather-bustier-and-fishnet-stockings line. But then again, he wouldn't be around to see it.

I hurried downstairs to let in the sitter, a plump, deceptively motherly looking Austrian in her sixties named Mrs. Bruegelstadler, known familiarly as Mrs. B. She toddled briskly in, lamenting about the "hot-rodders" on the Pacific Coast Highway, *ja,* they wanted nothing but to see her go crashing to kingdom come off the cliffs of Malibu, adding in the same breath, "You will be home by nine o'clock, *ja?* On a Thursday night, I don't wish to be going home so late." I resisted the urge to reply *Jawohl!* and click my heels, instead settling her in the kitchen with a cup of Lemon Zinger.

I found Chloe at the computer, staring at a blank monitor, from which issued a sound like a cat being disemboweled. "Miri Pleischer's downloading me Halloween sounds," she explained.

"You're going to scare the daylights out of Mrs. B.," I told her.

She wrinkled her retroussé nose. "Mrs. B. hates every single thing I do."

"That's not true. She just likes to kvetch." I squatted down to peer into a large glass tank on the floor. A little red-spangled snake lay coiled amid a moonscape of rocks and dead twigs on the bottom. My daughter is animal crazy: For years, believing that Kit was allergic, we'd allowed her no pets except a gecko named Gordon, who lived mostly on the lam beneath the furniture. But with the discovery that Kit's sneezing fits were spurred mostly by dog dander, Chloe's menagerie had grown to two Siamese cats, a chinchilla housed in a duplex cage, three bunnies named Squeak, Livingston, and Cookie Dough, a pair of lovebirds, and this latest addition, an adolescent rat snake who, revoltingly, had to be fed frozen baby rats. I tapped on the glass; the little serpent sleepily raised its head.

The computer gave out a prolonged death rattle that might easily have been lifted from a Jeremy Lord movie soundtrack.

From force of habit, I left by the kitchen garage door and nearly went hurtling into a gaping pit, having forgotten the garage had been temporarily sacrificed to the new construction. Skirting the excavation, I made it to the driveway where our three-car fleet was stashed and was climbing into my Grand Cherokee when my name was called.

"Hey, uh, Lucy!"

The contractor, Harold Davis, ambled up to the car window. He was thin to the point of gauntness, with a prophet's flowing brown hair and brown eyes that, disconcertingly, never seemed to blink. He possessed, in fact, a vague resemblance to Charles Manson, if Charles Manson's chosen métier had been, say, Benedictine monk instead of psychoserial killer.

"How's everything going, Harold?" I asked.

"Real good." This, I had by now learned, was his standard rejoinder and had nothing to do with the actual state of affairs. Thus, it could be "Real good, but that closet we knocked out turned out to've been a bearing wall"; or "Real good, but one of the carpenters just whacked off his left hand by mistake." I braced myself for the worst.

"We're gonna have to turn the water off sometime in the next coupla days. Two, maybe three, hours."

"No problem," I said with relief.

"The thing is, we're gonna have to regrade the drainage in the backyard and relocate the water main. I figure it'll add an extra twelve, thirteen thousand bucks."

Two Mexican men with chain saws hoisted on their shoulders sauntered by, their sunny grins belying their bandito appearance. "Is there any alternative?" I asked Harold.

"Gee, not that I can see."

"Then go ahead." Averting any further bulletins, I started the car and set off toward West Hollywood.

*

Twenty-five minutes later, I was idling behind an egg yolk–yellow Viper in the lengthy queue of luxury cars snaking up the side road to Spago.

From what I knew of Jeremy Lord, most of it through the Hollywood gossip grapevine, Spago was the perfect place to memorialize him. He'd eaten here so often, he had referred to it as his canteen, always occupying the same enviable table by the picture windows overlooking the gridlock on Sunset Strip. It was at Spago (or so rumor had it) that Jeremy had broken the news to Judie, ex-wife number one, that he was throwing her over for their nineteen-year-old nanny, Caitlin, having first presented her with a consolation prize of a diamond and sapphire Cartier bracelet. It was at Spago, too, that Caitlin, ex-wife number two, had Frisbeed an entire goat cheese and smoked duck-sausage pizza across the room after learning she was being dumped for Alison Wade.

And it was also at Spago that Alison, scarcely three months after the wedding, had chosen to flaunt her affair with her then-current costar, Chester Dorris, by soul-kissing him in front of Jeremy in the interval between the entree and dessert.

I finally surrendered my car keys to a sun-kissed young man who looked as if only minutes ago he'd been windsurfing, and joined the crush inside. Some six hundred of movieland's finest were jammed shoulder to shoulder in the main dining room. It's always a cause for some celebration in Hollywood when a major player drops from the top, whether by death or from lousy grosses; all around me lips were intoning phrases such as "So tragic!" and "What a terrible loss!" while eyes were broadcasting "Ain't this great!"

The room itself was awash with masses of white roses—an ironic touch, I thought, for a man who'd been so thoroughly committed to the color black. A larger-than-life-sized cutout of the Dark Prince himself dominated the front of the room, surrounded by a dozen TV monitors running clips of his films. I managed to extract a flute of Dom Pérignon from the packed bar, then wandered back to watch the monitors a moment, marveling at the sheer variety of ways Jeremy had devised to obliterate sophisticated machinery: On at least half of the screens, a train, plane, or nuclear submarine was going up in a fireball.

"Hello, you ravishing thing, you," crooned a smooth voice behind me. A hand snaked around my waist and pinched hard. With an indignant squeal, I whirled around.

The smoothie was Lane Reisman, who had recently, at the tender age of thirty-one, been named president of production at Keystone Pictures. At some time in his young life, Lane had been told he looked like Bruce Willis—mainly due to a similarly receding hairline—and he'd worked mightily ever since to cultivate the resemblance: lips curved in a perpetual smirk, baseball cap all but fused on his head, wiseass, hipper-than-thou attitude. Basically, he gave me the creeps. But Keystone was the studio making *A Merry Christmas to All,* meaning Lane was, at least currently, Kit's boss. For Kit's sake, I decided not to spit in his eye, but instead curved my own lips into a sociable smile. "I'm really sorry about Jeremy," I said. "I know you were a close friend of his."

"We were blood brothers under the skin. I'm hurting bad. The Wild Bunch just won't be the same without him."

I gave a noncommittal nod. The Wild Bunch was a loose-knit gang of thirty-something guys, all with heavy industry credentials, who had thumbed their noses at the current Hollywood devotion to home and family. They had shucked off any wives and families of their own in favor of barging off *en groupe* in such male-bonding pursuits as ice fishing in Alaska or big-stakes poker in Tahoe. They boasted of all-night drinking bashes and orgies with the highest-priced hookers. Women, of course, need not apply to join the Wild Bunch.

"Funny, isn't it, that you were the one who found his body?" Lane was saying. "It seems like it's getting to be kind of a specialty of yours."

"I'd rather think of it as just rotten luck," I replied crisply.

"Just between us"—Lane put his mouth so close to my ear I could feel his moist breath—"is it true he was wearing a Wonderbra and panties when he died?"

I gave a startled laugh. "No, it's not true at all."

"Too bad, it would've been just like the crazy kid. I'm gonna miss that bastard. He was the only guy I knew more decadent than me." His eyes shifted left. "Excuse me a sec, I have to say hello to Sally."

With a seamless motion, he slid off to waylay Sally Field, who was edging brittlely through the packs of happy mourners.

How did I despise Lane Reisman? Let me count the ways. I despised the way those predatory light eyes seemed always to be searching for fresh kill, and how, under the pretense of a warm greeting, he inevitably managed to cop a sneaky feel.

I hated the fact that he never went out with anyone his own age or even his own size, instead squiring an ever-changing parade of six-foot-tall, big-boobed, tiny-brained twenty-year-olds.

And I purely despised his fashioning himself as the ringleader of the loathsome Wild Bunch.

It was a relief to be rid of him. I glanced back at the TV monitors. On the nearest screen, the camera was panning up the seemingly endless length of a pair of exquisite legs. These proved to be attached to the torso of Alison Wade: She was lying on a black sand beach, wearing nothing but a dental floss bikini—unless, of course, you counted the eight-inch screwdriver embedded in the hollow of her throat. It was *Body Language,* the movie in which Alison and Jeremy had met and fallen in lust, leading to Alison doing her brief stint as Mrs. Jeremy Lord III.

The Baby Mogul rematerialized back at my side. In this sea of vastly bigger fish, why, I wondered, was he singling me out this way?

"I was the executive on that movie," he confided, gazing at the prone Alison. "When I was still over at Columbia. I told Jeremy not to get involved with her, she was a killer, but he was thinking with his dick, not his brain."

According to what I could tell, that had been his standard operating procedure. "I wonder if Alison is here?" I said.

"You've got to be kidding. She's well aware that anything she shows her ass at automatically becomes a red-hot event. She wouldn't give Jeremy that satisfaction, even with him rotting six feet under. But the other two have made the scene."

"His other ex-wives?" I glanced with interest around the crowd.

"See at that back table?" Lane turned me by my shoulders, getting in a sneaky quick massage. "The skinny blonde in the black straw hat . . . that's Caitlin, the second Mrs. Lord."

"The one who'd originally been his kids' nanny?"

"Correct. And that's her twin brother, Ralph Jones, sitting next to her. You've probably heard his name before—owner of the Tinseltown Café franchise. Or at least he's the front man. He's got a lot of silent partners."

I stared rather rudely at the pair. It was eerie to see two people of different sexes who looked so extraordinarily alike. Both had delicate features, with baby-doll round blue eyes and snub noses; both wore their golden hair in identical razor-shorn caps. In fact, about the only thing that distinguished Ralph from his sister Caitlin was a wispy, reddish-blond goatee.

"They look so ethereal," I observed. "Like they should have halos and wings."

"Yeah, a real couple of angels. Little Caitlin runs that quack herbs business of hers like an eight-hundred-pound gorilla. And Ralphie boy . . . everybody knows he's got bent nose connections."

"You mean the mob?" I tried to picture this golden angel hobnobbing with Mafiosi. It seemed ludicrous.

"Let's just say you don't want to look too carefully at those silent partners of his. You'll run into guys with names like Two-Fingered Tony and Vinnie the Chin."

The two blond heads inclined toward each other so that their foreheads were practically touching. "They seem pretty close," I remarked.

Lane issued a caustic laugh. "You know that old saying, 'Candy is dandy, but incest is best.' "

I glanced at him. "You're not serious?"

He shrugged and, just for a change, smirked. "My policy's always been, 'Don't ask and don't tell.' " He nodded to my left. "If you want a look at Judie, she's the babe in the pink jacket."

I followed his direction. Judie Lord Levritz was tiny, scarcely five feet tall—she and Jeremy must have made quite a Mutt-and-Jeff pair. Slightly cross-eyed, pleasant face. Salt-and-pepper pageboy. Though dressed in Chanel, she looked more like someone who might be featured in the *Ladies' Home Journal* for her jiffy tuna casseroles than the wife of a gazillionaire.

I'd seen her somewhere before. Recently. Though where or exactly when, I couldn't recall.

"A real dog, huh?" sneered Lane.

"I wouldn't say that," I bristled. "I think she looks charming."

"Yeah, and a terrific personality. Of course, she snagged Jeremy when he was just a babe in arms. Then Morty Levritz went for her because she was a Celebrity Ex. He gets to go to Rotary Clubs or whatever and brag about how his wife used to be married to a big-time Hollywood director."

Someone began clinking loudly on a glass. The crowd shuffled in a body to face the shrine of Jeremy's favorite table. A short, balding guy was perched atop it: chin fashionably stubbled, body Armani'd from collar to socks—he was practically the Platonic ideal of an agent.

"Friends," he boomed, as the hubbub of the crowd died down, "Romans, and fellow moviemakers! I come to praise Jeremy, not to bury him." He altered his tone to a bad imitation of Groucho Marx: "Which is just as well, since he was cremated this morning." He paused for the laugh; a thin chuckle obligingly rippled through his audience. "But really, my friends, as we all know, nothing could ever bury Jeremy in our hearts, or in the hearts and minds of his fans, who will continue to always cherish his movies."

The type of fan who would cherish Jeremy's brand of gore was not someone I'd care to meet in a deserted alley. I plucked some puff pastry hors d'oeuvres from a passing waiter's tray—I definitely needed sustenance to make it through the forthcoming platitudes.

"Jeremy Lord packed more into thirty-eight years than most people do in eighty," intoned our spokesman. "I've got a hunch that going out at the top of his game was just the way he'd have wanted it."

Yeah, right. And going out in the john, just like Elvis, was probably also his heart's desire. I washed down the puff pastry with a hearty swig of champagne.

"Jeremy was more than a client, he was a close friend and fellow rabble-rouser . . ." There now came a pause in the regularly scheduled programming to allow the announcer to wipe a welling mist from his eyes. "I guess I don't have to tell anyone here what I'm feeling right now," he faltered. This I believed was true: Life held few more poignant spectacles than the grief of an agent over the loss of an A-list client.

Something caused me to glance back at Caitlin and her twin brother, Ralph. Neither of *them* seemed exactly dissolved with grief. In fact, their identical eyes were identical in expressing no emotion at all; both gazed with the cold, hard indifference of sharks to a school of minnows about to be swallowed whole.

With a chill, I turned my attention back to the wrapup of the eulogy. We all raised a toast to the late, great director, the agent scrambled down from his makeshift pulpit, and the crowd resumed its frantic mixing. I had finally shaken Lane: he had thrust himself in front of an *Entertainment Tonight* camera, tearfully proclaiming that without Jeremy Lord on the planet life had utterly lost its savor.

I plunged into the melee and mingled for another hour. Yes, it was a terrible loss, I agreed with one and all. Yeah, it was really super that Jeremy had lived life to the fullest. Yes, Kit was absolutely certain the movie would go forward, the studio was still behind it a hundred percent. Then, figuring I'd fulfilled my wife-of-the-producer duty, I headed on out.

As I waited for my car to be brought up, I realized I was being stared at. It was a girl in her early twenties; I was certain I'd never seen her before. I was beginning to wonder if my bra strap was showing or if pastry crumbs were clinging to my chin when she stepped toward me.

"Excuse me, aren't you Lucy Freers?" She gave a deferential smile.

"Yes, I am," I allowed.

"My name is Denise Schumer. I'm Alison Wade's personal assistant."

"Oh, really?" I regarded her with greater interest. A wide face, with longish brown hair scraped back by a pink headband, the plastic kind, with scalp-nipping teeth. The plaid hip-hugger pants she had on, while no doubt the latest thing on Melrose Avenue, were an unfortunate choice for her pear-shaped figure. She was obviously one of the thousands of kids who pour into Hollywood each year fresh out of Yale, or Nebraska State, or USC Film School, hoping for a shot at the big time—*any* big time, be it writing, directing, or the fast track in an agency. But in a land where Appearances Count, I thought grimly, this Denise ought to invest in a subscription to *Savvy*.

"I suppose you're here representing Alison," I said conversationally.

Her eyes squinted a moment, as if she couldn't quite place the name. "No, actually Alison doesn't even know I'm here. But I sort of knew Jeremy when they were together and just thought I should pay my respects. And you know, this kind of event is great for networking."

Making contacts at a funeral—Denise was obviously more savvy than she appeared.

"Anyway," she went on, "the only reason I'm bothering you is because this is an amazing coincidence—I'm supposed to call you tomorrow."

"Me?"

"Yeah. Alison really loves your work. She thinks it's brilliant, and I do too, of course, totally brilliant. Every week, she has me tape your kids' show about the flying squirrel."

"It's a hedgehog, actually."

Denise stared at me, looking as stricken as if I'd just ordered her execution. "Oh, God, of course! Of course, I know it's a hedgehog. That was so stupid, I mean *I'm* stupid. . . ."

I had the uncomfortable sensation she was about to sink to her knees and perhaps kiss the hem of my garment. "It's okay," I said quickly. "A lot of people make that mistake."

She slapped her head with the heel of her palm. "Idiot! Anyway, the reason I'm supposed to call you is because Alison wants you to work on her next movie. It's this amazing script, where she plays a schizophrenic who suffers from delusions, and Alison thinks the delusions should be done in animation. It's a terrific idea, don't you think? So if you're interested . . ." She gave a deprecatory shrug, as if she couldn't imagine anyone actually signing on for anything as humdrum as a major motion picture.

I tried to keep my voice casual. "Yeah, I think I'd be interested."

"Fantastic! Then I'll go ahead and arrange a meeting at the house. Alison always has people come by the house first."

She hesitated, then blurted, "Maybe I shouldn't say this, but I think Alison kind of likes the fact that you saw Jeremy dead. Don't get me wrong, she really does adore your work. But if you want to know the truth, she really despised him."

So had her sister, Cheryl. And judging from what I'd seen of Jeremy's second wife, Caitlin, she wasn't heading up his fan club either. Jeremy Lord seemed to have had a singular talent for sending the women closest to him into fits of revulsion.

A breathtaking car glided up from the parking lot—a Bentley, the color of morning mist diffused by sunlight. Denise stepped forward to claim it.

"It's one of Alison's," she said rather sheepishly. "One of the perks of my job, I get to use the cars." She put out an awkward hand, which I pressed. "I'm really so glad to meet you, Lucy. I'll be speaking to you soon."

She slid into the Bentley and it whooshed away.

My Grand Cherokee roaring up right behind it suddenly seemed as exquisite as a municipal bus. I climbed in and turned down onto Sunset Strip.

I was immersed in thoughts of how exciting it would be to work on an Alison Wade movie, and maybe it could lead to raising the funding for another short film of my own, and where could I possibly have seen Judie Lord Levritz before, when someone suddenly popped up right behind me.

FIVE

You've probably seen this scene a dozen times in the movies: Unsuspecting driver tooling along in a motor vehicle is startled by someone springing up from the back seat. I'd even used it in one of my own animations: a sequence in which Amerinda, my flying blue hedgehog, pops up in a hay wagon behind a particularly slow-witted billy goat. In moving picture format, the driver's reaction is generally to gasp, maybe give a little shout or two, and skid the vehicle a bit before bringing it to a tidy halt.

My own reaction was somewhat different. I let out a blood-curdling scream, which caused my stowaway to scream back; and while we were both hollering at the top of our lungs, the car veered completely out of control, zigzagging into oncoming traffic. Through sheer reflex, I grabbed back the steering wheel and wrenched it sharply: The Cherokee swung a two-wheeled U-turn, narrowly missing a horn-blaring Miata, then went barreling the wrong way up a one-way side street. I slammed on the brakes; we skidded off the road, stopping inches from the scaffolding of one of those humongous billboards that tower over the Strip.

For several seconds, I could do nothing but breathe. Then gradually, I became aware of three things:

One, that I was still alive.

Two, the billboard that we'd nearly smashed into was the Marlboro Man on a white horse, which might have given new meaning to the phrase "tobacco kills."

And three, the face hovering in the rearview mirror belonged to Cheryl Wade.

I whipped violently around in my seat to face her. "For God's sake!" I yelled. "What the hell do you think you're doing?"

"I'm sorry," she whimpered. "I didn't know I'd scare you like that. Oh, rats, everything fell out of my pocketbook." She ducked behind the seat again.

My fingers, I observed, were still clenched in a death grip on the steering wheel. I pried them loose, then got out to check the state of the car. Any cruising cop who'd been fortunate enough to have witnessed my mini–Grand Prix maneuver could have filled his ticket-writing quota for a week, but miraculously, I'd pulled the stunt off with neither a moving violation nor major damage—just a small scratch or two on the passenger-side door.

I climbed back into the front seat and turned back again to my stowaway. She was scooping what looked like the contents of an entire Woolworth's up from the floor.

"How the hell did you get in my car?" I demanded.

"It was in your driveway, and you didn't have it locked."

My skin crawled. "You mean you've been hiding back there ever since I left home?"

"Yeah, and I was like terrified the valet was going to catch me. By the way, he used your car phone, and I think he called long distance. You really ought to complain." She began tossing handfuls of stuff into a purple suede backpack capacious enough for a Himalayan trek. For a moment I was distracted by the sheer quantity of things she evidently felt necessary to lug around: a Charles of the Ritz makeup bag, a roll of Altoids, a package of Famous Amos chocolate chip cookies, two or three lipstick tubes, a little plastic orangutan on a chain, one nude knee-high stocking, a Lucite church key, a dog-eared Filofax . . .

"I was going to talk to you back at your house, when you first got in the car," she said, interrupting my inventory. "But then that guy came over, and I didn't want him or anybody to see me. So I decided I'd better keep hiding till after dark."

"Who are you hiding from?" Knowing Cheryl, it was probably from someone with an incompatible aura.

"I'm in really big trouble," she said. "I'm the one who killed Jeremy."

I stared at her speechlessly. She suddenly started to cry, long sniffling sobs, punctuated with little mewing noises.

"What do you mean, you killed him?" I asked.

"He was poisoned, and I'm the one who gave it to him. Except I
didn't know I was doing it, I just figured it out later."

"I don't get it. Are you saying it was an accident?"

"No, it wasn't any accident," she squealed emphatically. "He was
murdered! And I've got something that can prove it."

"Murdered by who?"

"I can't tell you, or they'll get me too." She retrieved a wad of
crumpled Kleenex from out of her bag and blotted her wet eyes,
smearing black mascara in the sockets; it left an unfortunate skull-
like effect, unpleasantly reminiscent of the O'Keeffe print back at the
Chipotili Inn. "Look, Lucy," she sniffled on, "I can't trust hardly anybody I know. They're all ruthless and backstabbing and only out for
themselves. Like, they wouldn't help a drowning nun unless they
thought they'd get a TV movie out of it or something. But you're
different."

"How do you know?" I said. "Maybe I drown nuns as a hobby."

She shook her head vigorously. "I've seen you. I mean at parties
and things. You talk to people even though they're nobodies. You don't
care about all the bullshit. Plus, when Julia Prentice was murdered, I
heard how you kept on looking for the real killer, even when your own
life was in danger. So I figured you'd help me too."

"Help you how?" I asked with some exasperation.

She paused for a lengthy sniffle. "Somebody was in my house last
night. The alarm went off at like three-thirty in the morning, and the
security guy showed up and checked out all the doors and windows.
He said everything was all locked up and it was probably just some
short in the wiring."

"It probably was," I said. "Sometimes the rain or wind will set off
the alarm. I've had it happen to me before."

"Well, it wasn't raining or windy last night. And check this out.
When I came down to the kitchen this morning, things weren't in the

right place. I mean, like the Mr. Coffee maker was too close to the microwave, and I'm positive the toaster wasn't where it used to be."

I shot her a skeptical look. "So you think somebody broke in, shuffled around some breakfast appliances, then left, setting off the alarm, but otherwise leaving everything locked tight as a drum?"

"Well, yeah." Cheryl, the human jack-in-the-box, bobbed down and up again, retrieving what looked like a sixties-vintage Afro comb from under the front seat. She began tugging it through the tangle of her varicolored hair—which, along with the lime-green catsuit she had on, looked as if it had gone some days without hygienic attention. "When you've got tons and tons of money," she added in a conspiratorial tone, "you can get anything done that you want to."

"How do you know it's someone with tons and tons of money?"

"I can't *tell* you—I already told you that."

"Okay, fine," I said quickly, "but why would whoever it is *want* to break in?"

"Maybe they figured out I've got something that can prove it, and they were looking for it. Or maybe it was just to give me a warning. To let me know they could get me if I talked to anyone."

"Then why," I demanded, "are you talking to me? Why don't you take this proof you've got to the police?"

She yanked the comb down hard through a particularly ratted strand, jerking her head in the motion. "Because the cops are going to think I deliberately poisoned him. But you've got all those friends in the police, right? So maybe, if you could tell them it really wasn't my fault, they'd listen to you."

My mind reeled from attempting to follow this logic. "Believe me, Cheryl," I said, "there's not a cop in the world that's going to put two cents on anything I have to say."

Cheryl started to weep again. It was obvious that she believed what she was saying—but then again, this was a woman who also believed that the planet Pluto dictated her spending habits and that a crystal tchotchka could ward off deadly disease.

But then what about my own suspicions that Jeremy had died an unnatural death? . . . Wait a minute, I quickly told myself. You can't be crazy enough to look for corroboration from the Queen of Ditz.

"Cheryl," I said, in what I hoped was the voice of authority, "listen to me. Nobody killed Jeremy. He wasn't poisoned. He died of a congenital heart condition."

She peered dimly at me from under her sooty lids. "How do you know?"

"I talked to Kit just before I left. He's still in New Mexico. He said the autopsy left absolutely no doubt, it was definitely heart failure. The cops aren't going to be accusing anyone of murder."

"You sure?"

"Girl Scout's honor." I folded my fingers clumsily in the classic Scout sign.

She pressed herself into the back of the seat. "Thank God! You don't know what I've been going through. I thought any minute I'd be put under arrest."

"Tell me something," I said. "Why did you lie to me about how much Jeremy was drinking that night? You said he'd only had a couple of Coronas, but the autopsy showed he was smashed."

She emitted one of her little mewling sounds. "I didn't want anybody to know."

"Why not?"

" 'Cause they might think I was drinking, too, and it's not true, I only had a Diet Pepsi."

"Who might think that? Your sister Alison? Is that who you're afraid of?"

She didn't reply, but rummaged again in the enormous cavity of her bag and fished out a little vial. She shook a brightly colored capsule out of it and popped it into her mouth.

"What's that?" I asked irritably.

"It's these stress pills I've been taking. Want one?" She proffered the vial. It was marked with a prettily drawn logo of a peach—a perfect peach with one pale green leaf unfurled from its stem. "It's all natural," she elucidated. "Herbs and stuff. My nutritionist makes them specially for me."

"No, thanks." Most of my stress at the moment could be easily relieved by getting Cheryl "The Hysterical" Wade out of my life.

Forty feet above us, the Marlboro Man, bathed in a seductive amber glow, was firing up a cancer stick; a watery full moon rose poetically above his hunched shoulder. If I didn't get back soon, Mrs. B. would smear my name throughout the sitters' network, and I'd never be able to get out of the house on a Thursday night again.

"Where's your car?" I asked Cheryl.

"I don't have a car," she pouted. "It got repossessed, can you believe? You'd think Alison would let me borrow one of hers, but no-o-o! Last week, when I came back here to bring home Jeremy's kids, I called her up and she made me schlep over to her house and sit around for hours while she had meetings galore. Then finally all she says is she *needs* all her cars. I mean, la-di-da, she's got *six* of them!"

Including, I happened to know, a drop-dead Bentley that her gal Friday got to tool around in. "Look, Cheryl," I said, "I've really got to get back. Where do you want me to take you?"

"I've got a girlfriend who lives just off Sunset Plaza. Mind dropping me off?"

I'd have gladly dropped her off in Passaic, New Jersey, if it meant getting her out of my hair. I steered the Cherokee out of the ditch and, following her directions, wound up a series of increasingly steep and narrow streets, stopping at an A-frame chalet that would have looked right at home in the Alps if it hadn't been covered in scarlet bougainvillea.

Cheryl hopped out of the back seat, then pressed her face against my window, her big lips magnified by the glass to clownish proportions. "You won't tell anybody, will you?" she asked anxiously. "I mean about what I told you?"

"Not a word," I assured her.

She produced one of her tropical fish–like moues. "I know that nobody takes me seriously. They go 'Oh, it's just crazy Cheryl, don't pay any attention.' But I know what I know. And I have to tell you that you could be in danger too."

Leaving me with this cheery pronouncement, she hoisted her gargantuan backpack over her shoulder and marched off into the house.

Six

For none too mystifying reasons, my encounter with Cheryl left me jittery. My dreams that night were permeated with nightmares, the most vivid of which starred Jeremy Lord, outfitted like Death in an Ingmar Bergman movie, chasing me around what appeared to be the Beverly Hills branch of Barneys, wielding a bloody tomahawk. I awoke with a start, then screamed—a derelict was peering in at me from my second-story window. The derelict grinned and transmogrified into Harold the contractor. "Real sorry to scare you, Lucy," he yelled and continued climbing to the roof.

Even the short commute to my studio made me nervous. Every car that passed seemed to contain a suspicious character; an old man shuffling across Gretna Green appeared as menacing as if he'd been wearing a Ninja mask. With difficulty, I managed to concentrate on my work. I'd finally hit on a story concept for magnetism: Amerinda's pal, Sally the Seal (animal from the North Pole), tumbles head over tail in love with a dapper, tap-dancing penguin named Porter (animal from the South Pole); ergo, opposite poles attract. But then my drawing was interrupted by a terse call from Chloe's school requesting my immediate presence for a "conference."

*

The Windermere Academy for Progressive Education, known simply as The School by the mostly rich and famous parents of its student body, occupied an entire hillside off Mulholland, protected from potentially invading riffraff by a thick fieldstone wall. It boasted a riding ring, a Gothic assembly hall replicated stone by stone from a Gothic chapel in south

Wales, and as many English affectations as possible without actually
changing its name to Eton. Chloe was in the fifth grade, called fifth form
in Windermere parlance. I admit I had more than a few qualms about
her attending an establishment in which underprivileged meant getting a
Mustang instead of a BMW for your sixteenth birthday. But the education
was undeniably first-rate, and since Chloe had lately seemed far more
interested in cruising the Internet than lusting after her classmates' posses-
sions, we'd decided to keep her there at least another year.

I paced nervously in what the director, Ms. Baljur, referred to
as her study—a typical elementary-school principal's office that just
happened to have an Aubusson on the floor and a gilt-framed Mary
Cassatt on the wall. To distract myself, I picked up a copy of the current school bulletin and scanned the notices:

"There will be no story-writing class this Friday because the fourth
form will be at Astrocamp.

"Reminder: all permissions and deposits for the middle school's
Spring Break field trip to Japan and the Fiji Islands must be in by
November 15!

"Thanks to the generosity of Lila and Rick Murlman, Windermere
is proud to present a private screening of the new Warner Bros. motion
picture *Kids' Stuff.* . . ."

The door swung open. I glanced up, expecting Connie Baljur, the
director. But into the room sashayed Judie Lord Levritz.

Of course, I realized—this was where I'd seen her before. She was
a Windermere mom.

We gaped at each other in mutual astonishment. I searched for a
conversational gambit: *Hello, I'm Lucy Freers, you might recall that I
discovered your ex-husband's corpse.* . . .

But then Judie broke the ice with a rather Emily Post smile. "This
is a remarkable coincidence," she declared brightly. "Earlier this morning I was out scattering Jeremy's ashes."

This pronouncement left me even more tongue-tied. "How nice,"
scarcely seemed an appropriate rejoinder. "How interesting," I finally
muttered. "Where exactly did you do it?"

"Up in the hills right above the Hollywood sign. That was the kids' idea. If it had been up to me, I'd have just dumped them down the nearest sewer." She still maintained a tea party tone of voice. "Jeremy got the last laugh, though. The wind changed and blew the darned stuff right back in our faces." She gave a fastidious little wipe to the sides of her navy blazer, as if a few of the late director's remains might still be sticking to it. "Want my advice? If you ever intend to scatter anybody's ashes, make sure you pick a spot where the breeze only blows in one direction."

"I'll keep that in mind," I said, with a feeble laugh. On an impulse, I asked, "Was it your idea to have him cremated?"

She frowned. "Mine? No, it was specified in his will. Why do you ask?"

I shrugged. "If there was ever any future question whether his death really was from natural causes, it would now be kind of hard to tell."

"What makes you think he was murdered?" she asked sharply.

"Nothing. I was just speaking hypothetically."

She laid a dainty hand on the butterflied silk scarf at her neck and plucked at an edge of it. A diamond the size of a walnut coruscated on her ring finger. "Well, I have to admit that when I first heard the glad news, the thought crossed my mind as well. But maybe it was just wishful thinking. Jeremy had turned into such a total pig, it was a pleasure to think someone might have butchered him."

These cold-blooded sentiments were shocking, particularly coming from a woman who looked as if she'd just breezed in from the Pillsbury Bake-Off—though her slightly crossed eyes did have the unfortunate effect of also making her look slightly deranged.

I said gingerly, "He must have been a difficult person to be married to."

"He was a swine," she replied almost breezily. "Not to say that he always was. We went to high school together, you know, back in Orrelton, Utah. Back then he was your basic nerd, on the cheerleading squad and class treasurer, things like that."

"Jeremy?" I marveled. The thought of the self-styled Prince of Hollywood Darkness once leading locomotives was boggling.

"Believe it or not. We both came from strict Mormon families, no drinking, no smoking, no fun. It was a big rebellion thing for us to drop out of Brigham Young our freshman year and run off here and get married. That was about as far as my rebellion went. But Jeremy . . ." Her hand closed over the silk bow and crumpled it, as if crushing an actual creature. "The first thing he did when we got here was to look up this distant cousin of his, another black sheep, who was making soft-core porn movies. That was how Jeremy got started, carrying cameras for cousin Thomas. He was instantly attracted to moviemaking, but even more attracted to the sleaze. It turned out he had an enormous affinity for excess. And once he started to get successful on his own, there was no limit to his excess." She gave another fastidious little quiver.

Why was she telling me this? I wondered. But despite myself, I was becoming interested. "You stayed with him for a pretty long time, didn't you?" I prompted.

"Ten years. To the day. The son of a so-and-so chose our tenth anniversary to walk out on me. But what did I know, a simple little Mormon hick? Over the last couple of years of our marriage, reports started to get back to me. You know how some people are, they can't wait to let you know what's going on behind your back. Half of the things I heard, I just couldn't believe. As for the rest of it—I thought he'd get it out of his system. You know, sow his wild oats, then settle down. I just thank my lucky stars I don't have AIDS."

A child squealed from the soccer field outside. Judie suddenly seemed to realize that detailing her ex-husband's debaucheries in the director's study of a posh private school was not quite *comme il faut;* a ladylike blush deepened her already ruddy complexion. "I don't know why I'm telling you these things," she said, with a flustered laugh. "I just felt I needed to get it off my chest. Especially after this morning. I had to act sad and grieved for the children's' sake, when I really wanted to praise the heavens."

"Your kids must be pretty upset at losing their dad," I said.

"Oh, well . . . they hardly knew him."

"But they'd just spent a weekend with him. It seems like he was making an effort to be more of a father."

She had moved constantly closer to me as she spoke; now she thrust her face just below mine, the crossed eyes gleaming with unalloyed rage. "He won that round—I had to follow the court order. But I promise you, it was going to stop right there. The only way he was getting his filthy hands on those kids was over my dead body!"

I shrank instinctively back. Judie Lord Levritz might look like Betty Crocker, but I'd be terrified to have her as my enemy.

The door flew open again, and we both swiveled abruptly as more people started to filter into the room—five or six moms, their faces pinched with worry, and one dad, a TV writer type sporting a *Chicago Hope* baseball cap turned back to front. Hard on their heels was the director, Ms. Baljur, a bird-boned woman who carried herself as if she weighed three hundred pounds. She lumbered in state to the head of the room and regarded us gravely: I'd met Mother Superiors who were flightier than Connie Baljur.

"Thank you all for coming so promptly," she intoned. "I'm sorry to say your children were among those removed from their classes today."

We parents exchanged nervous glances. Had a riot broken out in the cafeteria? The entire fifth form been caught playing doctor in the cloakroom?

Ms. Baljur dropped the other shoe: "They failed a spot check for head lice."

It's impossible to describe the pandemonium that followed. A dozen people who were shelling out thirteen grand a year for what they thought was the crème de la crème of education had suddenly found out it was Tobacco Road. "Fuck me!" exclaimed the sitcom-writing dad. Judie Levritz, who was clearly the type who redusted after the maid had been through, looked as if she was going to faint. We listened in a stupor to our marching orders: All linens and curtains in the child's bedroom must be stripped and washed; every hair shaft on the child's head must be searched daily under a high-intensity lamp for nits. "There is an insecticidal shampoo," Ms. Baljur deadpanned, "but tests indicate it can result in minor brain damage. . . ."

At this, our hysteria reached a fever pitch. Shoving and elbowing each other, we stampeded out to collect our lousy kids.

Chloe had been sequestered with her fellow pariahs in the nurse's station. "We've got bugs," she declared to me, in a the-more-wild-life-the-merrier tone. "The nurse says I've got to put all my stuffed animals in the freezer."

"Just for a couple of weeks, till all the bug eggs are gone."

"Yuck," she said complacently.

Across the room, I watched Judie snatch up a girl with Jeremy's sharp features and gangly build. I'd so far managed to downplay with Chloe my recent corpse-encounter; fearing some awkward questions, I quickly spirited her away.

It was Thursday, and Thursday was my car-pooling day, which meant that twenty minutes later I was back on the open road, my Cherokee crammed with kids. Besides Chloe, I was chauffeuring three others: Tracy and Tristan Seigler, ages seven and six, who (to Chloe's awe) *each had their own nanny!* and who, as usual, spent the entire ride squabbling, and Skye Castaneda, whose father was a muckety-muck at Sony and who was given to retributory bouts of car sickness when he didn't get his way. Chloe, who'd been quarantined to the front seat, and who had anyway long since pronounced the other three hopeless geeks, had her ears plugged with the portable CD player she'd received for her tenth birthday. A tinny rap refrain whined from the headphones.

First stop was the Seigler residence, a Santa Fe adobe of a size inevitably referred to as palatial. The dual nannies were loitering as always under the thin stand of date palms in front. They were both fair-haired and young: As they started toward the car, something suddenly pricked at my memory.

"Tracy," I said, "did you ever have a nanny named Caitlin?"

She broke off informing her brother he was a dumb-ass retard. "I dunno." She shrugged.

She'd have only been about one or two—too young to remember. The siblings clambered out and were claimed by their respective nannies. I was almost certain my memory was right—that the second ex-Mrs. Lord, Caitlin Jones, had been a nanny here before going to work for Judie. I also seemed to remember she had left the Seiglers under the cloud of some scandal. . . .

My thoughts were interrupted by the sound of a beeper. Skye Castaneda dangled his shaggy head over the seat. "I have to use your phone," he announced.

"Don't be silly, we're two blocks away from your house," I told him.

"My mom says when she pages me I've got to call her immediately no matter what!" His complexion, I could see in the rearview mirror, was acquiring the interesting shade of split-pea green that generally presaged a vomiting fest. I floored it, and within seconds hit the drive to his family's neo-Georgian manse.

Patrice Castaneda came rocketing from the front door. Skye shot me a now-you're-gonna-get-it look and wriggled out, rump first. "*She* wouldn't let me use the phone," he piped.

"That's okay, darling. Go on inside—Mariella has your Fruit Roll-ups ready." Patrice fluttered excitedly over to my side of the car and bent to the window. "Lucy! I was paging Skye so I could talk to you." She had exceedingly wide-set eyes that, juxtaposed with an almost iridescent cap of pale hair, gave her the look of a glamorous insect. Her almost uncanny ability to pick up instantly on even the faintest trace of gossip in the air made it even easier to believe a pair of highly sensitive, if invisible, antennae waved above her head. "Did you hear about Cheryl Wade?" she chirped breathlessly.

I felt a tremor of alarm. "No, what about her?"

"She's at St. John's, in a coma. They think she's going to die!"

A sharp chill rose from my toes to the tips of my fingers. "What happened to her?" I asked hoarsely.

"Her cleaning lady came in this morning, well, I guess it was closer to noon, and found her still asleep, which wasn't that unusual for Cheryl. But after a couple of hours, the woman checked again, and Cheryl hadn't even moved, and then she noticed vomit on the pillow. So at that point she called the paramedics, who of course saw right away Cheryl wasn't sleeping but unconscious. They think it's suicide, that she took an OD of something. But they don't know for sure. I mean, they didn't find any empty pill bottles or anything."

"Was there a note? Anything to make it certain it was suicide?"

Patrice shook her shiny head. "Not that I heard of."

Nobody takes me seriously. Cheryl's last words to me reverberated as loudly as a shout in my mind; I saw her again hoisting her ludicrous backpack and marching gamely into her Alpine chalet. *You could be in danger too.*

I glanced at Chloe, who fortunately was still sealed up with Boyz II Men and hadn't heard a thing. "I've got to go, Patrice," I snapped.

"What?" The orthopterous eyes widened as, gunning the motor, I shot on past her.

At home, I hurried Chloe into the house, blessing the fact that Thursday was also one of my housekeeper's three regular days. Graciela nodded conversantly as I explained about the lice—*piojos* were apparently not an exotic phenomenon in her native Salvadoran village—and she and Chloe clattered merrily upstairs.

I propelled myself into the kitchen. Rummaged frantically through a drawer crammed with Thai takeout menus, ancient baby announcements, and crumpled grocery lists and fished out a business card. Dialed the number, shouted out a rather frantic message.

I was ensconced in the glamorous task of delousing my daughter's room, stripping off the Pocahontas sheets, imprisoning the stuffed toys in airtight plastic bags, when the gate buzzer sounded. I raced back downstairs and flung open the front door to Detective Teresa Shoe.

SEVEN

Terry Shoe hadn't changed much in the months since I'd last seen her. Same bunny rabbit–brown hair chopped off in a no-maintenance bob. Same hundred percent polyester wardrobe, today featuring a shapeless pants suit in a blend-into-the-crowd shade of buff. Same sensible shoes, in which she still walked with toes splayed out, like a duck. She gave a quick once-over to my own ensemble—vintage cowboy shirt printed with little lassos, sombreros, and cacti, paired with maroon clamdiggers. Judging from her knowing snort, it seemed I was pretty much living up to her own expectations as well.

She barreled into the house, squinting liberally around as if she were casing the joint. She was followed practically in lock step by another detective—not her usual partner, Armand Downsey: this one was a shortish, pock-marked Latino with weary, pouched eyes and the makings of what in several years would be a prodigious beer belly. If this had been a movie, he'd be the sidekick cop, the one who, ironically, gets gunned down with just a couple of days more to go before retirement.

"This is Detective Escovedo," Terry said. "Downsey's in court this week."

"A murder trial?" I asked eagerly.

"No, fighting a parking ticket. Yeah, of course a homicide. Hell of a case. Aggravating circumstances of necrophilia. Guy rapes and kills his next door neighbor, a surgical nurse and mother of three, buries her in his backyard. Then he digs her up the next day for the purposes of having intercourse again."

"Yuck," I said, echoing Chloe.

"It happened in the Mexican community, which is why it hardly even made the papers," Escovedo piped up. "If it was one of you movie people, it would've been front page."

We were silent a moment, contemplating the media frenzy that would no doubt ensue should some movie star or studio bigwig be caught having sex with a corpse. "Why don't we go into the kitchen?" I said abruptly and led the way.

"Hey, wait'll you taste this coffee," Terry told her partner. "She uses these special beans from Africa. It's as good as Starbucks."

It seemed that I was to be relegated to my old role of providing fresh-ground coffee for cops. Obligingly, I selected a Jamaican Blue Mountain blend, while the detectives settled at the recycled pine breakfast table. The shriek of the coffee grinder added to the outside cacophony of hammers, saws, and a jangle of *ranchero* music.

"Sorry about all the racket," I said, pouring filtered water into the Krups. "We're adding a few rooms on to the house."

"What, the place wasn't big enough already?" Terry asked bluntly.

Not for someone infected with The Hollywood Mogul Virus, was my sudden thought. The Taj Mahal wouldn't be big enough.

I explained to Terry the idea about wanting enough room to do my animation work at home. She nodded, then turned and nudged Escoveto.

"Hey, remember those cookie jars I told you about," she said. "They're on that shelf behind you."

He swiveled to check out my collection of old cookie jars in shamelessly kitschy shapes—begging Scotty dogs and acorn-noshing squirrels, an Uncle Sam with a chipped beard, a grinning, non-politically correct mandarin.

"They're a riot," Escovedo pronounced. "I guess you eat a lot of cookies, huh?"

"Mostly they're for display." I brought steaming Fiestaware cups to the table. "Look, I really didn't call you just to kibitz."

The two swiveled back, rather more, I thought, to attend to their coffee than to me.

"I think I might have uncovered a murder," I announced dramatically.

"Yeah, that's what your message said," Terry took a placid sip of her cup. "What gives you this brilliant idea?"

I slipped into a chair facing them. "You probably heard that a famous director named Jeremy Lord just died while making a film in New Mexico."

"Yeah, it was in all the news," Terry said. "And when I saw your name mixed up in it, I had to laugh." In fact, she laughed now, "hee, hee," the giggle that had more than once in the past made me fantasize throttling her.

"Then you probably also know," I pressed on, "that the official account was that he died of heart failure."

"Let me guess. You've got an *un*official account."

"As a matter of fact, I do. That he was murdered by some hard-to-detect poison. And if so, the autopsy performed in New Mexico totally overlooked it."

"Your small-time medical examiner's office is usually not the most thorough in its methods," pronounced Escovedo. "Or up to date. They'll run a standard toxicology scan but that might not turn up anything more exotic." Terry Shoe leveled an eye at him. He ducked his head and set to stirring the sugared sludge in his cup.

"You want to tell me who it was made this allegation?" Terry asked me.

"A woman named Cheryl Wade. Her sister's the actress Alison Wade, who used to be married to Jeremy." I filled them in on Cheryl's part of the story, through to her Jack-in-the-box impersonation in the back seat of my Cherokee, and her scoop that she had inadvertently caused the demise of the Maestro of Gore. "At the time, I didn't pay much attention," I finished. "I mean, she's practically the definition of the word *flake*."

"A flake how?" asked Terry.

"Scatterbrained. Never held much in the way of a job. And into astrology, faith healing, that kind of stuff. I wouldn't have been surprised if she'd told me the real murderer was an alien from Alpha Centauri."

Escovedo chuckled. Terry continued to regard me with a stone face.

"Now something's happened that does make me take it seriously," I went on. "Cheryl Wade was found in a coma this morning and taken to St. John's. They're calling it a suicide, but I don't believe it."

"Why not?" Terry Shoe demanded.

"For one thing, there was no reason for her to do it."

"I think that if I got the idea I'd killed my brother-in-law, whether accidentally or by intent, I might be remorseful enough to want to swallow a few pills myself."

"When I last saw her, she didn't seem remorseful. She seemed . . ." I thought for a moment. "Scared out of her wits." I picked up my own coffee cup and gripped it by its rim. "She believed Jeremy was killed by somebody rich and powerful enough to do anything they wanted, and she was terrified they were going to get her too. And now it sure looks to me like they have."

"I don't know," Terry said, shaking her head. "It sounds pretty far-fetched to me. And even if there was any hard evidence to back up any of this, I don't see there's anything we can do."

"But what about the whole tie-in with Jeremy's death?"

"You got an autopsy report listing natural causes. Even if you could prove it was incomplete, it's not like on TV—you just don't go exhuming a body at the drop of a hat."

"I'm sure you don't," I said. "Particularly when there's no body to be exhumed. It was cremated this morning."

Both sets of detective eyebrows shot skyward. "You know that for a fact?" Terry asked.

I nodded. "I ran into his first wife this morning. She's remarried, her name's now Judie Levritz."

"Levritz, like in all those housing developments out in the Inland Empire?" Escovedo asked.

"That's her husband. Anyway, she told me that this morning she and her two kids had scattered Jeremy's ashes in the Hollywood Hills. And she wasn't exactly in tears about it. In fact, she was practically whistling 'Zip-a-Dee-Doo-Dah.' "

"Then your only hope for real evidence is if the other victim dies," said Escovedo. Realizing how cold-blooded this sounded, he added flusteredly, "Not that anybody's hoping she dies, you understand. My hope is that she makes a full and complete recovery. . . ." His voice trailed off.

There was another ponderous silence. Mercifully, the phone rang. "Excuse me," I said and stepped over to the counter to pick it up.

"Hello, Lucy? It's Denise Schumer, Alison Wade's personal assistant. I had the pleasure of briefly meeting you last night?"

"Yes. Hi, Denise," I said. The two detectives both had ears cocked, unabashedly eavesdropping. In an attempt at privacy, I hunched over the counter and cupped the receiver.

"If it's not horribly inconvenient for you, Alison would love to have you come by the house tomorrow."

"Tomorrow?" I repeated with astonishment.

"I know it's, like, short notice, but with Alison's insane schedule . . ."

"It's not that," I said. "I just heard about Cheryl. I'd have thought that Alison would be far too upset to think about anything else at the moment."

"Well, naturally she's worried about Cheryl. But this movie's in preproduction, it's *got* to be delivered by March or we won't make a summer release."

"I see." I glanced back at Terry Shoe, imagining her reaction if she heard this: *There's typical Hollywood thinking for you. It doesn't matter who lives or dies, as long as the movie comes out on schedule.*

"Don't get me wrong," Denise pressed on. "Alison's extremely concerned about her sister. You might not have heard, but Cheryl's been pronounced brain dead."

"Oh, God," I breathed.

"Yeah." A weighty sigh issued from the other end of the receiver. "The doctors all advised pulling the plug. They said there's absolutely no hope she'll ever recover, but Alison won't hear of it. She's in*sisted* that Cheryl be kept on a respirator for as long as it's able to keep her breathing. Years, if that's what it is. And naturally Alison's picking up the entire tab."

"How generous," I said dryly. I could already visualize the tabloid headlines: DON'T PULL THE PLUG ON MY SISTER, CRIES HOLLYWOOD SUPERSTAR; SPARE NO EXPENSE TO KEEP HER ALIVE!

"So you see there's really nothing more to be done," Denise went on. "And Alison's really looking forward to meeting you. You can't imagine how much she respects your work. Should I tell her you'll be here?"

A new suspicion ticked into my mind. "Sure," I said. "I'm really looking forward to meeting her too." I jotted the Bel Air address Denise recited on the chalkboard beside the phone, then hung up and made tracks back to the table.

"I just heard some news," I announced. "Cheryl Wade's been pronounced brain dead."

"That's a damn shame!" Escovedo declared heavily, no doubt anxious to reestablish his compassionate-guy credentials. "A gal that young . . . that's a real tragedy."

"There's more," I said. "Her sister, Alison Wade, is paying to keep her indefinitely on a respirator, even though the doctors say there's no hope." My hands were trembling. To steady them, I gripped my coffee cup again. "Do you want to know how I see it?"

"It would make my life meaningful," Terry said.

I loftily ignored her sarcasm. "Let's assume for a moment someone *did* use Cheryl to poison Jeremy, and the same person has now tried to get rid of Cheryl. Alison Wade is the perfect suspect."

I knew enough not to expect any cries of *Eureka!* from Terry Shoe, but Detective Escovedo made no reaction either: Both continued to listen with faces carved of stone.

"Take a look at the facts," I plunged on. "Cheryl was deathly afraid of someone she said was rich and powerful, which of course Alison is. And from all accounts, Alison despised her ex-husband—possibly enough to want him dead." My words began to tumble out. "I also know that Cheryl had just been with her sister here in L.A. before heading back to New Mexico—so Alison would have had the opportunity of slipping her something lethal to pass on to Jeremy. And now Alison's conveniently prevented the possibility of an autopsy by keeping Cheryl on a respirator." I took a breath and sat back in my chair. "It all fits perfectly, right?"

"What about the first wife?" Terry remarked.

"Judie?" I gave a puzzled frown. "What about her?"

"She fits your bill too, doesn't she? Married to a rich guy. And seems to carry a grudge for the ex-husband—whose body she conveniently sent up in smoke."

This stopped me cold. "That's true," I admitted. "And Cheryl saw *her* that same weekend as well. She was bringing Jeremy's kids back home to her."

"So which one do you want us to put the cuffs on?"

I made an exasperated gesture. "Look, I know I haven't given you much to go on. . . ."

"That's the understatement of the year. We've got no bodies. We've got no jurisdiction. No hard evidence at all. Just hearsay from a witness who doesn't sound highly credible, not to mention can no longer testify."

The intercom between the kitchen and Chloe's room crackled and Chloe's voice piped up: "Mom, Ratty's escaped, and I can't find him anywhere."

I pressed the talk button on the monitor. "I'll be up in a few minutes to help you look." To the cops, I explained, "My daughter's got a pet rat snake. It seems to have gotten out of its tank."

"A pet snake?" Escovedo repeated.

"You still got that lizard under the bed?" Terry asked.

"Gordon the gecko." I nodded. "Last time I saw him, he was peeking out from behind an armoire in the dining room."

Escovedo had taken on the get-me-outta-here look of someone who was clearly convinced he'd stumbled onto the Addams Family. Terry rose to her feet, and he hurriedly followed suit.

"So that's it?" I said plaintively. "You're not going to do anything about this?"

"Like I said, I don't see there's a heck of a lot we can do." Terry shrugged.

"Look," I burst out, "the last time I saw Cheryl Wade, she warned me that I could be in the same danger she was. It might sound peculiar, but I don't happen to relish the idea of spending the rest of my existence in a vegetative state!"

Terry fixed her eyes on me. They were remarkable eyes, large, long-lidded, and deep-lashed, by far her best feature, with the extraordinary mood ring–like ability to change hues: At times they were a Bambi's Mom–ish mellow golden brown; at others, a rather flirty hazel; and, at their most disconcerting, they paled to the reflective yellow of a stalking cat's. At the moment, they hovered somewhere between the feline and the ungulate.

"I still think this sounds pretty far-fetched," she said testily. "But I'll tell you what. I'll do some asking around the station, just sort of casually. See if anything I hear lights up any buttons. In the meantime"—her eyes lightened ominously to a paler gold—"I strongly advise you to stay away from the whole shebang."

"I'd be delighted to," I said, "just as long as the whole shebang stays away from me."

✳

When they'd gone, I returned upstairs and joined in the hunt for Ratty the snake, who seemed, however, to have vanished into some hidden crack or crevice. Great, I thought—now we had two reptiles lurking beneath the furniture. Detective Escovedo was right, there was a distinctly Gomez and Morticia quality about my life, a thought that prompted me to return to Ms. Baljur's delousing program with greater vigor.

I had just finished imprisoning the last stuffed alligator in plastic when I heard a noise. A clack, as if someone had opened a cabinet door downstairs. But both Graciela and Chloe were in the adjoining bathroom, Chloe giggling and squealing while Graciela energetically scrubbed her scalp.

Just the cats, I told myself. But no—two puddles of fur on the freshly remade bed accounted for them both. Then perhaps the noise had come from outside, some last straggler of the construction crew packing up for the night. I peered out the window onto the darkening street. The crew trucks had all gone.

It was nothing, I assured myself—just my well-known hyperimagination running away with itself. And there was one simple way to prove it. I marched downstairs, making as much noise as possible with every step. At the foot of the staircase, I reached to the umbrella stand and grabbed the first handle I touched, listening hard. All was calm, all was quiet. I loosened my grip on my makeshift club, laughing at myself for my ridiculous paranoia.

And I was still laughing when footsteps started rounding from the living room.

EIGHT

"What in God's name are you doing?" Kit demanded.

I stared at him, still brandishing over my head what had proved to be a glazed Chinese parasol—a weapon that would have been singularly useless against any actual intruders, except for maybe slaying them with laughter. "Defending myself," I said, lowering it sheepishly. "I thought you were someone breaking and entering. What are you doing home, anyway?"

He was cradling a drink in his hand, tequila by the look and smell of it, a substance I felt I could well use myself. Now he raised it in a kind of Hail Caesar! salute. "The studio hired a new director. I'm here to meet him, get things jump-started. Then it's back to the set and get this damned movie on the road!"

Poor Jeremy, I thought; his ashes still swirling and swooping above the tiled rooftops of the Hollywood Hills, and already he'd been replaced. The great juggernaut of Hollywood moves on. "Who did you get?" I asked.

"An English guy, coming up from commercials. He did that great Bud Light ad in the last Super Bowl, the one where all the little beer cans colonize Mars. This'll be his first feature." Kit chuckled. "Lane says he'll be so grateful to be working with real actors instead of cats and dancing rolls of toilet paper, he'll do anything we tell him."

I gave a weak smile.

"You don't seem very excited," he said peevishly.

"It is exciting. It's just that I've had some bad news. About Cheryl Wade."

He nodded lugubriously. "I heard she'd attempted suicide."

"It seems it's no longer an attempt, but a *fait accompli*. She's only being kept alive by a respirator."

"Poor kid!" he sighed. "I feel like a complete shit for the way I talked about her. But hell, you remember what she was like, she seemed so totally flipped out. . . ." He downed a remorseful gulp of tequila. "God, I feel guilty."

Not half as guilty as I did. I resheathed the parasol in the umbrella stand and said, "Listen, something happened yesterday after Jeremy's memorial thing. I was driving back and Cheryl suddenly popped up in the back seat. She'd been hiding back there, waiting for me. Scared the hell out of me."

Kit regarded me with astonishment. "Cheryl Wade was hiding in your car?"

"Yeah. She wanted to talk to me undetected."

"About what?"

"She was convinced that someone murdered Jeremy, and that she might be next in line."

"Come on! You don't believe that, do you?"

I shrugged. "One's dead, and one's as good as dead. I find that a little suspicious."

"Then tell it to the police."

"I did. They practically yawned in my face. Said it sounded far-fetched."

"Which it does. If they see no cause to pursue it, then neither should you."

"Cheryl was scared stiff and begging my help, and I paid no attention," I said. "I think I owe her something. At the very least, to just ask around a little, see what I can dig up."

Kit's blond face flushed, as if with a sudden sunburn. "The last time you just 'asked around a little,' you nearly blew up my career and got yourself killed while you were at it."

"I find the order you put those things in extremely interesting," I flashed back.

"For sweet God's sake!" Kit glanced at his watch—a mogul-quality Rolex which had recently replaced his Goofy and Donald Duck

Swatches. "We don't have time to get into this now. Lane Reisman's taking us to Smithereens to meet this guy. We've got an eight o'clock reservation."

Lane, with his cop-a-feel hands and Perma-sneer—he was about the last person I wanted to see right now.

"I don't have to go, do I?" I said.

"Lane specifically invited you as well. It would be damned rude not to show up."

"I'll never get a sitter this late."

"I hear Graciela up there. I'm sure she won't mind staying." He bounded upstairs to go sweet-talk her in the idiomatic Spanish he'd picked up as a teenager when his family spent two years in Venezuela. I had no other excuse to wriggle out.

✳

Anyone who aspires to opening a trendy eatery in one of the ritzier districts of L.A. should be aware of one thing: that, while superb cuisine, an exciting ambience, and doting service might draw crowds in New York, Chicago, or San Francisco, what seems to really pack 'em in here is the celebrity status of the investors. Even who's cooking the food somehow takes a back seat to which stars have coughed up the hard cash to bankroll the kitchen.

Smithereens is a case in point. A breadbox-sized place tucked in a mini-mall off San Vicente, tables so jammed together you can participate in three conversations at once. The nouvelle Tex-Mex menu features twenty-one-dollar tostadas, refried turtle beans extra, and the minimalist decor is so reminiscent of Depression-era Automats you expect to see shabby men in fedoras slumped dispiritedly over chipped crockery mugs. Yet before it had even opened, the word had leaked out that among its investors were Sandra Bullock, John Travolta, and at least one of the regulars on *Seinfeld,* so that by its first week, there was already a five-day wait for reservations.

Lane Reisman, needless to say, had scored a table on the spur of the moment, a fact Kit had confided to me with a depressing measure of respect on our way over. A prime table, in full view of the door, so that Lane's was the first face registered by each new arrival. He had, I noticed, apparently managed to conquer his grief over his dear dead pal; in fact, he was in positively giddy spirits, regaling each table-hopper with the happy news that cameras were about to roll again. "We've got a brilliant first-time director," he repeatedly whooped. The Brilliant First-Time Director himself, a kid with a beaky nose and Sheriff of Nottingham facial hair, sat at Lane's side with the dazed expression of, say, Sylvester the Cat after being clobbered by the five-hundred-pound weight meant for the Tweety Bird.

Kit was trendily belting back Negronis, having detailed to the sullen young waitperson exactly how to make them ("Beefeater gin, just a splash of Campari, and orange *peel,* not a twist"), rather in the manner of James Bond and a martini. I'd opted for margaritas, rock salt, no ice, and downed three while picking at my swordfish tamale.

For distraction, I turned finally to Lane's date, a swan-necked brunette who'd been introduced only as Shawn and so far had opened her mouth only to insert a fork. "What do you do, Shawn?" I asked.

A look of intense concentration crossed her face, as if I'd asked her to compute pi to the first twenty decimal places. "I want to break into modeling?"

This came as no great surprise: The place was littered with models, actual or aspiring. At some recent point in time, the power date had switched from starlet to mannequin, but who exactly had blown the whistle and yelled, "Okay, all platinum blondes with significant cleavage out of the pool and all hipless six-footers with cheekbones in," I had no idea.

"That's great," I murmured, at which point our conversation seemed to hit an impasse. I returned to the more stimulating company of my drink.

Then, over Kit's shoulder, I glimpsed a familiar face working the room. It was Pamela Pemmel, an old film school buddy and former "men are the enemy!" radical feminist, now transmogrified into what the trades inevitably called the High Priestess of Publicity. She was heading full-bore our way, oozing her svelte behind through the needle-thin spaces between tables as effortlessly as if it were buttered. Back at NYU, Pam's daily uniform had been modeled on the bank-robbing attire of Patty Hearst—fatigues, combat boots, the occasional beret— but this ensemble had long since given way to the cutting edge of couture. This evening she featured a nubbly neon-orange top, paired with a hip-slung vermilion sarong, navel fashionably exposed. I was mildly interested to note it was an outie.

"Hello, you all," she cried. Her voice, richly cured by two and a half packs of Dorals a day, had the timbre and carrying power of a foghorn on San Francisco Bay. "You guys are the talk of the town! All the smart money said your movie would be canceled!"

"We're back on track and with a brilliant new director," Kit said, echoing Lane's rallying cry.

"I know, Frank signed with us last week." She blew an air kiss at the young director, who was gaping rather intently at the outie belly button. "Have you heard the news about Cheryl Wade?" she went on gaily. "She tried to off herself, and now she's been pronounced brain dead."

"How can they tell?" Lane quipped.

"For God's sake, Lane!" Kit said with disgust. I shot him a grateful look.

"I know, I'm bad," he said smoothly. "But this is a celebration," he added to Pamela. "You shouldn't be bringing us down."

"Believe me, I'm thrilled for you, darling. But speaking for myself, I've just lost a big, juicy client."

"Jeremy Lord was a client of yours?" I said.

She turned to me for the first time. Through the modern miracle of contacts, Pamela matched her eye color to her outfit; at the moment it was topaz, which lent her an odd kinship with Detective Shoe. "Yeah, he was one of my best," she said. "I worked on his very first film, and he stayed with me ever since, through thick and thin."

"You're the only woman in the known universe who can make that statement," spoke Lane.

I jumped up from my chair. "Pamela, let's go powder our noses." Before she could protest, I clamped her firmly by the arm and steered her toward the unisex bathroom.

"This is very nineteen fifty-six," Pamela remarked, as we entered the cubicle. "But of course, you've always been retro, haven't you?"

"Right from the cradle," I said, shutting the door behind us. The rest room, in curious contrast to the spartan dining room decor, was fitted up like a Tijuana bordello, strident pink-and-gold embossed wallpaper, Mexican tiles, brass faucets in the shape of perky bare-breasted mermaids.

Pamela turned to peer at her reflection in the rather murky mirror. "My eyes are itching like all hell," she said and deftly plucked out her contacts. Denuded of the lenses, her eyes were of two different colors—one hazel, the other a brilliant aquamarine, a phenomenon that had lent her a certain fame back in film school days. Seeing them now, I suddenly had an intense and displacing image of the Pam Pemmel of yesteryear: a sturdy girl in frizzy braids who had once advocated the cultivation of body odor as a feminist political statement.

Then she squirted Ocurest into the two-toned irises, reinserted the topaz discs, and the image disappeared: Here was once again the Pamela of today, the one who, the very *day* after her husband and partner, Jack Schwartzman, had dropped dead of a stroke while haranguing a valet outside Le Dome, had managed to revamp every logo in the office from the Schwartzman-Pemmel Agency to a brisk Pamela Pemmel & Associates.

I decided to get right to the point. "Pam, I've got reason to suspect that Jeremy was murdered."

Hot-breaking celebrity gossip was Pamela's favorite intoxicant: She whirled to face me, shimmering with ecstasy. "Tell, tell!" she commanded.

If I wanted to extract any information from Pamela, I knew I'd have to dole some out first: With the High Priestess of Publicity, it was strictly tit for tat. "I saw Cheryl Wade just yesterday," I said. "She told me that she had evidence that could prove Jeremy had been poisoned."

"Really?" Pamela's breathing suddenly became audible. "What kind of evidence?"

"She didn't tell me that. And now"—I paused for dramatic effect—

"she'll *never* be able to tell. It seems that whoever did in Jeremy also wanted to keep her mouth shut."

"My God! Did she give you any hint at all who it could be?"

"Only that it was somebody rich and powerful."

Pamela's eyes bugged out so wide, I was afraid the topaz lenses would go pinging across the room. "This is thrilling!" she gasped.

"I don't think Cheryl is too terribly thrilled about it," I retorted acidly.

"No, of course not, poor darling." She pulled a professionally long face, but the greedy excitement couldn't be suppressed for long. "And now I suppose you're going to investigate!"

"No, I'm not," I said firmly. "I'm just trying to dig up a little more information, so that maybe I can get the police interested." I rested a haunch against a piece of painted furniture, a sort of breakfront that served no discernible purpose other than to take up what little space remained in the room. "Since you worked with Jeremy for so long, I thought you might have some idea about who might have wanted to kill him."

"That's a no-brainer. Just about every woman in town under forty. He was an equal opportunity sexist pig." The corners of Pamela's mouth tightened with what seemed like nostalgic regret. "Most of my time for him was spent keeping his escapades out of the *National Enquirer*. You wouldn't happen to have a cigarette, would you?"

"Sorry, I quit years ago."

"And I can remember when you used to smoke like Vesuvius." Her voice threatened to become downright sodden with nostalgia.

"Getting back to Jeremy," I said crisply. "Does anyone more specific come to mind?"

"If I had to point my little finger, it would be in the direction of one of those ex-wives. Each one of them loathed him truly."

I felt a thrill, hearing my own suspicions echoed. "I know that Judie certainly did. She seems never to have gotten over being ditched for nanny Caitlin."

"Ah yes, Judie, our little cross-eyed Saint of Suffering. But you know, of course, it wasn't just that he ditched her that made her his mortal enemy. It was all the added Jeremy touches."

"What do you mean?"

"Well, to begin with . . ." Pamela boosted herself by her palms and perched on the edge of the sink basin. She had, I noticed, acquired a tattoo, a tastefully delicate rendition of a dolphin etched just above her left ankle. "You know Caitlin Jones?" she said.

"I know who she is. The second Mrs. Lord. Ascended to the title after being the nanny."

"Right. Well, Caitlin had originally been working for this couple, the Seiglers. Gail and Saul. He's some kind of accounting mojo at Disney."

I nodded. "The Seigler kids are in my car pool. And today, while I was dropping them off, I remembered that she'd worked there. Also that there'd been some kind of scandal."

"Yeah. Gail started to notice things were missing around the house. The odd piece of sterling here, a vase or a figurine there. Eventually she figured out that Caitlin was swiping them and passing them on to her twin brother, Ralph, and Ralphie, in turn, was fencing them to his underworld pals."

I recalled my glimpse of that angelic pair, two golden foreheads so innocently touching. "As I remember the story, though, nothing was ever proved."

"That's true. Caitlin hysterically maintained she was as innocent as the driven snow. But Gail wasn't having any of that and sent her packing. At which point, Judie Lord, the original bleeding heart, took her in, the way somebody else would take in a lame puppy. She even went traipsing all over town defending the honor of her new pet. And you know how she got rewarded? She came home one sunny old afternoon and found Miss Nanny going at it with Jeremy. Doggie-style, I believe," Pamela added coolly. "In the baby's room, right beside the bassinet."

I whistled. "I guess even the sainted Judie didn't stand for that."

"Hell, no. Caitlin once again got the immediate sack. Jeremy, though, was forgiven. Judie had long before this decided to turn a blind eye on all his tomcatting. Keeping the marriage together for the sake of the kids, blah, blah, blah. But also, I strongly suspect, to hang on to her title of Mrs. Hottest Young Director in Hollywood."

"Except, of course, she *didn't* hang on to it."

"Nope. Jeremy opted for the nineteen-year-old. Surprise, surprise. But here comes the beauty part. First of all, he delivers the news to Judie on their wedding anniversary."

"Yeah, she told me that," I said. "But I also heard he softened the blow with a sapphire and diamond bracelet from Cartier."

Pamela sniggered. "It was a fake. Rhinestones and zircons that he stuck in a Cartier box."

"So he was a tightwad on top of everything else?"

"Hell, no, it had nothing to do with money. He was already starting to rake in millions and throwing it around like confetti. But he knew that Judie would immediately march back to Cartier in a high dudgeon and try to return it, and she'd be told, 'I'm so sorry, madam, but this is paste' by those ultra-snotty clerks they breed there. Which is precisely what happened."

I could imagine the scene, Judie slinking out in disgrace before a store full of Beverly Hills matrons, browsing sugar daddies, and gawking Japanese tourists. "I can sure see why she nursed a grudge," I said. "But then, of course, Caitlin got dumped herself for Alison Wade."

The doorknob rattled. *"Occupado,"* barked Pamela. The rattling stopped abruptly.

"But again, it wasn't just the dumping," she continued eagerly. "It was the very special way he did it. You see, Caitlin desperately wanted kids. I mean, after all, she *was* a nanny. Finally, about two years after becoming Mrs. Lord, she managed to become pregnant. But it was an ectopic—very serious, she almost died, got rushed to the operating room just in the nick of time. But then while removing her tube, the doctors find she's got some hideous, runaway endometriosis, and they insist on doing an entire hysterectomy. So now get this. . . ." Pamela practically smacked her lips with the juiciness of her info. "While his wife's in surgery, having her womb sliced out of her body, Jeremy takes some gossip reporter to lunch and announces he's in love with his leading lady, Alison Wade. That they plan to get married and have scads and scads of kids!"

"He really was a world-class bastard!" I exclaimed. I was beginning to feel a sneaking sympathy for the person who had removed Jeremy Lord from society. "But that brings us to Alison. What did he do to earn her abiding hatred?"

"I don't know." Pamela pouted. Obviously this yawning gap in her intelligence net rankled her pride. "But there's one thing that's for sure. He sniffed out some particular weakness of hers and used it to humiliate her. That's what he was *really* into."

"Humiliating people?"

"Yeah, and particularly women. Probably some Freudian revenge thing on his mother." Pamela began swinging her crossed ankles, producing the optical illusion that the tattooed dolphin was actually leaping. I flashed on her late husband, Jack Schwartzman, a guy of the old school who'd thought Doris Day the pinnacle of feminine desirability; I wondered how he would have taken to finding himself suddenly mated to Lydia the Tattooed Lady.

"You know what Jeremy would do when some girl resisted his advances?" the Tattooed Lady was saying.

"I take it he didn't just send flowers."

She gave a snort. "Not exactly. He'd show up somewhere she was alone, like in an office after hours. Then he'd come on like the ultimate big brother, listening to her problems, all very sympathetic and hands off. And just when she thinks everything she's heard about Jeremy Lord is a dirty lie, that he's really this kindly supermensch, and she's ready to trust him with her life, he excuses himself to go to the little boys room. And then he pops out buck naked."

I lifted my head. That cleared up the mystery of Jeremy's pantsless corpse in the Chipotili john—Cheryl had obviously been about to get the director-in-the-raw surprise.

"It's a brilliant ploy, when you think about it," Pamela added. "You're trapped, you've got a naked man standing between you and the door. What are you doing to do?"

"How about calling the cops?"

"Yeah, right, and have the entire Wild Bunch on the warpath against you? You'd be dead meat in this town. Those guys stick together like Krazy Glue. You know about the scavenger hunts, don't you?"

I shook my head. "What scavenger hunts?"

"It's a Wild Bunch thing. Part of those debauched get-togethers of theirs. They make each other lists of tasks to be accomplished—mostly getting well-known women to do something pretty compromising. And there has to be photo documentation of it. They go off in teams of two or three, and the team that comes back with the most Polaroids wins. I was on the last list," she added. "Three of them showed up at my house at one in the morning. The task was to get 'Pamela Pemmel kissing ass.'"

"Did you do it?" I asked dubiously.

"You bet I did. There's a snapshot in wide release of me planting a big wet one on Lane Reisman's butt. After all," she said smoothly, "you're nobody unless you've made it onto a Wild Bunch scavenger list." She shot me a smug look, no doubt to underscore my own inherently nobody status.

The doorknob-rattler changed tactics and began an importunate rapping. "I think we better get out of here," I said.

"Yeah, you're right. I've got a table full of Brit journalists who've probably got their bloomers in a bundle thinking I've stuck them with the check." Pamela slithered her butt off her perch, gave a perfunctory pat to her sleek-as-a-seal dark hair. "Speaking of darling Mr. Reisman . . ." she said, "what about him? Maybe *he* sent Jeremy into Never-Never Land."

"Lane?"

"Why not? *A Merry Christmas* was the first movie he green-lighted as head of production, and everyone knew that Jeremy was sending the budget way out of control. Plus the scuttlebutt was that it was headed for major flopville. Lane had everything to gain from Jeremy's death and everything to lose by his staying alive."

"Do you really think Lane is capable of murder?" I said.

Pamela arched an expertly tweezed eyebrow. "Babycakes! You don't get as far and as fast as our darling Lane has without being a killer at heart."

She nonchalantly pushed open the door.

"It's about time!" A guy stood pacing irately in front of the door. With a shock, I recognized the golden cap of hair, the wispy gold goatee.

"Why, Ralph Jones!" Pamela boomed, "I was just bandying about your name!"

He stared at her. From his sudden change of expression, I had the certainty that, had he happened to have a switchblade handy, he would have slit our throats, effortlessly and without a single twinge of remorse. I hopped a self-protective step backward. Then instantly, his features softened; he appeared once again as guileless and beneficent as any Fra Angelico angel. "Good things, I hope," he said, smiling.

"Only the best. Send my love to your fabulous sister." Pam smacked the air in his general direction and led me away. "Everybody now probably thinks we're a couple of lesbians," she declared in a tone probably intended to be discreet, meaning it only carried to the immediate three or four tables. "I hope so. It's so chic to be a dyke these days. Now remember, Lucy, my love, we've got a pact. The *second* you get any leads on this, you call me. Any time, night or day."

Exactly when I'd entered such a pact escaped me. But Pamela had already veered toward a table occupied by five men who had reached that stage of drunkenness where such items as the salad fork, the pepper mill, and the waiter's shoes had become objects of high hilarity. "My God, they've probably cleaned me out of cigarettes," she cried and scurried off.

I returned to my own table and found it now wreathed in smoke. Everyone including Shawn was puffing on a cigar. For reasons I found baffling, cigars had become the hottest rage in Hollywood: People who hitherto had consumed only the purest of bottled waters and permitted only the most pesticide-free foodstuffs to pass their lips were suddenly lighting up phallic sticks of tobacco; starlets who, on a fat day, weighed in at a hundred and five pounds were affecting stogies that would have been the envy of Edward G. Robinson. It had become *de rigueur* to have a source for contraband Cubans, preferably some shadowy figure referred to only by his *nom de tabac,* such as Duardo or Habana Bill, the way hippies used to score pot from dealers known as Electric Larry.

"So what were you two doing in there?" Lane asked with a leer.

"You know Pamela, she loves to dish," I said evasively.

He extended a small humidor to me. "Don Ramons, in eighteen-year-old Cameroon wrappers, each one signed and numbered by the employee who rolled it. Rated outstanding by *Cigar Aficionado.*"

I shook my head, wondering if I was meant to smoke it or have it framed and hung on the wall. Then I glanced at Kit, who was rather self-consciously conveying one to his lips. "When did you take up smoking?"

"I haven't taken up smoking. I just like to indulge once in a while in a good cigar." He added, a little too quickly, "Lane thinks he can get me into The New Cubana."

"The what?" I asked.

"It's the club with all the movie stars that you have to be a member to get into," piped up Shawn. An entire sentence issuing from the formerly mute lips made us all start.

"There's at least four hundred names on the waiting list, but I can leapfrog Kit right in," Lane declared. "Ralphie Jones is a silent partner and he owes me a couple of favors."

I stared at Kit across the table. Could this really be my husband? I wondered. The same guy who habitually dashed off checks to the Sierra Club and couldn't pass a panhandler cold? The former non-hot shot whose most exclusive membership to date had been with Blockbuster Video?

And if it was, would that part of him ever find its way back?

*

When we returned home, Kit quickly undressed, gave a token pass to his dazzling teeth with the electric brush, and tumbled into bed. "I feel a little woozy," he muttered. "Must have been the cigar. Go ahead, say, 'I told you so.'" He fell instantly asleep.

I, on the other hand, lay awake for hours, ticking off a list of my anxieties. I was afraid that (1) the fertility pills were definitely making my feet expand to the size of Bozo the Clown's, and (2) it was all for nothing since, at the rate our sex life was currently going, any baby we had would have to be by immaculate conception, and (3) before even that could happen, Kit would get seduced by the Wild Bunch into shucking off his family in favor of such testosteronal activities as heli-copter skiing and bimbo-nailing, which wouldn't matter anyway, since (4) whoever dispatched Jeremy and Cheryl was about to come after me as well. . . .

Unless somehow I could manage to find out who it was first . . .

Kit murmured something that sounded like "Rin Tin Tin" and heaved over onto his side; as he did, a slight reek of stale cigar smoke wafted up from his hair. I suddenly had a vivid recollection of Jeremy Lord's dead face: the eyes bulging like grapes in stark terror, the con-torted, horrified rictus of the mouth . . . I squeezed my own eyelids shut, willing the gruesome portrait out of my mind.

But it stubbornly refused to go away.

Part

2

NINE

A rattletrap Ford pickup with Montana "Big Sky" license plates was pulled over to the shoulder of Sunset Boulevard, reeled in by a waving Hispanic teenager and a sign shouting MAPS TO STARS' HOMES. The Montana folks were in for a letdown, I thought, as I passed by. These roadside maps were notoriously out of date—most of the stars they featured had long since relocated to that great celebrity estate in the sky, their homes now occupied by the newest rich: talent agents, cardiologists, and music video directors. For a moment I entertained the notion of stopping and informing the truck's passengers that they were scarcely a half mile away from the bona fide current address of Alison Wade. But in the end, I continued on and turned through the portals of Bel Air's West Gate.

The fact that Alison Wade had almost single-handedly brought glamour back to Hollywood was by now a cliché, dragged into every article and interview written about her. There were probably even a few doctoral dissertations being churned out on the subject: How, after several decades in which leading ladies seemed intent on making themselves as frumpy as librarians, Alison looked always ready for her close-up. Never showed her face unless it was as flawlessly made up as Dietrich's. Hair always sensational, either tumbling in rich cascades to her shoulders, Rita Hayworth-style, or swept up in a beware-the-temptress loose French twist. And she always dressed to kill: little gem-colored couture suits that molded to her splendid curves, gowns that plunged and swirled and sparkled, hats with sweeping brims à la Garbo.

Even the story of her rise to stardom seemed the concoction of an old-time studio's publicity machine. Grew up in a dying little town at the foot of the Rockies, single mom struggling to make ends meet on disability. Knocked about after high school in a series of dead-end jobs, outstandingly as a bowling shoe dispenser at a Denver Snack 'n' Bowl. Then one dazzling autumn afternoon, she attended a Broncos game. During a lull in the action, a bored cameraman swept the bleachers and picked out a stunning girl in a flamingo-pink tube top, dreamily lapping a strawberry ice cream cone. He flashed her up on the big board. The crowd went wild.

Within a week, the producers of the daytime soap *Southampton* had tracked her down and cast her in the unlikely part of an idealistic marine biologist, no doubt because it called for her to sport a wardrobe consisting almost entirely of wet suits. Alison proved so sizzling in the role that the other actresses (at least, according to Alison) banded together and demanded the character be terminated; after one season, young Dr. Liddy Calhoun perished tragically in a freak tidal wave off Montauk Point.

Alison had been knocking around B movies for five or six years when Jeremy Lord began casting *Body Language.* The female lead was the part of a bisexual D.A. with a penchant for first bedding her defendants, then deftly slitting their throats; the role demanded a brief but steamy girl-to-girl seduction scene, and no star would touch it. A career killer! gasped their agents. You'll be branded a lesbo for life!

So Jeremy took a chance on the relatively unknown but indisputably ravishing Alison Wade, and once again the crowd went wild. Far from being branded a lesbo for life, she shot instantly to the top of the A-list, vaulting over Julia Roberts, leaving Michelle Pfeiffer in her dust . . . and incidentally scooping up Jeremy Lord in the process.

I did a quick mental review of all this as I pulled up to Alison's imposing gates. I was feeling somewhat nervous, possibly because my own glamour quotient at the moment was approximately zilch. The phones had begun chiming importunately for Kit at 7:00 A.M.; the hammering started thirty minutes later. Then Chloe, climbing into the dragoness Halloween costume I'd spent the better part of a week constructing, ripped the tail off. I patched it back on, then raced her to school and waited anxiously in the nurse's station while her scalp passed muster under a high-intensity lamp. Then back home, through a heat wave that had already soared to ninety degrees, to discover the builders had knocked through a back wall, and everything, including the clothes in my closet, was frosted with a fine whitish dust. As an additional surprise, this was the day Harold had selected to shut off the water, the upshot being that my hair now hung in a harridan's stringy mop and my clothes gave off little poofs of dust with every movement.

I announced my name into a phone mounted into a miniature sentry's station; with a great creaking and groaning, the gates parted. A sycamore-lined drive propelled me to a massive Norman-style stone mansion—an architecture no doubt intended to invoke romantic *Wuthering Heights* allusions, but that made me rather more suspect that Igor would open the enormous iron-grilled door.

The door was opened, however, by a fat Mexican woman wearing a HAPPY BIRTHDAY, MICKEY T-shirt. She executed a wordless sidestep, which I took as an invitation to enter into a sepulchral atrium. *"Momentito,"* muttered the woman and left me alone.

Alone metaphorically though not in actual fact. It's often struck me how extremely unprivate the private lives of celebrities generally are, and Alison's was no exception. The joint was jumping: Women with Dustbusters and electric brooms puttered in and out, passing men with claw hammers and tape measures. A FedEx messenger clambered downstairs, followed by a stately old lady cradling a bouquet of dead flowers. Frenetic young people ran in and out, without a glance in my direction. From outside issued an equal amount of activity, leaf blowers and lawnmowers, the grumble of a car engine turning over, and the familiar *whack, whack, bam!* of construction.

After some minutes of cooling my heels, I decided to explore and wandered into an adjoining room. It was also vast, the ceilings high enough to cause nosebleeds, the rough-hewn granite fireplace fit to roast an entire cow. Some hapless interior decorator had labored hard to warm it up with cabbage-rose chintz divans and muted Chinese rugs, but the Valhalla-like proportions defeated all efforts: The room was about as homey as a bank vault.

Several dozen framed photographs were crammed on a mantel. And every one of them, I discovered, was of Alison. Alison in soft focus. A laughing Alison on skis. Alison in shades, lounging in a director's chair. In a few, she shared the limelight with a costar, friend, or fan. Nothing of Jeremy, which was hardly surprising.

But also nothing of her sister, Cheryl.

"God, I'm so sorry to have kept you waiting!" Denise Schumer came bounding into the room. She was wearing another trendily trashy outfit, this one a clash of plaid separates, and once again she had paired it incongruously with the same plastic headband. If she found my own Harriet Homeless appearance disconcerting, she tactfully kept it to herself.

"Aren't those pictures fabulous?" she gushed. "Alison is so incredibly photogenic."

"Yeah, and so incredibly self-effacing," I returned.

Denise removed her headband and raked her hair from browline to crown. It was apparently a nervous tic, since the gesture effected no appreciable difference to her lank hairdo. "You've got to have an enormous ego to become a star." She shrugged, snapping the band back on the top of her head. "I could never do it. I mean, like fat chance anyone would ever make me a star anyway." She let out a little laugh that culminated in a snort.

For some reason, a song suddenly ran through my head. "Too many fish in the sea . . ." An old Motown hit that was a regular on the oldies station that provided my favorite driving soundtrack. I even knew the name of the group who had done it—the Marvelettes. But why Denise Schumer should make me start mentally humming a sixties girl-group tune was mystifying.

"Come on upstairs," she said, leading the way. "Alison's dying to meet you."

We trudged up a steep stone staircase, meant no doubt to seem baronial but somewhat more reminiscent of a dungeon.

"It's kind of a gloomy house, isn't it?" I remarked.

"Well, it was really Jeremy's choice. They bought it right after they got married."

This made sense. Jeremy's aesthetic had definitely leaned toward the dungeonesque.

"If you think it's gloomy now, you should've seen it then," Denise went on. "It had been empty for a long time before they bought it, and it was a real pit. I mean, disgusting. Rats everywhere—you could hear them scrambling around in the walls. And the plumbing was so bad that sometimes when you turned on the faucets in a bathroom, shit would come out. I mean real shit, you know, human waste. Plus there were nests of black widows in the cellar, and they'd come crawling up out of the heating ducts."

"Very homey," I said.

"Of course, everything's been totally redone now. And besides, Alison's hardly ever here. Half the time she's off on location, and then she's got three other places—the house in South Beach, the ski place in Sun Valley, and now she's fixing up a loft in TriBeCa. Same building as De Niro's."

I murmured something meant to sound suitably impressed.

The stairs led up to a thickly carpeted hall. "This entire wing is Alison's bedroom suite," announced my tour guide as we padded down the hall. She flung open a set of double doors; we stepped into a boudoir done entirely in varying shades of champagne.

A wiry black woman sat in a rosé satin upholstered chair, thumbing through a copy of *Men's Health;* she glanced up and scrutinized me as warily as if I'd just wriggled in through a window.

"This is Laraine, Alison's bodyguard," Denise said brightly.

"I'll have to look in your bag," Laraine said.

I handed her the vintage green crocodile clutch I was carrying. She rummaged briefly, then thrust it grudgingly back at me, obviously disgruntled at not being able to expose me as a secret assassin.

"You're clear," she grunted.

"Laraine used to be with the Cincinnati police force," Denise informed me as we moved on. "Alison hired her away by offering her triple her salary. It was after Alison had a stalker last year."

"Didn't it turn out to be just a kid?" I said. "Fifteen or sixteen, and went to high school in the Valley?"

"Yeah, but he managed to get into the house twice, which freaked Alison. Anyway, the younger they are, the crazier."

We headed into the bedroom proper, dominated by a huge bed so tented with gauze I almost expected Omar Sharif to pop his head out of it. It did not surprise me that I was meeting Alison in her boudoir, since she was notorious for conducting business in *intime* circumstances: She had once demanded that an interviewer from *Esquire* join her in a spa bath of cornmeal and rose essence, and reportedly she'd fired her last agent while having her legs waxed. I was prepared to find her wearing nothing but a towel or peek-a-boo lingerie, or even nothing but her birthday suit.

What she happened to be wearing was an evening gown.

It was a frothy concoction of lilac blue, with a gathered strapless top and billowing from the waist in at least a hundred yards of tulle. Some dozen other equally sumptuous dresses were strewn like rags on chairs or the carpet, as Alison stood before a three-fold mirror, turning herself this way and that.

"What do you think of this one?" she asked me, as if in the middle of an ongoing conversation. "Do you think this shade makes my skin too yellow?" She stroked a creamy arm. "I've got a feeling I look like I've got what's-it-called, hepatitis B."

"You look fine," I said. This was an understatement. She looked utterly and depressingly sensational.

"Alison's been invited to dinner at the White House," Denise piped up. "The designers all want her to be seen in their stuff, so they send her samples."

"The rich get fucking richer," Alison declared with a mirthless chuckle and corkscrewed at the waist to glimpse her flawless back. I studied her for a resemblance to Cheryl. Both were tall, with full mouths and slightly tilted gray-green eyes, but where Cheryl's long limbs always seemed to be flailing in two or three directions at once, Alison moved with the fluid grace of a panther. And in contrast to Cheryl's clownishly overblown lips, Alison's perfect bow would make strong men weep.

"This sucks," she pronounced. "It looks like prom night in Bakersfield."

"Maybe you should go back to the Lagerfeld," Denise suggested.

"Go back to the Lagerfeld?" Alison's voice was corrosive with scorn. "Exactly which Lagerfeld would that be? The one that made my hips look like the seventh wonder of the world? Like the great fucking wall of China? Is that the one you mean?"

"You're right, dumb idea," Denise gasped. "Which one do you think?"

"I'll decide later. Get me out of this frigging thing."

Denise scrambled to undo the zipper. The gown shimmered to the floor. Alison, now clad in the black lace undies I'd expected in the first place, stepped out of the ocean of lilac tulle and gave it an indelicate kick to one side. Another of what seemed a legion of Mexican women appeared from a hidden antechamber with a chiffon robe, which Alison shrugged on. "Five years ago I didn't know Chanel from shit, and now I'm supposed to be their walking clothes hanger," she sighed. Over-whelmed by the burden of advancing the cause of *haute couture*, she sank languidly onto a daybed.

"Here, Lucy, sit here." Denise pulled a tufted chair from a dressing table and placed it opposite the prone Alison. I awkwardly took a seat.

"How come my guest has nothing to drink?" Alison demanded.

"But Alison, you're on that fast," Denise whimpered. "You're not even allowed water before noon."

"Excuse me, but does that mean my guest has to fast as well?"

"I just thought—"

"Just a glass of water," I quickly told Denise.

"Tŷ Nant or Perrier?"

"Either one."

She turned and fled. Suddenly I was alone in the room with Alison Wade, world-famous movie star and possibly also cold-blooded dis-patcher of family members both former and current. I had a flash of paranoia. What if this was a trap? Perhaps she knew what I suspected, and this was all just a pretense to lure me here where I'd meet with some precipitous and regrettably fatal accident. Maybe a plunge off those steep stairs . . . or more likely a drop of something slow-acting and undetectable in my glass of Perrier. . . .

"Lucy Freers," Alison murmured.

I glanced up, startled. She was eyeing me thoughtfully. "You are a genius," she pronounced.

I gave a tinkly I-wouldn't-exactly-say-that laugh.

"You are," she insisted. "Your films are brilliant. They display a natural lyricism in the use of color and line, combined with an even rarer talent for storytelling."

"Thanks," I said uncertainly: What she'd said sounded eerily like something I'd heard before. Then I realized I *had* heard it before: in a *Hollywood Reporter* review of a short film I'd had at Sundance several years ago. Alison had simply learned her lines. I began to have the even eerier suspicion she'd never seen my animations at all. My paranoia rose several degrees.

"Tell me about Jeremy," she said abruptly.

I gave a start. "What do you mean?"

"I mean, how did he look when he died? Did it seem like he suffered much?"

"To be honest, yeah, it did. It looked to me like he died horribly. There was an expression on his face I can't even describe. And I can't seem to shake it out of my mind."

I watched her own face for some telling expression, such as satisfaction or triumph; instead, she sighed again, this time with a dramatic heave of her bosom.

"Poor boy," she said heavily. "I cried like there was no tomorrow when I heard the news. And then I went on an eating binge, stuffing my face for the rest of the week. That's why I'm on this miserable fasting thing now. I'm supposed to stick my body in front of a camera three weeks from today, and it would be a damned lousy career move if I looked like the Goodyear Blimp."

It struck me that Alison and her late ex-husband had had at least one thing in common: the ability to deflect any topic of conversation instantly back to themselves.

"I'm a little surprised you were so upset by Jeremy's death," I ventured.

"Why?" she said sharply. "It's because of the media, isn't it? All that crap they write about me. They always paint me as this cold, un-feeling bitch, and it's not true. I happen to be a very sensitive and generous person. As long as someone's not trying to screw me, I'll do the *world* for them."

"I'm sure you would," I said. "But frankly, I'd always heard that you hated Jeremy's guts."

Her lips pursed into a startlingly Cheryl-like moue. "Jeremy and I . . . well, it's kind of hard to explain. What we had was a love-hate relationship. We were desperately, passionately in love, but if we'd stayed together, we'd definitely have killed each other. In fact," she added briskly, "he did try to kill me once."

I leaned forward. "He did?"

She tilted her head back, closed her lids. "It was on one of those white-water rafting trips with those pals of his. You know, that gang of Wild Bunch assholes who are always trying to prove their *cojones* by shooting the rapids and crap like that. Of course, they all had about six guides apiece to keep them safe and sound." She opened her eyes and sniggered.

"I thought no women were allowed on those Wild Bunch jaunts," I said.

"And just who was going to stop me?" she shot out. I shrugged, conceding the point. "Anyway, there were about a dozen of us crammed onto this raft, getting tossed down the goddamned Colorado River, and naturally Jeremy and I got into one of our drag-outs. Christ knows about what—it could have been the price of tuna fish, anything would set us off. Suddenly we hit the most treacherous part of the rapids, what they call number four white water. Most of those guys were so pissing scared, I thought they were going to start crying for their mommies." She laughed, relishing the memory. "But then suddenly I felt Jeremy's hands on my shoulders, gripping me hard. And the next thing I knew, I was being thrown into the water."

"Are you sure? I mean, maybe he was trying to hold on to you, and it was the bucking of the raft that threw you off."

"No," she said evenly. "He wanted me to die. At least at that point in time. Luckily I was swept right to the banks, and then about a dozen guides came jumping in after me."

I hesitated, then, what the hell, took a chance: "There must have been a few times you wanted to kill him, too."

She grinned tightly. "About ten times a day. But only when we were actually married. Once we were divorced, we became the very best of friends. I could always go to him for anything, any kind of favor."

"Like getting a job for your sister?"

The grin stretched to its limits. "Yeah, just like that."

We were interrupted by Denise bearing a tray that bristled with a forest of small, colorful bottles. "There wasn't any Perrier, so I brought a selection to choose. There's Solé, Pellegrino, Tŷ Nyant, some Danish one. . . ." She set these waters of the world at my feet, glancing optimistically at Alison for a flicker of approval.

I chose a bottle at random and poured a glass, but with visions of strychnine still bobbing in my brain, stopped short of actually taking a sip. "I'm really very sorry about Cheryl," I continued to Alison. "There's no chance of a recovery at all?"

"None." She gave a resigned little shrug. "What can I say? My sister was determined to self-destruct sooner or later."

"You think she really did attempt suicide, then?"

"Of course she did," Denise piped up. "It's plain as day."

"But for what reason?" I pursued.

"The obvious reason." Alison paused dramatically. "Because she could never be me, no matter how hard she tried. Her last pathetic attempt to have an affair with Jeremy was so typical. When even that failed, I think she just gave up."

"I don't think she was trying to seduce your ex-husband," I said. "I think it was the other way around."

"Oh, I'm sure Jeremy was willing and able. He couldn't keep his prick in his pants for more than two seconds at a time. But I hope you weren't taken in by my sister's Poor Little Miss Innocent routine. Cheryl was a real user." Alison quivered indignantly. "Even when we were kids, she had the act down pat. She'd come on all klutzy and helpless, while I went out and fought all the battles, and in the end, she'd get exactly what she wanted. The Barbie dolls, the darling little outfits, the pony rides, you name it!"

"She didn't get what she wanted the other week."

Alison cocked an eyebrow.

"I mean when she came to see you before going back up to New Mexico. And you refused to keep up her car payments."

She shrugged again, this time defensively. "The only time she ever showed up here was to try to grub some money. So she was finding it tough to work for a living—my heart was bleeding for her. *I* had to fight tooth and claw to get where I am now, but Cheryl seemed to think it was my natural purpose in life to keep her alive."

"Then it's kind of ironic, isn't it, that now you are?"

This time I'd gone too far, I thought. I braced myself for an attack.

But to my surprise, Alison's eyes moistened. Her voice acquired a grieved little catch. "What else could I do? She's my baby sister. I'm really the only one she has left in the world. And naturally I'm staggered by guilt. If I'd had the *least* suspicion she'd actually go through with something like this, I'd have given her a car. I'd have given her anything her heart desired."

The trouble with investigating a murder in the Hollywood community, I'd previously discovered, is that you inevitably come across actors. If your suspects are limited to, say, manicurists, or lion tamers, or nuclear engineers, it's probably a snap to detect the classic signs of lying. A damp brow. Shifting eyes. The patently phony tone of voice. But when you're dealing with people who get paid to convincingly fake being serial killers or nuns, you never quite know where you stand.

And I supposed I *was* investigating murder, since I'd definitely blown any chance I'd ever had of working on Alison's movie.

"Uh, Alison . . ." Denise was glancing at the screen of a pocket-sized computerized datebook. "It's twelve thirty-five. You're meeting Jack for lunch at one o'clock."

Alison sprang to her feet. "You wait till now to tell me, you idiot? Marta," she screamed, "get me dressed!"

A middle-aged woman whose white pants suit lent her the incon-

gruous look of a dental hygienist scurried in from whatever antechamber had also produced the Mexican maid: with an air of almost operatic
drama, she began flinging open closet doors.

"I called the Bel Air and told them exactly what you can and cannot eat," Denise said. "They won't even give you a menu."

Alison whirled. "And what's Jack going to think? I'll tell you
what—that he's having lunch with a gross, fat pig who goes out of
fucking control at the sight of a menu, that's what!"

"I'll call them back and change it!" Denise fairly shrieked.

"And where the hell's the script? Why haven't you given Lucy a
copy of the script?"

Denise now looked as if artificial resuscitation would momentarily
be required. "But the latest revisions haven't been incorporated, so I
didn't think . . . I mean, they're back at the offices. . . ."

At a glance from Alison, her mouth snapped shut.

"My Cro-Magnon assistant will deliver the script to your home by
the end of the day," Allison said to me. "I'm so thrilled you're going to
be joining us on this project."

She turned abruptly to her dresser. Denise was already huddled
with a phone, frantically trying to rectify her menu gaffe. "Don't worry,"
I said to no one in particular, "I'll just see myself out."

I was trudging my way down the grim stairwell when words echoed
from upstairs: ". . . to keep her goddamned mouth shut!" It was Alison's
voice, strident and agitated. I stopped, straining to hear more. After
several fruitless minutes I continued on, wondering, with a shiver that
wasn't caused by the dank stone, if she had been talking about me.

T EN

I'd been home for scarcely an hour when a car pulled into my driveway. It was a white Range Rover, a vehicle built to sustain mighty treks across the savanna, now become Hollywood's choice for navigating such rugged terrain as Rodeo Drive. This one, though, did appear to be fresh from safari, since three huge animal heads were nosing out the back windows. I headed out for a closer look. The jungle beasts metamorphosed into dogs, two slavering Weimaraners and a Great Dane. Denise, looking even more harried than usual, jumped out of the driver's seat, waving a maroon-covered script.

"Those Alison's dogs?" I asked.

"Yeah. Revolting beasts—they've got the run of the whole house. Alison finally noticed they've torn up half the furniture, so now I've got to haul them to the vet to get their toenails clipped." The dogs, as if understanding, began to bark in furious complaint. "Shut up!" Denise screeched. "They've been like that the whole way over."

"It's none of my business," I said, "but it seems like you put up with a lot from Alison."

"You mean I act like her slave? You don't have to tell me that." She gave a self-effacing shrug. "It's been my dream all my life to work in movies. I've got no talent—I mean, to act or write or anything—but I'd love to break into the production side. Like, me and a hundred thousand other guys, right? But this way, being personal assistant to Alison Wade, I meet everybody, and I hear everything that's going on, all the stuff they don't teach you in film school. I can do favors for people, stuff that might pay off later. So if I have to take shit for a while, well, everybody's got to pay dues." She added with almost pathetic eagerness, "I met this guy at Bar Marmont the other night, he's now a VP at Paramount, but you know how he started out? His job was to make sure the pens on Francis Ford Coppola's desk were exactly lined up by size."

"You know how I started out?" I said. "I was an inker for a comic book artist. He thought he was Michelangelo painting the Sistine Chapel, the only difference being that instead of God, he had a super-hero with scorpion powers called The Sting. My main job was to assure him he was brilliant about twenty times a day."

"Then you understand!" Denise gazed at me with newfound devotion. "So here's the script," she said, presenting it to me. "I'm such a complete idiot not to've had it before—I should've *known* Alison would want you to see it right away."

I accepted it gingerly, wondering if this was somehow connected to making me keep my mouth shut. "Does this mean I'm hired?"

"Well, there'll have to be a meeting at Keystone to tell them your ideas, but I wouldn't worry about that. If Alison really wants you, the studio's not going to put up a fuss. Lane Reisman's an even bigger toady to Alison than I am." Denise sniggered.

"But are you sure Alison really wants me?"

"Absolutely. I told you, she adores your work. Anyway, she won't want to go making any changes now, because she's kind of distracted." Denise plucked off her headband and did a quick scalp-rake. "Can you keep a secret?" she asked.

"Sure," I said quickly.

"Alison's getting married!"

"Oh," I said, a bit flatly—I had expected some darker revelation. "Who to?" Since she had separated from Jeremy, her name had been linked with almost every leading man in town.

"His name's Jack Jampol. He's a dermatologist. After Alison's last movie, when she got back from location in Cuernavaca, she came down with this disgusting rash. This oozing, crusty stuff all over her face and body. She went to four different specialists, and nothing. Then finally she went to Jack, and he got rid of it right away."

"How erotic." I grinned.

"Oh, but he's a really sexy guy. You know how he proposed? He chartered a private jet and had it totally filled up with orchids, and then they flew to a private island in Hawaii, where he'd rented this gorgeous villa overlooking a waterfall. And when Alison walked in, it was filled with wedding gowns and wedding cakes and bridal bouquets. Isn't that like awesomely romantic!' Denise's face blurred with a wistful Some-Day-My-Prince-Will-Come expression. "Anyway, she's going to announce the engagement officially on Leno next week. That's why it's gotta be kept a secret."

The construction crew, back from a break, started in suddenly, and the dogs, not to be outdone, put up a fresh ruckus. "Would it be too much trouble if I got some water for the dogs?" Denise asked.

"Of course not. Come on in." I led the way into the half-demolished disaster area that was currently my kitchen.

"Sorry everything's such a mess," I said. This had become my automatic refrain. I began rummaging for an old bowl that would serve as a dog dish.

"I'm used to it," Denise said. "Alison's always having stuff done on her houses, tear this down, put this up. You'd think she'd want some peace and quiet for a change." She took a peek into the dining room, which I'd festooned with Halloween decorations of my own design, strings of jitterbugging skeletons, witches, and ghosts. "Cool decorations! God, I wish I was just one-tenth as creative as you."

"I'm sure you've got plenty of your own talents. It's just a question of developing them." Even to my own ears, this sounded like the smarmiest of platitudes; in embarrassment, I reached for a dented aluminum mixing bowl from the recesses of a bottom cupboard and carried it to the sink.

"Um . . . the dogs aren't supposed to get tap water. Only Sparkletts or bottled."

"This once isn't going to kill them," I said firmly and filled the bowl from the faucet.

Denise looked dubious. She shifted her weight from one fashionably clunky-shoed foot to the other, then said abruptly, "Can I ask you a question?"

"Sure."

"I kind of heard, from around town, that you think Jeremy was murdered and you're investigating it."

Einstein was wrong: There is a phenomenon faster than the speed of light—Pamela Pemmel's transmission of red-hot news.

"I guess you could say that," I replied hesitantly.

"And Cheryl too, right? That's why you were pumping Alison about her?" Denise, in her earnestness, jutted her round face forward from her body, exactly, I imagined, like one of the Weimaraners picking up a jackrabbit's scent. "There's something you ought to know," she said. "The last time Alison saw her sister, the day Cheryl came to try to borrow a car? They ended up having a blowout fight."

I glanced up. This *was* an interesting tidbit. "What about? Cheryl wanting to freeload again?"

"I don't think so. I mean, I wasn't in the room, I was down in the kitchen having a glass of chocolate milk, but I could hear them. Everybody in the whole *house* could hear them, mostly Alison, screaming at the top of her lungs, things like 'You little c-u-n-t,' except she didn't spell it out, and Cheryl yelling back something like 'Why the hell should you give a damn?' Then Cheryl came barging downstairs, looking all discombobulated, you know, in that way she had?"

"Like her arms and legs were all going in different directions?"

"Yeah, exactly. And she was in hysterics, like she just wanted to leap out of the nearest window. I felt real sorry for her, so I drove her home."

"She didn't tell you what they were fighting about?"

"Uh-uh. All she did on the way was go on about some kind of numerology thing about her birthday and Alison's. I was, like, 'Earth to Cheryl, he*llo*?' but she just wouldn't make any sense. Then, of course, when I got back I caught holy hell from Alison for being gone so long. Not to mention the fact that I took the Bentley." Denise began to reach again for her hairband, but then, as if intent on curing herself of a bad habit, she crossed her arms across her chest and clenched her fists.

"From what you're saying," I put in, "it sounds like all Alison's sisterly concern over Cheryl is just a sham."

"It's more like Alison always found Cheryl a huge embarrassment. Like having this klutzy sister attached to her kind of spoiled her glamorous image."

"Like having a zit on her otherwise perfect complexion."

"Yeah," Denise giggled, "I guess you could look at it that way." She hesitated, then plunged on. "You know what I really think? With Alison's movie going into production and now the wedding, I think she's probably kind of relieved to have Cheryl out of the way."

"Is she that cold-blooded?" I said slowly.

"Oh God, yeah. You should see her when she gets really mad. She goes completely nuclear. And when she does . . ." Denise took a breath. "I wouldn't put anything past her."

"What do you mean?"

"Well . . . if it came out that Alison had something to do with what's happened to both Cheryl and Jeremy, I guess I wouldn't be too surprised." Denise shot me one of her please-don't-kick-me looks. "You won't tell Alison I said any of this, will you? I'd get fired so fast it wouldn't be funny."

Or possibly murdered. I could again hear Terry Shoe, my personal Jiminy Cricket, cackling in my ear: *There's a typical Hollywood reaction—more scared of losing your job than losing your life.* "I'll never breathe a word," I assured Denise.

"I know that. I know I can totally trust you. And hey," she said eagerly, "I can be kind of like your spy. If I hear anything or see anything that might, like, be important, I can let you know, okay?"

Denise, it appeared, was one of those people with a desperate need to devote themselves to someone else. It also appeared that she was more than ready to transfer her servitude from Alison to me. I didn't quite feature myself as a slave owner, but I had to admit, the idea of having a mole within Alison's *ménage* was tempting. "Okay, great," I said. I handed her the bowl of water. "Better get this to the dogs. They must be dying of thirst by now."

"Oh, yeah, right. And you've probably got Halloween parties and stuff."

"Trick-or-treating after my daughter gets home. You can keep the bowl, it's a throwaway."

"Oh, great. Thanks." She awarded me a last, lambent gaze of devotion, then finally took herself out the door.

＊

I fixed myself a gourmet meal of instant ramen noodles and a fistful of Oreos, then dug into the script. It was the tale of a dedicated young gymnastics teacher who starts hearing voices, which she thinks come from the Board of Education trying to control her thoughts and desires; it's all downhill from there as she develops into a full-blown schizophrenic. Not what you'd immediately target as an Alison Wade role, which I knew was exactly why she was itching to do it. It's a basic rule of thumb that no sooner does an actress hit it big in steamy thrillers or frothy romantic comedies than she begins to get restless. She discovers it's no longer enough just to be fabulously paid and publicly adulated: She also wants to be Taken Seriously. To be mentioned in the same critical breath as Meryl Streep. To work with real auteurs, the Scorseses and Altmans and Woody Allens. To win awards for her acting rather than the size of the checks she dashes off to the Fresh Air Fund.

All of which means courting the kind of gritty, not-afraid-to-look-plain-or-even-downright-unattractive roles that automatically do get taken seriously. Prostitutes are good, with or without a heart of gold, outlaws even better, and a significantly handicapped character is guaranteed Oscar bait. Alison had needed only a glance at the scene in which her character, now filthy and disheveled, wanders the mean streets of New York, peeing in doorways, scrounging the remains of Egg McMuffins from Dumpsters, and spieling florid nonsense at alarmed passersby, to begin composing her acceptance speech to the Academy.

But I was hooked as well. I began rapidly sketching ideas in the margins: a fractured mirror, each fragment reflecting a different distorted face; a wedding cake exuding roaches and rats, fireflies and ladybugs . . . I was annoyed when the phone interrupted and snapped it up with a brusque "Hello."

It was Kit. A fresh crisis had erupted. "Some of the actors are stalling at going back to the set. There've been two deaths connected to the movie, so they're beginning to think it's some kind of cursed production."

I could believe that. The average actor was only slightly less superstitious than the average ninth-century Saxon peasant. "What are you going to do?"

"One of the agents seriously suggested I get an Indian shaman to do some kind of ritual and take the curse off. It's fine with me, but where the hell do I find a shaman on the spur of the moment? They don't exactly advertise in the Yellow Pages. Anyhow, I'm going to have to deal with this, so I have to pass on the trick-or-treating."

"But Chloe's been counting on your coming. She's been telling all her friends how cool you're going to look as Zorro."

"Hey, I'm sick about it too, but there's nothing I can do. I'll catch you later at the Castanedas'."

Before I could protest further, he was off the line. "You crumb!" I hollered into the phone, "putting some ridiculous movie ahead of your own daughter!"

My righteous indignation was cut short by the toot-toot of a horn signaling the arrival of Chloe's car pool. Composing myself, I went back outside to meet her.

It was the Seiglers' car pool day: One of the two fair-haired nannies manned the wheel of a sleek green Lexus. I could hear Tracy Seigler's strident voice informing her little brother precisely what species of dog turd he reminded her of, and his less discernible riposte, which seemed to feature the word *Tampax*. Chloe, carefully protecting her silver-scaled dragon's tail, eased herself out the back seat. "You're not in your costume yet!" she complained to me.

"I've got time. We're not going out for a couple of hours yet."

The nanny waved at me and called "Happy Hallows." She was the older of the two and the blonder, her head as flaxen and fluffy as a dandelion gone to seed. She was from Johannesburg, I recalled, and studied transactional psychotherapy on her days off. I searched for her name: Ellie. On an impulse, I went up to her window.

"Ellie," I said casually, "by any chance were you working for the Seiglers when Caitlin Jones was there?"

She shook her fluffy head. "I was hired to take her place. Right after the suicide."

"What suicide?" I asked quickly.

"Caitlin Jones's. I mean her attempted suicide. I guess not many people know about it, it was kept pretty hushed up at the time, but it's been years now, so I guess it's okay to tell."

"How did she do it?"

"Some kind of poison, from what I heard."

I felt a frisson run up my spine. "Do you remember what kind?"

"I don't think I ever heard. I do remember, though, that they said she took exactly enough to make it look like she meant business, but not enough to really do herself in. I guess it was supposed to make the Seiglers feel sorry for her and forgive her for robbing them blind. It almost worked until Gail found out it was just a fake. After that, she wouldn't let Caitlin set foot back in the house. Had all her stuff packed up and sent to wherever."

I rolled this news excitedly in my mind. Caitlin Jones, Jeremy Lord's ex-wife number two, was versed in poison—which would seem to put her smartly in the running, along with exes numbers one and three, as a suspect in his death. I bent closer to Ellie, intending to pump her further.

Tristan Seigler suddenly delivered a swift left hook to his sister's shoulder, which his sister countered with an impressively professional right cross to the rib cage; it immediately degenerated into a round of free-form pummeling.

"Knock off, you little horrors," Ellie snapped, adding to me, "I'd better get these two home before they beat each other to bloody pulps. Have a good one." She waved a toodle-oo, then backed the Lexus out.

"Mom!" Chloe yelled from the door. "Come on, I want to see your costume."

"Coming," I said and ambled back into the house just as the phone rang. As before, it was the second line, the unlisted number we never gave out. Meaning it would be Kit again.

I picked it up, said, "Did you change your mind?"

On the other end, there was faintly audible breathing against a background of . . . what? An unearthly sound that made my skin crawl . . .

Then a click as the phone hung sharply up.

ELEVEN

I clicked immediately for a dial tone, hit the preprogrammed call return, and waited nervously as the line on the other end began to ring. It continued to ring, eighteen, nineteen, twenty times, until it became obvious no one was going to pick up. I dropped the receiver back in its cradle.

A Halloween prank, I told myself. Some twisted teenager, dialing numbers at random, happened to hit on our unlisted line.

But what about that hideous noise? It gave me the crawling jitters just thinking about it . . . like someone torturing a small animal, twisting the ears off bunny rabbits or macerating gerbils in a blender. I wondered if I ought to notify the police or the ASPCA. . . .

I'd sound like a lunatic, I decided. The only thing I could do was put it out of my mind and attend to more pressing matters—like getting myself into costume sometime before Thanksgiving rolled around.

I've always loved Halloween for the same reason I love animation—I can let my imagination run totally amok without anyone actually eyeing me as a candidate for the funny farm. I always begin planning our costumes directly after Labor Day, Chloe changing her mind about hers on a daily basis ("A hippopotamus! No, a fairy princess!"), Kit agreeing to anything so long as it involves wearing neither kilt nor codpiece. I naturally opt for an animated character, this year the Wicked Queen from *Snow White*. It promised to be one of my best efforts. A moth-eaten opera cape rummaged from a bin in an Arthritis Foundation thrift shop had converted nicely to the queen's cloak. I'd whipped up her five-pointed crown from the same gold foil that had produced Chloe's dragon tail and fashioned a snood from an old black slip. To complete the look, I sketched two thin black parabolas over my eyebrows to approximate the queen's vintage 1933 brows and painted my lips a cruel dark red.

But that gruesome phone call continued to disturb me. I suddenly thought of my father. One February day when I was nine, my mother and father, while crossing an icy road, had been hit by a skidding trailer truck. My mother was killed outright. My father lost his left leg and more than a few of his marbles; and throughout my life, he had been given to making odd, semicoherent calls to me at unpredictable hours of the day or night.

Then I started to think of the first dreadful Halloween after my mother's death. Dad, having shucked his thriving practice as a tax accountant, decided to run for alderman. In the name of "campaigning," he replaced his artificial limb with a wooden leg he'd acquired from God knew where, slapped a homemade black patch over one eye, and hit the trick-or-treat rounds of our little Minnesota town—the only grown-up among the throngs of costumed kids. At each door, he stomped his wooden leg and growled, "Yer candy or yer life!," then presented a hand-printed flyer: PEGLEG STAN KELLENBORG "STUMPING" FOR ALDERMAN. I had been so utterly mortified, I wished I could simply disappear.

But Dad was now far too gone with Alzheimer's to even remember my number. Besides, I knew that tortured bunny shriek had not come from him. That was nothing I'd ever heard before and something I sincerely wished never to hear again.

With a shudder, I blotted the vampirish color on my lips, gave my snood a final tug, and hurried out, making sure as I left that the house was well locked and the security system fully armed.

✳

There were plenty of grown-ups among the dozen families gathered outside the Castanedas'. In these days of well-publicized child molesters, serial killers, and assorted deviants, none of us parents was about to let our kids traipse through urban streets unchaperoned; I, for one, had nightmares of finding myself portrayed by Brett Butler in a CBS movie of the week entitled *Trick or Treat Horror: The Real Story of the Hollywood Halloween Kidnappings*. Us parents were also, I noticed, just as elaborately costumed as our kids, and sporting somewhat better accessories.

A black stretch limousine hogged the bulk of the Castanedas' crushed limestone driveway. "Cool, a limo!" Chloe cried. "That's what I want to ride in!" She made a beeline to it, conveniently forgetting her opinion of Skye Castaneda as Super-Geek of the Year to grab the jump seat beside him.

Patrice Castaneda fluttered up to me. "Lucy," she trilled, "thank God you're here—everybody was so late I thought they'd never come. I love your costume!" she added in the same breath. "Phantom of the Opera, right?"

"Actually, I'm the Wicked Queen from *Snow White*." I brandished my prop mirror. "You know . . . 'Mirror, mirror on the wall . . .' "

"Oh." Patrice blinked vacantly; I recalled that, before snagging Paul Castaneda, she had been not a rocket scientist but an herbal wrap technician at the Golden Door. Her own costume consisted of a green suede tunic, tights, and a saucy green cocked hat, meant, I presumed, to portray Robin Hood—though with her buggy features, the first and most durable impression was of a grasshopper.

"Where's Kit?" she asked.

"Tied up in last-minute craziness." I attempted a breezy chuckle. "You know how it is. He'll try to get here later."

"I'm in the exact same boat. Paul got called away to an emergency meeting in New York this morning, leaving me to deal with this entire thing all by myself." Her eyes dimmed in panic, as if she'd been stuck single-handedly coordinating an operation on the scale of, say, the invasion of Normandy.

"We're going to have a terrific time," I assured her.

A stocky man in full Indian-chief regalia drifted over, squinting at the harvest moon that bloomed hazily just above the horizon. "We ought to get hopping," he stated. "They're predicting rain later tonight and we don't want to get caught."

"Rain?" Patrice gasped, as if this were some dangerous, possibly even fatal, phenomenon. "Oh my God! We better get going right away. Lucy, you get everybody into the cars." She pressed a computer-printed map into my hand. "Here's the route that I thought we could take. We can all follow the limo."

I've never considered myself a take-charge type, usually preferring to hover on the sidelines while bossier people did the organizing; however, I wasn't me at the moment, but Snow White's rather more assertive stepmother, and so I efficiently began piling the kids into the limousine and consolidating the grown-ups into a half-dozen cars. At my direction, doors slammed, engines started, and we wagon-trained it out, the limo forging the lead, trailed by a straggle of Jeeps, Mercedes-Benzes, and Volvo station wagons, with a Hummer bringing up the chuck wagon position.

Patrice had traced a route through only the most upscale streets, her theory being no doubt that the richer the household, the more lavish the treats. We skipped the places that were curmudgeonly dark, snaking up the private drives of those that were lit, at times becoming ensnarled in traffic jams with other trick-or-treating convoys. We amassed at the front doors, shouted our ragged chorus of "Trick or treat!" and duly collected our goodies from bemused Mexican or Guatemalan or Filipino housekeepers. Popular this year were little gold-beribboned boxes of Godiva chocolates, anything Cadbury's, as well as the homier candy bars like Almond Joy and Snickers, but only in the gigantic movie-counter sizes. Definitely out were just about any of the things I remembered from when I was growing up: candy apples (could contain razor blades or other harmful substances), gingerbread men (ditto), Cracker Jacks, and candy corn (far too plebeian).

After each foray, I caught a ride with a different set of grown-ups. After some forty-five minutes, I found myself in the back seat of a Volvo, haunch to haunch with an adolescent girl dressed in jeans and a Porno for Pyros T-shirt. "No costume for you?" I asked conversationally.

"Costumes are for babies," she declared with a sullen pout.

Her mother, who was done up as Cat Woman, complete with a snapping whip, and whom I vaguely recognized as a mover and shaker on numerous Windermere Academy committees, leaned across my chest to address her daughter. "That's exactly what I mean by attitude," she snapped. "No wonder you didn't get picked for the Welcome Squad."

A sound like a tomato being squished issued from the daughter's thorax. Her face took on the current socially correct expression of teenage alienation: head bobbling to one side, mouth falling slackly open, eyes glazing with the stupor of a poleaxed cow.

Her Cat Woman mom turned her attention to the window as our convoy lurched into a cul-de-sac. "It looks like Judie Levritz has really gone all out," she remarked.

"Is that where Judie Levritz lives?" I said with interest. I didn't have to ask which house she meant. You couldn't miss it—an immense, newly built Mediterranean that managed to be both grandiose and ordinary at the same time, rather like one of Morty Levritz's tract houses on steroids; but what was particularly eye-catching about it was the sweeping front lawn, populated with enormous, automated Halloween figures. Gigantic witches bobbed on broomsticks; black cats the size of water buffaloes arched and hissed; Casper-ish ghosts taller than street lamps raised and lowered attenuated white arms. The entire production basked in orange and white floodlights, and it had a soundtrack: amplified moans and groans that resounded for blocks away.

"Judie's neighbors must love this." I grinned.

"They used to kvetch like crazy," Cat Woman said. "But this year, what with Judie on chemotherapy, they had to keep their traps shut."

The grin froze on my face. "Does Judie Levritz have cancer?"

The front seat was occupied by other Windermere parents, Sy and Becky Cronin, he in a red neoprene devil's suit, she a rather anorexic belly-dancer. Becky now swiveled to join in the conversation, the tiny bells on her costume tintinnabulating with her movement. "Breast," she pronounced lugubriously. "She had a lumpectomy last month. I told her she was out of her mind—if it was my decision, I'd have said cut them both off, don't take any chances."

"Has anybody noticed that all of a sudden *every*body seems to have breast cancer?" mused Cat Woman. "It's like it's contagious or in the water or something. Half the gals I know have been diagnosed."

"Sy's whole family is riddled with it," put in Becky. She glanced at her husband, who nodded.

"Mom, aunt, two sisters," he said.

All the adult women instinctively wrapped protective arms around our own bustlines.

"What's Judie's prognosis?" I asked. "Is she going to be okay?"

Cat Woman made a flipping so-so gesture with her hand. "The doctors say so far, so good. But you never know, it's a sneaky disease. One year you're fine, the next it pops up in all your glands and *phfft!* You're gone."

"With Sy's cousin, Hella, they told her she was in a hundred percent remission," Becky said. "Six months later, we're flying back to her funeral in Great Neck."

A gloom had descended over us as the Volvo cruised to a stop behind the limousine. We wordlessly emerged into Judie's All Hallows' extravaganza and followed a lane marked by candlelit jack o' lanterns and arrows.

My thoughts were racing. So Judie Levritz had had a brush with death! Which had to mean that the foremost thing on her mind would be what would happen to her kids if she were gone. The prospect of having them end up with the loathed and debauched Jeremy must have tormented her out of her mind. I remembered the way she had turned on me so fiercely in Connie Baljur's study and hissed, "The only way he was getting his filthy hands on those kids was over my dead body!"

One thing I knew for certain—she would have killed him first.

I was distracted by something plopping on my head. A raindrop! It had been eight months since the last rain had oozed from the Southern California skies; the unfamiliar feeling of precipitation caused us all to fairly stampede to the door.

An elderly Asian woman opened the door and, beaming bravely at our numbers, motioned us inside. We herded into a travertined atrium dominated by an enormous hollow plastic pumpkin that was brimming with every conceivable kind of candy. A whoop of delight arose from the kids and they made a charge; with some chagrin, I watched Chloe muscle several others aside to begin shoveling monumental Hershey bars and ultralarge Butterfingers into her bag. I dictated a silent memo to myself: Have heart-to-heart with Chloe on Unselfishness, Patience, and Waiting Your Turn.

As the kids stocked up, I couldn't resist a peek into an adjoining room. A dining room, done in unstylishly massive Spanish Colonial— twenty could be seated at the rectangular table and still have plenty of elbow space. Nosily, I stepped in to examine a mahogany breakfront. A reproduction—gazillionaire's wife or not, Judie was obviously still thrifty to the bone.

"Not in there . . ."

I gave a start. The voice had come from what must have been the kitchen at the other side of the dining room—and it had sounded like Judie's. Odd, I thought—I had assumed the Good Mother would be out with her own children on the Halloween circuit. But as long as she was around, I might as well say hi. And while I was at it, maybe hint that I suspected her secret. . . . Let her know that as a mom myself, I could well understand how she'd want to slip her ex-husband something lethal, rather than chance his getting his clutches on their kids. . . .

I could practically hear her choking but unrepentant confession as I barged through the saloon doors into the kitchen. "Judie . . ." I began.

There was no one there.

I glanced around as if expecting to find her crouching beneath a counter. But the kitchen was definitely empty—which meant I'd either imagined I'd heard her voice or she'd just slipped out another door. I continued to gaze around the kitchen out of sheer nosiness. In keeping with the rest of the digs, it was a cavernous room, with acres of custom cabinetry, granite and marble laid with high abandon, and two of every major appliance—two dishwashers, two Sub-Zero fridges— except for sinks, of which there were four, and ovens, of which there were countless, including microwave, convection, and an eight-burner Wolfe restaurant-quality range. It was also spotlessly clean: Every surface and cranny, every appliance, gleamed as if it had been scrubbed with Kit's sonar-powered toothbrush. I found it impossible to imagine anyone sullying such a temple of immaculateness with an activity as messy as cooking.

On an impulse, I opened a few cupboards at random. Cans and boxes of foodstuffs were stacked with an almost terrifying neatness, the labels all primly facing front. "Probably all alphabetized as well," I giggled to myself. One cabinet housed a lazy Susan on which small jars were aligned as smartly as storm troopers on drill parade. I gave it a desultory spin.

Then stopped it with a sudden slam of my hand.

On the top rung of the lazy Susan was a grouping of vials somewhat smaller in size than the rest of the jars. Each was marked with a simple logo of a peach—a perfect peach with one leaf unfurled. . . .

The same logo that had been on Cheryl Wade's packet of stress pills the night she had jack-in-the-boxed up from the back seat of my Cherokee.

I reached for one of the vials. A hand-lettered label on the back listed the contents: lobelia, goldenseal, Siberian ginseng. Inside were large ovoid pills, pale yellow and exuding, when I held the jar to my nose, a faintly grassy odor. I snapped the cap back in place, then, on yet another impulse, tossed the vial into my trick-or-treat bag.

Okay, I thought, now that I was a bona fide snoop and petty pilferer, I might as well go the distance. I began rapidly opening and closing cabinet doors, finding nothing more exciting than precision-stacked towers of dishes, and bowls arranged meticulously from the gigantic to the small. A sudden sound made me whirl: Judie, catching me red-handed! But it was just the automatic ice-maker in one of the Sub-Zeros spitting out fresh cubes. With a breath of relief, I turned to head back to the group, whose shouts and squeals I could hear from the foyer.

Then, at the back of the kitchen, I noticed a set of wood-framed pocket doors that were partially opened to a glassed-in service porch. On the porch were several trash cans, the jumbo-sized kind you always spot in alleyways behind the mansions of Beverly Hills—the idea being, I suppose, that the superrich have more garbage than you and me. I remembered reading somewhere that you could learn volumes about a person by examining what they threw away. Just a quick peek, I decided. With a flutter of excitement, I pushed one of the pocket doors fully open and stepped onto the porch. I pried off the lid of the nearest can.

A stench of rotten vegetables and pizza sauce considerably past its prime assaulted my nostrils. "Yuck," I exclaimed and slammed the lid back on. Lucy Freers, Finicky Investigator.

With somewhat less enthusiasm, I tried a second can. Better luck here: Judie Levritz's help, as might have been predicted, separated the wet garbage from the dry, and this one contained the dry stuff. I began to shuffle through it, fascinated by what the Levritz household had discarded. There were the usual catalogs, empty cereal boxes, the shards of a broken teacup. I could understand why the still-sealed can of LeSueur Baby Peas had been tossed out—it was dented and botulism could lurk within—but why the unopened box of De Cecco vermicelli? Or even more mysteriously, the brand-new video of *All Dogs Go to Heaven II* still in its shrink wrap?

I dug down even farther, as if into a Christmas grab bag, and yanked out something cylindrical. A vase, the kind that comes with floral deliveries, made of thick, bubble-marred glass. I had a good assortment of them at home, the sort of thing I found too cheap-looking to actually use again, but somehow too good to throw away; how was it that the ostensibly thrift-minded Judie had no such qualms?

As I was pondering this, something hard jabbed against my spine. I turned with a startled sound.

Then froze.

TWELVE

I was staring into the barrel of a gun.

It was a shotgun, actually, double-barreled, with a plain polished walnut stock and no doubt a hairpin trigger, the sort of weapon favored by John Wayne in his more mature films—the difference being that this one was being wielded by a young Asian man in baby-blue pajamas. He was slightly built, with the kind of slicked-back patent-leather hair rarely seen since the early talkies, and a delicate, high-boned face that, under modified circumstances, I might have found rather exquisite.

He was standing in the doorway between the glassed-in porch and the kitchen. "No move," he ordered.

I realized I was trembling; worse, I realized that so was he, enough to cause the gun to go off accidentally, a fact that made me shake even harder. I tried to raise my hands, a gesture to convey either surrender or "I come in peace."

"No move," he yipped again.

"Okay," I yipped back. We remained at a standoff, staring at each other in stark alarm. He seemed particularly unsettled by my Wicked Queen cloak, perhaps assuming that in this particular country, this was the housebreaker's uniform of choice.

"Look," I said finally, "I think you are making a terrible mistake." I spoke in the loud, slow voice that's supposed to make foreign speakers magically comprehend English. "I'm a friend of Judie's. Mrs. Levritz's."

The name didn't seem to ring any bells. I pointed with my chin toward my Halloween bag perched on a counter in the kitchen directly behind him. "You know, trick or treat?"

I was still clutching the florist's vase; his eyes flicked first to it, then to the bag, then back to the vase. Terrific, I told myself: Now he probably thinks that's how I'm collecting the loot. "My friends are out in the front hall," I said. "Go get them. They'll tell you who I am."

"No one here," he said. "Everybody leave."

I realized with dismay I could no longer hear their voices. While I was rifling through the trash, they must have trooped on out. It was a large enough group that it was possible no one would immediately notice my absence.

The Asian edged several steps backward. "I call police," he declared.

"Good idea." I moved gingerly back into the kitchen and sidled toward a phone mounted on the wall. "Let's call the police, so we can get this whole thing straightened out."

"No move!" The Asian tightened his grip on the gun.

I froze again.

"Police coming," he elaborated.

For several interminable minutes, we stood engaged in a silent staring contest. Then footsteps clumped onto the service porch I had lately vacated and two uniformed cops burst through the pocket doors. One was tall and burly, with a pumpkin-shaped head that seemed to sit on his shoulders without benefit of neck. His partner was a good foot shorter, with a squished-in face like a Pekinese, chin and jowls scribbled with a bluish five o'clock shadow. Their guns were drawn, held in a two-handed ready-for-business grip. It struck me as almost hilarious that there were now three deadly weapons pointed in my direction.

"Everybody freeze!" the no-neck cop commanded.

Since I was already in freeze position, this command presented little problem for me. The Asian, however, seemed not to understand he was included in the general indictment. He flashed a broad thank-God-the-cavalry-has-arrived smile and advanced several steps toward the cops.

They both swiveled in chorus line–worthy tandem. "Freeze right where you are," hollered the little Peke-faced cop. "Lay the weapon on the floor!"

This time the Asian quickly got the gist. He deposited the shotgun on the floor, then straightened and thrust his hands over his head, as if this were a stickup. No-Neck Cop produced a pair of handcuffs and with fluid efficiency cuffed the young man's hands behind his back.

His partner edged up to me, gun still poised for action. His small, narrow chest made his badge seem outsized, like a kid playing deputy sheriff. But what he lacked in stature, he more than made up for in vocal volume. "You," he boomed. "Put down that vase."

I obligingly set the vase down on the nearest counter.

"Put your hands behind your back."

"If you'll just let me explain—" I began.

"Hands behind your back!"

It's amazing how effective an order can be when bellowed by an officer of the law holding a gun: My arms whipped out from the folds of my cloak and flew behind my back. Before I could realize exactly what was happening, handcuffs clamped over my wrists. "This is all a ridiculous mistake," I protested.

"That's what we're here to determine. What's your name?"

"Lucy Kellenborg Freers." Full disclosure seemed the prudent choice of action. His own name, I noted from the outsized-looking badge, was O'Neal. Over his head, I watched No-Neck Cop lead the terrified-looking Asian out of the kitchen.

"Do you have an I.D.?" roared Officer O'Neal.

"My wallet's in the bottom of my bag." I delivered another chin point to the Nordstrom's bag.

Officer O'Neal edged cautiously toward it as if suspecting a trap and plucked it by the looped black-cord handle. "You mean this?" In his incredulity, he forgot to raise his voice: The question came out in almost subdued tones.

"Yes, that," I replied. "It's for trick-or-treat. Halloween, re-member?" I added with a peevish edge, "Isn't it obvious that I'm in costume?"

He seemed to have to consider this. "So what are you supposed to be? Wonder Woman?"

"No," I said icily. "Phantom of the Opera."

He gave me a hard look. Then, with his weapon-free hand, he rummaged briskly through the bag and pulled out my wallet, a hand-tooled buffalo-hide number Chloe had picked out for me in a gift shop at Yellowstone. He flipped it open, sloughed out the driver's license from its plastic slot, squinted dubiously at the picture. "This on the license is your current address?"

"Yes, it is."

"You don't live here."

I confirmed this brilliant deduction.

"Can you identify the address of this residence?"

"You mean right here?" It occurred to me unpleasantly that I couldn't. "I don't know the *exact* address," I said. "I was with a large group trick-or-treating. They're probably still on the block."

"Nobody's out on the block. The rain's sent everybody home."

For the first time, I realized it was raining hard. I could hear it sheeting outside the window, plus O'Neal's cap had a glistening wet sheen. Which gave me my first real twinge of alarm. The downpour had probably sent my group scurrying into the various cars. It could be a good while before anyone realized I wasn't in any of them.

"Look," I said hurriedly, "I came with a group of people to trick-or-treat and left them for a second to see if I could get a glass of water. Then suddenly I was accosted by that guy with the gun who refused to let me leave. My friends must have gone on in the meantime."

O'Neal grunted, not unreceptively.

"My daughter's with the group," I continued. "She's only ten—she can't be left on her own. I've got to go get her. So could we please just go catch up with them? I'm sure they're still in the neighborhood."

O'Neal squinched his brow, as if about to relent. Then his partner strode back in, the young Asian in tow behind him, unshackled now and smiling with smug triumph. "Mr. Trinh checks out with the rest of the staff," said the cop, whose badge ID'd him as Linik. "He's some kind of butler or houseboy here. Says he saw an intruder burglarizing the kitchen and called 911."

"That's ridiculous!" I burst out. "I am not a burglar. I've never stolen anything in my life!"

All eyes immediately focused on the florist's vase perched on the counter.

"She taking," declared Trinh.

Linik picked the vase up as gingerly as if handling the crown jewels. "What do you think?" he said to his partner.

"Could be valuable," O'Neal shrugged. "Maybe Waterford."

"Valuable," affirmed Trinh. "Very valuable."

"No it's not, it's junk," I said forcefully. "It was in the trash can. It was being thrown away." Neither cop showed signs of buying this story. "Look," I went on, "I'm a friend of the woman who lives here. Let's get hold of her and put a quick end to this nonsense." How I was going to explain to the testy and houseproud Judie Levritz exactly how I came to be prowling in her garbage I really didn't know, but I figured I'd cross that particular bridge when I came to it.

"Out of town," spoke up the Asian. "Mista, Missis Levritz in Hawaii."

Both Linik and O'Neal narrowed eyes at me. "I think you'd better come down to the station," said O'Neal.

"I'm under arrest?" I gasped.

A spasm of horror turned my knees to Silly Putty. My legs buckled, and an insect seemed to have become trapped inside my forehead, buzzing angrily in that space between the brows where Hindus postulate a third eye. But I wasn't experiencing enlightenment—rather something between giddiness and the desperate urge to throw up.

There was a whoop of a siren outside and a second brace of cops blew in, one a policewoman with the sort of problem hips that kept Jenny Craig well in the black. She conferred briefly with Linik, then marched over to me and briskly patted me down, the paraphernalia on her belt clanking and jangling against her ample proportions. She nodded an all clear to Linik and O'Neal.

Officer Linik gripped me firmly by the elbow. "Okay, let's go," he said and hustled me out the kitchen door. We marched several steps in a drenching rain to a black-and-white parked in the alley. He ducked me into the back seat and rather tenderly strapped me into my seat belt. "Okay?" he asked in a paternal voice.

The back seat had the same rancid peas and carrots stench that always lingered in my Jeep Cherokee after one of Skye Castaneda's car sickness bouts, and the floor was sticky; there were shooting pains in my arms from having them wrenched so long behind my back, and I was on my way to jail. How, I wanted to shriek, could you possibly think it's okay?

"I need to contact my friends," I insisted. "My daughter's going to freak when she finds out I'm missing."

"You can straighten all that out at the station," Linik said. He slid into the driver's seat and O'Neal hopped in beside him, carrying my trick-or-treat bag and the incriminating vase. We pulled away at a rather leisurely pace, with neither flashing lights nor sirens, O'Neal manning the static-plagued radio. "No wants or warrants on you," he reported to me with a congratulatory smile.

I beamed back almost giddily, as if I'd been recognized for some rare and extraordinary accomplishment. The cops then launched into mutual commiseration over a café on Lincoln that had recently changed hands, gone all fancy-shmancy, a fondly recalled hot pot roast with gravy sandwich now become some gourmet ripoff involving little mushrooms and those namby-pamby French rolls. It occurred to me that they hadn't read me my Miranda rights, but I couldn't quite see barging into their gripe session to ask about this oversight.

Instead, I stared miserably out into the rain, my mind a muddle of desperate thoughts: that in the Windermere yearbook, which ran photos of parents as well as students, mine would be the only one with a number under it; and that, from now on, I would now have to feel solidarity with such fellow arrestees as Leona Helmsley and Tammy Faye Bakker, and if I *had* to be arrested, why couldn't I be wearing something more dignified than an opera cape, snood, and tin-foil crown?

We turned onto Pico, cruised past Fast Kids, Chloe's favorite clothing store. We'd been there just last week; I'd bought her a little cropped green cotton sweater with a monkey appliqué—back in those halcyon days when I was still an Honest Citizen.

Self-pity flowed through me, more drenching than the weather. I burst into tears.

THIRTEEN

I sobbed freely for the rest of the ride, pulling myself into sniffling shape as we reached the station house. With the same paternal solicitousness as before, Linik unfastened my seatbelt and, grasping me by my upper arm, steered me into the building. We trudged through a locker room and down several drab corridors, visions of Jimmy Cagney walking the last mile to the electric chair flickering through my head.

As we passed a door marked DETECTIVES' ROOM, it flew open, and out stepped a tall black man in a stylish houndstooth sports coat. It was Terry Shoe's partner, Armand Downsey. I instinctively ducked my head—being force-marched in handcuffs through the business end of a precinct was not precisely the way I wished to recultivate an old acquaintance. But then it occurred to me that he could clear up this ludicrous mistake, tell Officer Linik I was no petty thief but an upstanding citizen. I turned my head to call him.

But the corridor was empty. He had already gone.

Linik steered me into a cinderblock room. "Here we are," he pronounced with a rather uncalled-for heartiness.

I gazed desolately around. It was a starkly lit little chamber painted a dull, abandon-all-hope gray. By way of decor, a metal counter, a mounted phone and intercom, and an incongruously cheery keep-kids-off-drugs poster starring Yogi Bear in snappy yellow shades. Also three ominous metal doors, each with a small grate-covered window. From behind Door Number One, a man was screaming something about spiders with claws; from behind Door Number Two, someone else bellowed back at him to shut the fuck up, the two alternating in a kind of lunatic call and response.

"The spiders, they're crawling at me on their claws!"

"Shut the fuck up, you fuckin' asshole!"

"Halloween's always one of our busiest nights," Linik told me. "You're lucky it's still early. By midnight, this place'll be really hopping."

"Will I still be here at midnight?" I asked with alarm.

He glanced at his watch. "Hope not," he said cryptically. The diminutive O'Neal unlocked my handcuffs. I stretched my arms luxuriously as the blood tingled back into my numbed fingertips.

Linik counted out the money in my wallet. "Twenty-four dollars and thirty-six cents," he declared, in a rather disappointed tone, as if he'd expected me to be packing a more impressive bankroll. I signed for it, handed over my rings and watch, an antique gold Timex. These, along with the wallet, were sealed in a plastic bag. A frizzy-haired policewoman bustled in and treated me to a more thorough pat-down, probing under the elastic of my bra, shaking out my shoes.

"I'll have to take that tiara," she said, plucking it off my head. "We can't have you trying to hurt yourself." I must have reacted with a particularly sour expression, for she scrunched her own face in sympathy. "Hey, don't feel so bad. We get all sorts of folks in here. Actors, rock stars . . ." She added with wistful nostalgia, "We even had the deputy mayor once."

The L.A. city jail—where the elite meet. For some reason this didn't significantly cheer me up.

"What happens now?" I asked faintly.

"We gotta put you in the tank while we check out the rest of your story," O'Neal said.

"You mean I'm not being booked?"

"Not yet."

I breathed out with some relief. "Can I make my phone call now?"

"Like I just said, you're not being booked. You're not entitled to it yet."

"Please!" My voice rose to the same frenzied pitch as the spider claw man's. "Please, just let me make one call."

Linik and O'Neal traded what-the-hell facial expressions. "Okay, one call," Linik said and handed me the receiver.

I hesitated. Exactly whom was I supposed to call? Kit, obviously. But I didn't even know where he was at the moment; besides, I wasn't thrilled at the prospect of telling him what had happened. And it was too soon for the group to have returned to the Castanedas'. . . .

In the movies, people always get in touch with their lawyers. Of course, in the movies, people always *had* lawyers—and specifically the Perry Mason kind, who made it down to the jailhouse lickety-split and got things rolling immediately. The only attorney that sprang immediately to my mind was Ronnie K. Moscowit, who negotiated Kit's contracts: He was a partner in the ritziest entertainment firm in town, billing four hundred bucks an hour plus disbursements. He was a killer when it came to scoring gross points in a deal, a whiz at obtaining an extra million or two on the back end; studio heads quaked at the sound of his adenoidal voice, and hardened business affairs chiefs fell quivering to their knees. But what did he know about springing clients from the poky? I suspected the only time he'd ever seen the inside of an LAPD station was on reruns of *Hill Street Blues.*

Still, he *was* a lawyer. Besides, I happened to know his home number: Chloe and Ronnie's daughter Penelope had become best friends at circus camp last summer, and I was forever ringing up the Moscowit household to arrange playdates. I dialed, troubling the heavens with another frantic prayer, this time for him please to be home.

An Englishy accent answered, snootily declared the Moscowits were "entertaining," would madam care to leave a message? I replied that madam's husband was an important client and that madam had a dire emergency that couldn't wait. Within seconds, Ronny was on the line.

"Lucy, what's up? You calling for Kit? They're not trying to kick him off the movie, are they? Cause let me assure you, he's got an airtight pay-or-play deal. If those bastards try to can him, I'm gonna make them bleed through the nose."

"It's not about the movie," I cut in. "I'm at the police station. I'm being held, and I need you to come and get me out."

"Jeezus!" he breathed. "What did you do? DUI? Anyone seriously hurt? My God, no one was killed, were they?"

"It's not a DUI. I didn't do anything!"

I gave a quick and substantially edited rendition of the night's events. "It's just a ludicrous mixup," I said. "I need you to come and get me out. It's only five minutes away from you."

"I'm in the middle of a dinner party." He lowered his voice to a hiss. "I've got Candice Bergen here."

"I don't care!" I shouted. "I don't give a damn if you've got James Dean, Yasir Arafat, and the Pope!"

The spider claw guy, who'd been taking a short breather, was spurred by my raised voice to a fresh and more robust performance. "The spiders have legs and all the legs have claws on them!" he shrieked.

"Shut the fuck up, you asshole," bellowed his faithful echo.

"What the hell's going on there?" asked Ronnie. "It sounds like a riot."

"Almost. There are people on drugs here and they're freaking out. Listen to me, Ronnie," I added. "If you value Kit as a client, you'll get your ass down here immediately!"

A moment of silence. I could sense him frantically trying to weigh which course of action would be the more expedient, to piss off the celebrity dinner guest or the hotshot producer client. "Okay," he said grudgingly. "I'll be there in about twenty minutes. In the meantime, I'll make some calls and get a judge to stay late so you can be immediately arraigned."

"Arraigned?" I said in a small voice.

"Sure, so you can walk. You don't want to be detained overnight, do you?"

I assured him that I certainly did not, thanked him profusely, and hung up.

"Okay?" said Linik.

"Yeah, hunky-dory," I said glumly.

He unlocked one of the metal doors and ushered me into a cinderblock cell furnished with two wooden benches, one of them occupied by another detainee. I trudged in, the door shut behind me, the lock turned with a solid clink. I sank onto the free bench and pulled the homemade snood down off my head, freeing my matted hair.

To ward off another crying jag, I focused on my cellmate. Nearly six feet tall. Acne-pitted white complexion. Semi-beehive of brass-colored hair. Fifties-style knockers, large, pointy, and jutting skyward. And modeling an outfit in which the slutty and the demure competed for equal opportunity: silver stiletto sling-backs, slutty; ribbed beige pantyhose, demure; orange vinyl miniskirt, slutty; pink polyester-blend twin-set, demure.

Transvestite was my immediate guess: The annual Halloween Gay Parade would be kicking off on Santa Monica Boulevard just about now, and it always brought the drag queens out in force—though from what I recollected, they generally came dressed as either Jackie O or prima ballerinas. Besides, would they have put me in the same tank as a man, even though he did happen to be wearing a skirt and heels?

I realized I was staring rudely. I covered up this social gaffe with a tremulous smile.

Bored brown eyes thickly ringed with black liner fixed on my face.

I faltered. Should I introduce myself? Or was it the proper cell-block etiquette to preserve anonymity?

"What'd you do?" my cellmate suddenly asked. Her voice was husky, but with a decidedly feminine timbre.

"Why was I arrested, you mean?" I attempted a carefree laugh; it came out a desperate cackle. "Technically, I guess, for burglary. But it's all a ridiculous misunderstanding. I'm just waiting to get it all cleared up. . . ." I broke off under her impassive stare. Naturally, all us felons always proclaimed our utter innocence. Jeffrey Dahmer, when he was busted, had probably insisted it was all a simple mix-up; if they'd just give him a minute, he'd ex*plain* how all those severed heads came to be in his Frigidaire. "So what got you here?" I asked quickly.

"Sellin' shit."

What sort of shit? I wondered: drugs, stolen jewels, her body? She didn't elaborate. But I felt a compelling need to fill the silence. "I have to admit I'm a bit anxious," I chattered on. "I mean, nothing like this has ever happened to me before, so it's kind of intimidating. What about you, have you ever done this before?"

"What do you think?"

The question, I decided, was rhetorical. I pulled my cloak snugly around my shoulders, more for the succor of a security blanket than for warmth.

"I like your manicure," my cellmate offered.

I looked down at the blood-red talons on my fingertips, cheap press-ons that had seemed to jibe with the queen's character. "They're just fakes," I replied with a dismissive wave. "But I love *yours*. They're really terrific."

"You think?" She dangled her left hand toward me. The nails were so long they curled like Fritos, each painted a different rock-candy color topped with a little white squiggle. On closer scrutiny, the squiggles turned out to be letters, spelling out the succinct message: EAT ME.

"Very nice," I murmured.

"I do them myself," she confided.

Our little *kaffee klatsch* was interrupted by the sound of footsteps approaching our door. I sprang to my feet, thinking for one fuzzy moment that Ronnie Moscowit had made it here in supernaturally record time.

But the face that appeared at the window grate belonged to Terry Shoe.

"Downsey said he thought it was you," she chortled, "but I had to see this for myself."

"Thanks a lot," I said bitterly.

"What's that black stuff on your face?"

I touched my cheek, then examined the black smudge on my fingertips. The black arched eyebrows I'd drawn on must have run in the rain. "Nothing," I said. "Just part of the makeup I was wearing for my costume. This *is* a costume, you know," I added.

"Sure, from *Snow White*, right? The wicked stepmother? It used to be my daughter Sunny's favorite video. I must've watched it with her a hundred times. She was crazy about Dopey."

Another time, I might have found her daughter's preferences in toon characters fascinating, but at the moment I had more pressing issues on my mind. "Look, this is all a ridiculous mistake!" I burst out. The phrase seemed to be quickly becoming my mantra.

"Oh yeah? I hear you're under suspicion of stealing a Waterford vase. Something that valuable makes it a felony. Nothing too ridiculous about that."

"It's not Waterford," I fairly shrieked, topping even the spider claw guy. "It's not even crystal! And I wasn't stealing it, it was in the garbage. For God's sake, you don't think I make it a habit of burglarizing houses, do you?"

She gave a little snort, implying she might not put it past me. "You want to tell me what you *were* doing?"

I ran my smudged fingers nervously through my hair. "I was out trick-or-treating with Chloe and a group of our friends. We ended up at Judie Levritz's home. You know, Jeremy Lord's first wife."

"Somehow I figured that name would come up," Terry said.

"Did you?" I remarked icily.

"Yeah, I did. Go on, what happened next?"

"I thought I heard Judie's voice coming from the kitchen. I'd just found out she'd had breast cancer, and she was scared she was going to die and Jeremy would end up with custody of the kids. I figured that would have given her a pretty good motive to kill him."

I shot a look at Terry, expecting at least a flicker of acknowledgment. The yellow cat's eyes remained locked on me without expression.

"Anyway," I continued, "I thought I'd go say hello and maybe try to sound her out a little. So I went into the kitchen to find her. But I was wrong about having heard her. There was nobody there."

"So knowing you, you decided to snoop around."

"I wouldn't say that," I bristled. But I'd forgotten how that tawny stare could propel me into an unstoppable babbling state. "Okay, maybe I did a little," I conceded. "I mean, I just peeked into a few cabinets. But then I saw some trash cans out on the service porch, so I decided to see if there was anything in the garbage that might prove significant.

"Hee-hee," she giggled.

"What's so damned funny?"

"What did you expect to find? Body parts? Or maybe a bottle marked 'poison' with a big skull and bones on it?"

"Okay, it was a dumb idea, I can see that now." I stuck my face close to the window, my nose almost rubbing the grate. "I promise to God I'll never do anything like it again. So can you please get me the hell out of here now?"

"No, I cannot."

"Why not?"

"What do you think, I'm the governor, I can just spring anybody I want to? Besides which, this is a very good lesson for you. You want to become a detective, join the police force. Otherwise stick to cartoons."

In the course of my acquaintance with Terry Shoe, there had been times I had loathed her, times I could take her or leave her, and even times when I'd almost been fond of her. Loathing was definitely what I felt now, and in spades. The glint of her gold wedding band caught my eye, dazzling as a sapphire amid the bleak fluorescent lighting. I recalled that Terry Shoe's husband was a Korean American and also a Presbyterian minister; I marveled that someone ostensibly committed to the Christian values of charity and mercy could be hooked up with a woman who, back in Inquisition days, would've been Torquemada's first draft pick.

"Hey, cheer up," she said dryly. "First offense, you probably won't have to do any real time."

Before I could let her know just how vividly I detested her, she disappeared from my view.

I remained peering out into the desolate room, listening to the racket of Spider Claw Guy, whose hallucinations were becoming baroquely convoluted, now incorporating snakes with claws and fangs and leeches with teeth. My arms and shoulders had intermittent shooting pains, my wrists still felt raw from the bite of the cuffs, my head throbbed. This can't possibly get any worse, I thought miserably.

A hand suddenly grabbed my buttocks and gave a firm, even professional, squeeze.

I whooped and took a little skip, clutching myself in front and behind, like Popeye doing the hornpipe. Then I whirled to face my cellmate, who was hovering rather expectantly behind me.

"Don't touch me!" I croaked. "Stay away."

She gave a blasé shrug and sashayed back to her bench. I retreated to my own, and, squeezing back fresh tears, huddled down to wait.

FOURTEEN

Time is relative, as Albert Einstein pointed out; it's particularly relative when you're locked in a cell with a person of indeterminate gender who's already groped you once. Hours seemed to ooze by as we sat in our opposite corners, she studying the information on her fingertips, while I kept a wary watch on her for any sudden moves. It seemed to me to be well after midnight when Officer Linik's Pekinese face reappeared at the window grate.

"Okay, we're releasing you," he said. The lock turned, the door opened.

I bounded to my feet and scurried out of the cell, as if afraid he might change his mind.

"One of the detectives looked at that vase and said it was just a piece of junk," he said a bit sheepishly.

"So I'm free to go?"

"We're not booking you now. But the homeowners can still file charges if they want. They've got up to a year. Just so you understand."

He produced my property bag, counted out my money again, gave me back my wallet, rings, and old Timex, as well as the now-crumpled tiara. According to my watch, I'd been locked up for less than forty minutes. Impossible, I thought; it must have stopped. I held it to my ear: It was faithfully ticking.

"We had to throw away your bag of candy," Linik said. "It's regulations—sorry. We have to discard all comestibles."

"Perfectly okay," I assured him gaily. What was the loss of a few chocolate bars compared to earning my freedom?

"There's someone waiting for you out front," he said. "Follow me."

*

Ronnie Moscowit was standing by the front desk, looking as if someone had sprinkled itching powder down the back of his silk Versace shirt: His shoulders twitched, his hands jingled the coins and keys in his pockets, his feet tapped an in-place soft shoe on the filthy floor.

"Jesus Christ, you look terrible!" was his greeting.

"Thanks," I said. "It's been kind of a rough night."

"Did they give you any grief? I've got a friend who specializes in police brutality cases, just won a half-million-dollar judgment against the city of Glendale."

"They treated me just fine," I said quickly.

"Oh yeah, good," he said, with a dubious squint. His was a baby face, with plump pink-skinned cheeks and a squalling little mouth; a dab of what looked like pesto sauce above his upper lip now heightened the impression that he was usually fed by a spoon. "So what gives?" he went on. "I just got here, and they said you were being let go."

"I wasn't exactly the career criminal they thought I was," I said sourly.

"No charges?"

I shook my head. "Like I told you, it was all a mistake."

An ambitious look came into his eyes. For a moment I was sure he was going to suggest another buddy who was the king of false arrest litigation, but he contented himself with saying, "Fine, so now if you don't mind, I'd like to get back to my guests."

"Can you drop me off at the Castanedas'?" I asked. "It's on your way."

"I'll have to bill for this," he snapped.

We filed out into the rain-slicked parking lot. Ronnie's silver Mercedes glittered exotically within the pack of shabbier cars. I sank with a sigh of pleasure into the butter-soft leather seat. "You can't possibly know how wonderful this feels," I murmured.

"Eighty grand, it better feel damned good," Ronnie grunted. He turned the key. An easy-listening selection burbled into the air, a soupy blend of voices crooning about love lasting forever and all time: The hang-'em-high and take-no-prisoners Ronnie K. Moscowit was a secret softie! This was evidently an unintended revelation—with a rapid shot of his palm, he ejected the CD.

"So what do we tell Kit?" he said, as we pulled out of the parking lot.

A fascinating question. "I'll tell him the truth," I said. "There's no reason not to. I was out trick-or-treating and was mistaken for an intruder by a non-American who didn't quite get the concept of Halloween. That's all there was to it."

Ronnie shot me a sidelong "yeah, right" look. "This wouldn't happen to have anything to do with Jeremy Lord, would it?" he said.

I glanced at him uncomfortably. "What makes you say that?"

"First you find his body. Then you go around town spouting off that you think he was murdered. And now you get caught prowling around his ex-wife's pad. When I smell fish, I look for flounder." He pursed his tiny mouth. "On second thought, don't tell me—I don't even want to know. I'll give you this advice, though. Anything to do with that scumbag is bad news." He began squirming in his seat, as if the very memory of the dead director reactivated the itching powder, this time under his pants. "Major-league bad news," he repeated.

"Really?" I said, all wide-eyed innocence. "I've heard he was pretty nasty in his private life, but I've also heard that he made a very good client."

In his agitation, Ronnie actually began to bounce in his seat. "You want to hear about good? Let me tell you. I put together a financing deal for a movie the bastard had committed to direct. I logged a hundred-plus billing hours, busted my balls to pull a hundred percent of the money in, and then at the last minute, the last *second,* the bastard threatens to back out! Hands me some manure about having artistic problems with the script." Ronnie produced an old-fashioned but nonetheless eloquent raspberry. "Here's a guy who couldn't look at the *Mona Lisa* without picturing a bullet hole between her eyes—you know, just to wipe that smirk off her face. And he gives me artistic crap."

"He did win an Oscar," I pointed out.

Another raspberry, this one, I presumed, in honor of the collective critical faculties of the Motion Picture Academy.

"What happened to the deal?" I pursued.

"I got lucky. He dropped dead."

"Why was that lucky? Being dead, he still couldn't direct the movie."

"No, but it let me off the hook with my investors. The main source of the funding was Jeremy's former brother-in-law, Ralph Jones. He was putting in fifteen million bucks on behalf of the Tinseltown Café consortium."

I raised my brows. "From what I've heard, that's got organized crime connections."

"Not exactly classified information," Ronnie snorted.

"So let me guess. Ralph and his pals were skimming money off the top of the café receipts and wanted a way to launder it."

"Not to my knowledge," Ronnie said crisply. "As far as I knew, the funds that were committed were perfectly legitimate."

It was my turn to make a "yeah, right" expression. "So okay, then, what was the problem?"

"The problem," Ronnie continued, with exaggerated emphasis, "was that when you're dealing with people like Ralphie Jones's partners, it's not a healthy idea to back out at the last minute. I was sweating, I'll tell you. Every time I picked up the phone, I kept worrying it would be some guy named Paulie talking in a gravelly voice. So when I got the word that Jeremy Lord was dead, it was great. My ass was off the line."

By kicking the bucket, Jeremy seemed to have gladdened many a person's day. "Do you think it's possible he was killed by the mob?" I asked. "You know—rubbed out for having double-crossed them?"

"Nah." Ronnie impatiently waggled his head. "A mob execution's not known for its subtlety. You get the three shots, blam, blam, blam! behind the ear, or else you just disappear off the face of the earth, like what's his name, Hoffa."

"Then what about Ralph himself?" I said eagerly. "It seems to me he'd have been in even more hot water than you were. He could have been very motivated to get rid of his ex-brother-in-law."

Ronnie suddenly hit the horn, a long, nasty blast at a Celica that had had the temerity to merge into our lane. "Listen, Lucy," he said curtly. "I'm just telling you all this to make my point. Jeremy frigging Lord was, and posthumously continues to be, bad frigging news. As far as I know, and as far as you should be concerned, he died of natural causes. *Finito,* okay?"

"Yeah, okay," I said, equally curt.

Heavy rain suddenly whomped the car, a stingingly knitted blanket of water sheeting and spattering the windshield with alarming intensity.

"I can't see a goddamned thing," muttered Ronnie, stepping on the gas.

I tightened my seat belt. This was the way nature behaved in California: months of boringly placid sameness, punctuated by brief but violent bursts—tropical downpours, eucalyptus-felling gusts of wind, earthquakes. The rain continued to pound, until, just as it seemed it would go on all night, turning streets into raging rivers and sidewalks into moats, it subsided into barely a sprinkle.

By the time we reached the Castanedas', there was only the kind of spritzing mist that's supposed to give Englishwomen their peaches-and-cream complexions. Ronnie glanced at my door, clearly eager to be rid of me.

"Listen, Ronnie," I said. "How about not mentioning this to Kit at all, okay? You can send the bill directly to me."

"I always respect the confidentiality of my clients," he said loftily. "Just don't forget what I told you. Bad news!"

Scarcely waiting for the door to close behind me, he peeled out.

I hurried up to the house and rang importunately. Patrice answered and let out a little hiccup of relief at the sight of me. "Thank God, there you are!" she squealed. "What happened? We got back here thirty minutes ago and finally realized you weren't in any of the cars. I had the horrible intuition you were run over, the way we kept dashing across the street."

"I popped into the john at the Castanedas', and when I came out, everybody was gone," I improvised. "It took forever to get a cab, with the rain and all."

A pathetically lame story: It meant either the longest pee or the most severe taxi shortage in Los Angeles history. Patrice peered closer at me. I could sense those invisible antennae of hers beginning to tauten, picking up the vibrations of a plum piece of gossip. "Where's Chloe?" I asked quickly.

"All the kids are in Skye's playroom, checking out what they got. We didn't tell them you were missing yet."

"Good." I elbowed past her, repeating my ridiculous alibi to anyone else who accosted me on the way to the playroom. There it was bedlam, *Halloween V* in full volume on a big-screen TV, The Fugees blasting from a boom box, and the shrieks and screams of a half-dozen children on a candy rush. Cartons of take-out Chinese were congealing in neglect, while the kids stuffed their mouths with processed sugar.

I dragged Chloe out of this orgy and drove home, enduring a nonstop whine about how it wasn't *fair,* all her other friends got to stay up as late as they wanted, even on school nights! More protests of cruel and unusual punishment got logged in when at home I confiscated her trick-or-treat bag.

"You know the rules. One piece a day from now on." I realized suddenly that I'd had no dinner and grabbed a Reese's Piece from the bag.

"That's mine!" Chloe squealed indignantly. "Why don't you eat stuff from your own bag?"

"I must have left it back at the Castanedas'," I said. Lying at the tick of a clock was a skill I was rapidly honing. "Look, it's a Reese's, and you can't have it anyway. It's got peanuts."

"Oh," Chloe said, somewhat mollified. Her peanut allergy was swift and virulent, raising furious red welts all over her body and making her wheeze like a rusty bellows.

I stashed the bag in a cupboard so high that even I needed a stepstool to reach it. To compensate for my cruelty, I let her take in the second half of *Halloween V* while I stripped out of my now-hated costume. The opera cloak I balled up and stashed in the garbage, never wanting to see it again.

Chloe was asleep, and I was curled in bed with an Elmore Leonard, when Kit came barging home, flush-faced and ebullient. "It's all systems go again," he crowed. "We actually managed to rustle up an Indian shaman! A member of the Nez Percé tribe who's supposed to be a bona fide medicine man. He's agreed to perform some kind of purifying ritual in return for a speaking role in the movie. Turns out he's already got his SAG card." He laughed a little too gleefully.

"It sounds like you went to celebrate again," I said, hating the tone of my voice—like a comic strip wife in hair curlers, fuming at the top of the stairs and brandishing a rolling pin.

"We stopped off at The New Cubana for an Irish coffee. By the way, I've been accepted. I'm now a full-fledged member." He began to undress, peeling off his natural-fiber designer wear, carefully slipping off the Rolex and setting it on his dresser.

Meet the Freers Family. Him: internationally acclaimed film producer and *bon vivant,* into fine wines, rare cigars, and sculpting the perfect bod. Her: jailbird.

"But I want to hear about the trick-or-treating," Kit was saying. "How was your night?"

My night? Well, let's see. . . . I was detained at shotgun point by a nervous butler, hauled off to the slammer in handcuffs, and slapped into a cell that had all the charm of an execution chamber. I was patted down by two lady cops and felt up by a person of indeterminate sex; my candy was thrown away, and I employed a four-hundred-dollar-an-hour contract attorney as chauffeur. "It was fine," I said stiffly.

"Chloe had a good time?"

"Terrific. Except for being disappointed that you didn't make it."

"I'm disappointed too," he said.

"Are you really?"

"Of course, what do you think?" He wriggled one cashmere sock off a foot.

"I don't know what to think anymore." The rolling pin–brandishing tone clung obstinately to my voice.

He paused in mid-divestment of the other sock. "What's that supposed to mean?"

"I mean I just don't know what you care about anymore besides your damned movie career. Obviously it's not me or Chloe. And I might as well stop taking those fertility pills, since you don't seem to care about having another baby, either."

"That's absurd," he said. "Look, I'm really sorry about tonight, but I honestly was up to my neck in crap until about forty-five minutes ago. By that time I knew it was too late to catch up with you, so a quick drink didn't seem to make any difference. And I really don't think my missing one Halloween is going to scar Chloe for life."

I made a noncommittal sound.

He clambered up beside me on the bed. "Hey, why don't I show you what I care about?" he murmured. Like an overgrown puppy, he began to playfully nuzzle me. His body no longer felt as rock hard as it had a couple of weeks ago—in fact, there were the beginnings of love handles at his waist. It was the pre-Virus, pre-Navy-SEAL-toned body that was so familiar to me.

All my resistance instantly melted away. I began kissing and stroking my husband voraciously back.

✳

At 3:00 A.M., my eyes shot open. Just for a change, I was wide awake, with little hope of falling immediately back to sleep.

I slipped out of bed, taking care not to wake Kit, pulled a robe over my naked body, and tiptoed downstairs. In the den, I poured myself a stiff shot of Calvados and curled on the sofa. Furball, the more social of our cats, sprang onto my lap; his brother, Howard, whose claim to fame was having seven toes on each of his front paws, draped himself behind my head.

I scratched Furball's ruff, then picked up the remote and began to channel surf: *Real Stories of the Highway Patrol* . . . Click. Elayne Boosler doing shtick about penis lengths . . . Click. Erotic movie, a couple writhing in soft focus on what appeared to be a trampoline . . .

Click. Infomercial, lithe blond woman in a tigerskin leotard prowling with a mike in front of a giddily enthusiastic audience . . .

I was about to click, when, with a start, I realized I recognized Ms. Tigerskin—it was Caitlin Jones, former nanny to the elite and second ex-wife of Jeremy Lord.

I turned the sound up a notch. Caitlin had selected an audience member to join her on stage, a fiftyish woman with what's known as a "Lockheed lift"—the kind of face-lift that makes you look like you're perpetually caught in the blast of a jet engine. The gist of her testimony was that her sufferings throughout menopause had been epic: hot flashes you could toast marshmallows on; mood swings that would have made the average manic-depressive look serene; reflexive gagging at the mere thought of sex.

Caitlin was taking this in with a solemn, I-share-your-pain expression, occasionally dipping her golden head in sympathy. "But this was before you began my VitalHerb four-step regimen, is that correct, Lila?" she asked, in the probing but tender manner of a surgeon palpating a post-op patient.

"That is correct, Caitlin," beamed Lila. "I began the VitalHerb regimen two months ago. After one week, my hot flashes diminished to the point where I hardly noticed them at all, and my mood swings became completely manageable. And I'm pleased to say that now my husband and I enjoy a full and satisfying sex life."

The audience cheered and whooped. Caitlin applauded, kathump, kathump, kathump, with the mike. Lila flushed crimson, as if having a sudden relapse into one of those barbecue-starting hot flashes. A silky male voice-over came on the line: "As personal nutritionist and diet counselor, Caitlin Jones has helped hundreds of Hollywood celebrities to lose weight and maintain peak physical performance. But now you too can order her amazing, one hundred percent organic products, once only available to her celebrity clients. . . ."

There followed a list of the available regimens. VitalHerb seemed to offer a pop-a-pill solution to just about anything that might ail you, from insomnia to flabby thighs, from stress and anxiety to postnasal drip. The fact that at the moment I seemed to be able to check off at least eighty percent of these categories made me an ideal candidate for VitalHerb Regimen numbers one through six inclusive.

I'll stick to booze, I thought. I drained my Calvados as the 800 number floated onto the screen, backed by an attractive grouping of the miracle products. I gave another start, nearly choking on the last swallow of my drink.

VitalHerb came to you in vials, small, medium, and family size. Each was decorated with the VitalHerb logo, which appeared to be a peach—a perfect peach, with one tender green leaf unfurled.

Which meant that Judie Levritz had an entire lazy Susan stocked with Caitlin Jones's line. And that Cheryl Wade had been popping VitalHerb pills like candy kisses.

But so what? Maybe they were both simply aficionados of ordering from late night infomercials. Maybe they both also had closets crammed with veggie juicers, ThighMasters, and the entire series of "Sweatin' to the Oldies."

The bottles of herbs on the TV screen had now given way to a doctor with a Marcus Welby knock-off hairdo and a checkerboard of illegible diplomas behind his desk. As I listened to him drone on, something else suddenly struck me: The TV vials all had the words VITALHERB clearly printed beneath the logo. But neither Cheryl's nor Judie's vials had been marked with anything but the simple peach—I was certain of that—and the contents labels on the back had been elegantly hand lettered, not printed up for the infomercial masses.

I recalled Cheryl in the back of my Cherokee, offering me one of her stress pills: "My nutritionist makes them specially for me. . . ." Not even Cheryl Wade could have been flaky enough to believe that a product ordered from an 800 number on the tube was customized for every caller.

I got up for a refill of brandy, Furball mewling in protest at being summarily disturbed. You're just picking at straws, I told myself. Even less than that, you're just picking at gossamer threads. I reached for the Calvados bottle on the wet bar.

I suddenly had the unsettling feeling that something about the way the bottles were arranged on the bar was not right: They all seemed turned around, the Scotch where the tequila should be, the liqueurs switched with the tonics and Rose's lime juice.

So what? I told myself. Perhaps Graciela had been a little too zealous in her cleaning.

Except that she hadn't been in today. . . . I shrugged, then poured an even stiffer shot of Calvados and put it to my lips, where it froze.

Directly at my eye level hung a cel from one of my short films, a drawing of an imaginary animal with a zebra's body, webbed feet, and the head and neck of an ostrich. It had decorated the wall above the wet bar for so long I rarely noticed it anymore.

And I wouldn't have tonight except for the peculiar fact that it now appeared to be hung upside-down.

FIFTEEN

Harold Davis stood in the demolished breakfast room with one of his Mexican crew, both gazing at the jagged top of an exposed pipe and rather systematically shaking their heads in such a way that I had absolutely no desire to inquire about it.

"Good morning, Harold," I said, coming up to him.

"Hey, morning, Lucy," he replied. The melted chocolate eyes slid placidly to me.

"Um, Harold . . ." I motioned him several steps away from his crew member and in a discreetly lowered voice went on, "Have any of your crew been coming into the house? I mean," I added quickly, "they're perfectly welcome to come in and get sodas and stuff from the refrigerator. And of course they can use the bathroom. But I'd prefer it if they didn't mess around with anything else."

He continued to fix me with that benign, never-blinking stare. I often had the creepy sensation, when talking to Harold, that he was only here collecting information for his real planet—perhaps one circling Betelgeuse or Orion.

"Can't happen, Lucy," he said cryptically.

"What?"

"My crew knows the house is off limits. I supply them with beverages, and the food truck stops here twice a day. And they don't use your facilities. We've got the two Brite-O-Sans."

"Oh," I said. "Well, if you're sure . . ."

"Positivo."

"That's fine, then. I'll see you later."

"Real good."

I headed on to my car, unconvinced. Harold, despite his Alien from the Planet Bizarro demeanor, was neither all-knowing nor all-seeing. The most likely explanation for what I'd noticed the night before still was that a couple of the guys had sneaked in to cadge a few quick drinks, and while they were at it, took down the animation cel to have a good guffaw at what these gringos considered art—then carelessly replaced it upside-down.

Why else would someone just come in the house, move a few items around, then leave?

Which was exactly what I had told Cheryl Wade the night before she checked out of the conscious world!

At this thought, I felt as if a hand was smothering me: Suddenly I could hardly catch my breath. It was even distorting my vision—my Cherokee on the drive looked like it was listing to one side.

I forced a deep breath, but the Cherokee still appeared to be atilt—for the simple reason, I realized, that it actually *was* atilt. Both left-side tires were completely flat.

The temperature of my paranoia soared to the boiling point. "Harold!" I yelled.

He came ambling languorously toward me; the outbreak of World War III wouldn't make Harold Davis break into a brisker stride. Several of the crew, attracted by the prospect of an interesting calamity, sauntered up behind him. "Looks like you picked up a couple of nails," he observed, then spoke in rapid Spanish to his crew, who listened with the same inscrutable cheerfulness with which they seemed to greet both disaster and success. "I told the guys to make a clean sweep of the driveway," Harold said. "You'd better take care of those flats."

I called Triple A and had them tow the listing Jeep to a service garage; then I grabbed the keys of Kit's mid-life-compensation Corvette and zoomed off to my Culver City studio.

I cruised down Sepulveda, where Christmas decorations had already begun to materialize, plastic Santas slogging through the eighty-nine-degree smog, snowflakes looking startled to find themselves strung between coconut palms. I soon noticed an interesting phenomenon: I was no longer just a routine mom making the rounds in a regulation sports utility vehicle. Now I was a Babe in a Vette. At every stoplight I was flanked by solo men in cars, from a tidy, silver-haired gent in a Lamborghini to a grinning slacker in a bestickered VW convertible, all of them gunning their engines like long-horned steers pawing the ground. But the Vette was a whiz off the line; I left them all in my dust.

Except for one car, a suntan-colored Caprice that had managed to stay clamped on my tail. I was about to floor it, show them just what this baby could do, when I heard the brief whoop of a siren and a disembodied voice: "Please pull over."

"Hell!" I muttered aloud and cruised to the curb, the Caprice gliding up behind me. A speeding ticket meant a stint in traffic school, an endless Saturday spent listening to a failed stand-up comic desperately trying to find the hilarity in parallel parking. I looked up sullenly as a cop trundled to my window. Female, plain clothes . . .

My sullenness bloomed into overt hostility when I realized it was Terry Shoe.

"Nice wheels," she remarked. "Kind of a new image for you, isn't it—hot-rodding mama?"

"Are you following me?" I asked icily.

"Uh-uh. We saw you shoot by, so we took a U-turn and caught up. Which wasn't easy, the way you were hitting the gas."

"Funny that you seem to just happen to be everywhere I am. It's like being stalked."

"Depends on how you look at it. If it was me, I'd say it's like having a guardian angel." She leaned in closer to the window. "We were just going to stop and grab a cup of java. Care to join us?"

"I suppose this isn't just a social invitation?"

"You suppose right. There's a coffee shop four blocks up, north side. We'll catch you there."

The two detectives were already ensconced in a leatherette booth when I entered the restaurant. With old-fashioned civility, Armand Downsey bobbed to his feet as I slid into the seat opposite them.

It was one of those places that reflected the changing demographics of a neighborhood. On one hand, it had lima bean–green leatherette booths and a six-page laminated menu, and was named Moishe's; on the other, the waitress had streaked magenta hair and a nose stud, and took my order for a double caffè latte without blinking. I knew from previous experience what the detectives would have: black coffee for Terry Shoe, no milk and extra sugar for Downsey. With Terry's, the waitress set down a blueberry muffin the size of a grapefruit, a glistening masterwork of congealed lard and crystallized sugar.

"See, I picked up the health bug from you," Terry informed me. "I gave up doughnuts and switched to muffins. I still don't think too much of the bran kind, but the blueberries and the granola ones they got here are pretty tasty."

"That blueberry muffin," I said with vindictive glee, "is loaded with refined sugar and saturated fat. It's got just as many calories as a Whopper and probably more cholesterol."

I was gratified to see her face fall. "Well, waste not, want not." She shrugged philosophically. She broke off a large hunk of the sticky pastry, squashed a pat of butter on it, and conveyed it to her mouth.

"I have no illusions at all about this cruller," announced Downsey and took a jaunty bite, reminding me disconcertingly of Kit with his cigar.

I crankily stirred my latte. "If you've brought me here just to gloat about last night, I can tell you right now I'm not in the mood."

"That's the kind of gratitude we get?" Terry said.

"What am I supposed to be grateful for? Learning what a bummer it is to be groped by a complete stranger? Thanks, but I used to live in Manhattan and ride the subways. I've already absorbed that particular life lesson."

"Who groped you?" Downsey asked, sternly knitting his bow.

"My cellmate. She very expertly goosed my behind." I added plaintively, "And I don't even know if she was really a she or a he."

"She had to be technically a female," Terry said didactically. "We don't put a suspect in the ladies' tank unless we've made sure they've got no penis. Sometimes they've had the breasts done, but they've still got the dick. In that case, we put them in with the men."

"You could file a complaint, you know," Downsey said. "We take things like that very seriously."

I shook my head. "I just want to put the whole God-awful experience behind me."

"Which is why you ought to be thanking Downsey," Terry said. "Who do you think got you released?"

"That was you?" I beamed him a look of newfound appreciation.

He shrugged. "I told them the vase was a worthless piece of junk. It was like arresting somebody for lifting an empty peanut butter jar."

"Downsey's like you, a pack-rat, always collecting stuff," Terry said. "He's got a lot of fancy glass at home."

"Mostly Waterford and Steuben, and one or two pieces of Venetian." He gestured dismissively with the cruller, spritzing a fine spray of sugar over the table. "I wouldn't really call it a collection."

"Believe me, I'm enormously grateful," I said. "I don't think I could've survived another ten minutes in that place."

"If they had shipped you off to Sybil Brand, that would've seemed like the Hilton," Terry declared airily.

"What's Sybil Brand?"

"The county pen. They haul you off on a bus in ankle chains and throw you into this huge holding tank chock-full of gal gang-bangers. After that, you're on your own."

The idea that I might have been shipped off to Sybil Brand set a school of hyperactive polliwogs squirming in my stomach. I leaned back in the booth a moment and stared at the actors' composites that lined the wall beside us. A pretty typical lineup: studly young guys glowering like Brando or grinning with the elation of someone who's just discovered a new brand of deodorant soap; pouty girls with upper-class-hooker makeup, reclining come-hitherishly on sofas or hearth rugs; the requisite character types: a jolly fat guy, a foxy grandpa in a spotted bow tie. These photos were everywhere in L.A., a ubiquitous and rather forlorn fresco; they hung in shoe repair shops and dry cleaners, mingled with Preparation H ads in Rexall's and adorned the brick ovens in pizzerias, all in the hope that. Oliver Stone, while picking up his freshly laundered jeans or grabbing a quick knish between editing sessions, would spot that one special face and cry "Eureka!"

Or if not Oliver Stone, then Jeremy Lord—before, of course, his sudden and untimely demise.

I grimaced at the thought of the dead director. "You'll be happy to know that I'm giving up on the whole Jeremy Lord thing. It's a dead end. There's nothing more to be known about it."

Armand Downsey sidled a quick glance at his partner.

"What?" I said, adding eagerly, "Did you find out something? From your pal investigating Cheryl's suicide attempt?"

"Actually, I did a little investigating on my own," Downsey said. "Just out of curiosity, I shmoozed the intern who pumped her stomach. He told me the lab report revealed the presence of Valium and Scotch, a nice enough combo to do yourself in with. Not optimum, but it can work. Except there didn't seem to be a high enough concentration of either the drug or the alcohol to do the dirty."

"What about poison?" I asked eagerly.

"Apparently nothing of significance turned up."

"Some people are extremely susceptible to even low doses of drugs," Terry put in. "Every year you hear of some poor kid going through frat rush, he chugs a lot of booze, but no more or less than any of the others. But for some reason this one kid drops dead. It's just the way the body chemistry works."

"From what I'd heard about Cheryl Wade's body chemistry," I said, "it was sturdy enough to let her drink most of her dates under the table. Besides, she swore to me that she was on the wagon. She said she was in AA and using chocolate as a substitute high."

"If she was depressed enough to try to knock herself off, she probably wasn't worrying too much about staying sober," Terry observed.

"Maybe," I said dubiously.

"That's the first place it gets wiggy," Downsey said.

"There's more?"

"Possibly. It seems there was another unexplained death associated with Jeremy Lord."

"When?" I breathed.

"About four years ago, while he was directing the movie *Body Language*."

"Which starred Alison Wade," I pointed out. "That's when they began having their affair. The second the cameras stopped rolling, Jeremy dumped his second wife, Caitlin, to marry her."

"The thing is, Alison apparently wasn't the only one on the set he was having an affair with," Terry said. "There was another gal, what do you call it? The one who fills in for the movie stars on the naked shots?"

"The body double," Downsey supplied, with urbane smoothness.

"Right. She was Alison's body double. Name was Marcy Callow. They were shooting down in Alabama, some hick town, middle of nowhere. Callow was found dead in her motel room, suffocated on her own vomit. The autopsy was inconclusive: she'd been drinking, but blood alcohol levels were not particularly high. There were a couple of marijuana roaches in the ashtray, a prescription bottle of Halcyon that was still half full. Not exactly a lethal combination. But not withstanding, the coroner ruled an OD."

"It's almost the same way Jeremy went," I said excitedly. "Dropped dead from no specific cause, while filming in the boondocks. It can't be just a coincidence! That proves I'm right, doesn't it? There is a murderer out there."

The detectives took simultaneous sips of their coffee. Armand Downsey set his cup meticulously in its saucer and said, "With no hard evidence, it's still merely speculation."

"I don't think it's speculation," I burst out. "I think it's obvious. Somebody used Cheryl Wade to kill Jeremy by giving her something poisoned to pass along to him. Then in order to shut *her* up, they broke into her house and poisoned something she later ate—although it proved to be just enough to put her in a coma instead of fatal." I glanced at my companions; they were attentive, if not exactly encouraging. I plunged on. "Cheryl seemed certain she knew who this person was— somebody with the money to literally get away with murder. Somebody that she must have seen the day she brought Jeremy's kids back home from the *Merry Christmas* set." I gave a little chuckle. "The problem is that Jeremy was such a prince among men, it seems impossible to find anybody who *didn't* want to kill him. Practically everybody he ever met is a possible suspect."

My humor didn't exactly double up my audience. In fact, Joe Friday would have envied them their deadpans.

"At least we can narrow it down to whoever Cheryl was with that day," I continued. "We just have to trace her movements."

"What do you mean 'we,' kemo sabe?" Terry said. "Weren't you the one who just told us you're giving up on this thing? Or is there something wrong with my hearing?"

"But if I'm in a position to find something out . . . I mean, I just feel like I owe it to Cheryl."

"You owe it to Cheryl to let us do our jobs without worrying about protecting your butt as well."

Downsey gave me an avuncular pat on the wrist. "If anything solid does turn up, we'll make sure we'll follow it through."

Terry signaled the actress for the check. "By the way," she said to me, "this time the coffee's on the LAPD."

*

After leaving the detectives, I continued on to the somewhat shabby little office space I used for a studio. It was on the second floor of a seen-better-days commercial building in Culver City. I unlocked the door, gathered up several days' accumulation of junk mail from the floor, then shimmied open the one thick-sashed window.

Outside was a vista of low warehouses, many empty, their former occupants victims of the reeling Southern California economy; the rest were leased by businesses so marginal they rarely featured signs of activity. At the end of the block, a small van marked Pinky's Party Supplies backed laboriously out from a loading dock; with a painful grinding of stripped gears, it disappeared around a corner, and the road was deserted once again.

Even my own building, once teeming with tenants, was now almost entirely unoccupied. For years, the office across the hall had been the rehearsal space of a pair of comic magicians; all day long, snippets from their act would come filtering through our partially opened doors: ". . . My God, ladies and gentlemen, her head is floating right off of her torso!" But the two had come to blows over an effect that involved

vanishing a mink coat, a dressmaker's dummy, and a dirty-talking par-
rot; they had dissolved the act, one partner slinking back home to Sche-
nectady in a high funk, the other hooking up with the Cirque du Soleil,
and now I was alone on the floor.

It was eerily still, as if a neutron bomb had been detonated, wiping
out all forms of life in Culver City except for me. For company, I
snapped a tape into the boom box, mid-seventies Rod Stewart de-
manding an opinion of his sex appeal, and turned the volume to one
notch below deafening. Then I moored myself at the animation board.

As was my usual MO, I was significantly behind deadline on my
Amerinda the hedgehog magnetism episode; I set myself to sketching
out Porter Penguin, the amorous South Poler who falls for the Nordic
Sally Seal. What I was going for in his character was an air of devil-
may-care sophistication, like Fred Astaire, but I was having some
difficulty: After some fifteen minutes, all I was achieving was a dirty-
old-man leer, unsettlingly like Benny King.

"Do ya think I'm sexy?" Rod Stewart was rasping. "You're a real
sex machine, Rod," I muttered, rubbing out another lecherous bird
from the board.

Someone giggled right behind me.

I spun in my chair, heart pounding, to find Denise Schumer lurking in the doorway. "You might have knocked!" I snapped. I was getting
spooked by the way people suddenly seemed to keep materializing without warning.

"I did," she said, cringing, "but I guess you didn't hear me. You
said I could come by, remember? But if this is a bad time, I'll get lost."

"No, it's okay. Come in." I got up and shut off the cassette, then
turned to Denise, who had lost no time in embarking on a tour of
the premises. She was sporting another eye-poppingly trendy outfit:
chartreuse vinyl biker's jacket that must have been saunalike given the
day's heat, a pair of flared Carnaby Street–redux striped purple pants,
and thick-soled clodhopper shoes suitable for mining coal.

"Wow, this is fabulous!" she exclaimed, shuffling between the animation board and computer. Her jacket, when she moved, made an
unfortunate squeaking noise, like the high note of a harmonica. I

couldn't decide which I wanted more—to get her out of my hair or treat her to a head-to-toe makeover.

She paused, mouth agape, in front of a statuette of a silver-plated kangaroo brandishing a paint brush in its paws like some Asian martial arts weapon. "First prize from the Sydney Animation Festival," Denise recited. "Awesome! I mean, like how did you get to be so incredibly creative?"

"Piece of cake," I said airily. "All I had to do was sell my soul to the devil."

"Right, stupid question." She awarded the side of her head a stiff whack with the palm of her hand. Then she plunked herself down on the edge of my drawing table, her broad bottom squashing several of my incredibly creative sketches. "I really shouldn't be here," she confided. "I'm going completely crazy. Alison's having a bridal shower, and I'm in charge of all the details."

"Alison's throwing herself a shower?" I laughed, a trifle caustically.

"Oh, no, not really. It's being given by Bobbie Lomato, you know, the agent? But Alison's lent me to her to get everything organized." If Denise resented being swapped around like a mohair sweater or the latest bestseller, it wasn't apparent from her blithe tone.

"I thought the marriage was supposed to be hush-hush."

"Well, word kind of leaked out. And besides, Alison wants to speed everything up. She's decided she wants to get pregnant right away. She's going to start taking fertility hormones, just like you are."

I stared at her. "What did you say?"

"I said she wanted to get pregnant."

"I mean about the fertility hormones. How did you know that I was taking hormones?"

Denise's round gray eyes opened wide. "Gee, I don't know. I guess I heard it from Alison. You must have told her about it."

"No, I didn't," I said brittlely. "Kit and I agreed we wouldn't tell anybody until we knew if it was going to work or not." Damn Kit! I thought. He must have broken his word and blabbed the news—probably to his new best buddy, Lane Reisman.

"I won't say a peep about it, I swear," Denise said and made a cross-my-heart gesture. "Anyway, I didn't just come here to sit around and bother you. I wanted to tell you about something I heard. About Alison, I mean."

I sat down in the ersatz Eames chair at my desk, still seething about Kit. "What did you hear?"

"I was talking with her business manager yesterday, and he said he was about to get rid of everything in Cheryl's house. Alison's ordered him to sell whatever was worth anything and then throw the rest away." She peeped at me anxiously. "That could be significant, don't you think? Like she was trying to cover up something?"

I felt tempted to quote Terry Shoe: *Like what? A bottle with a big skull and bones on it?* "I'd say it shows she doesn't really expect her sister to ever recover," I replied.

"But don't you think that it's suspicious she's not saving anything? Like to remember Cheryl by?"

"My impression of Alison is that she's not someone whose finest hours are spent strolling down memory lane. Of course I could be wrong."

"No, you're right," Denise said. "She never keeps anything from the past. It's like she always wants to wipe out anything that happened more than a week ago."

"How long have you been working for her?" I asked.

"Since the movie *Body Language.* I was a gofer on the film. It was my first job after graduating from Mills. I met Alison and kind of started doing things for her, errands and stuff. Afterward, she hired me as her personal assistant."

I could well picture Denise unctuously flattering her way into Alison's favor. *Wow, you're so incredibly gorgeous! God, if I could just be one-tenth as talented as you, I'd cut my head off!* How could someone as completely self-absorbed as Alison resist?

"If you worked on *Body Language,* you must have known about Marcy Callow," I said.

"Who?"

"Alison's body double? The one found dead of an OD?"

"Oh, yeah," Denise said shortly. "That pig."

I looked at her, startled.

She flushed. "I guess that's a shitty thing to say about somebody who's dead. But that Marcy was a real piece of work. She tried to steal Jeremy from Alison. It was so pathetic, really, the way she chased him. She'd practically give him blow jobs right on the set."

"From what I know of Jeremy, he was never one to pass up the offer of a blow job," I said.

"Oh, he screwed her a couple of times. She did have a pretty good body, if you go for that big-tits type. I thought they were pretty gross, myself. And she had a really trashy face, Miss Trailer Park of 1994. There was no way Jeremy was going to prefer her to Alison."

"Though of course," I pointed out, "he was actually still married to Caitlin at the time."

Denise gave an airy wave of her hand, as if that were a detail too trivial to be even considered.

"Speaking of all this," I said, "the last time you saw Cheryl, when you gave her a lift after her fight with Alison . . . where exactly did you take her?"

"Didn't I tell you? She was going to see Caitlin Jones."

"I thought so!" I crowed. "So Caitlin was Cheryl's personal nutritionist. It seems kind of peculiar for somebody with a multimillion-dollar business."

"She still does private consultations if you're important enough. Cheryl and Alison were both hooked on her treatments. I think it's all bullshit, myself, all that New Age homeopathic stuff." She eyed me furtively to make sure I recognized her superior level-headedness.

"It's still strange that Caitlin would take on Alison as a client. Alison stole Jeremy from her. You'd think she'd consider her her mortal enemy."

"Are you kidding? It was Caitlin who came after *Alison*." Denise hooked a strand of drab hair from beneath her headband and nibbled it meditatively. "Look, she knew that having big-time movie star clients was the way to make her reputation. And it worked. Now she can say she's the diet guru to the stars on those infomercials of hers."

A thought tweaked my mind. "Did you say that Caitlin is into homeopathic remedies?"

"She's into all of that stuff, you name it."

"Doesn't homeopathy use poisons? Things like belladonna and arsenic?"

Denise shrugged. "Does it?"

"Yeah, I'm sure it does," I said excitedly. "I once dated a guy who swore by it. Whenever he had anything wrong, a headache or if he even sneezed twice, he'd go rushing off to see some homeopathic doctor and get some kind of potion." A vivid picture of Richie Woodriff suddenly appeared in my mind's eye. He'd been one of a fairly hefty variety of lovers I'd gone through one wild and confused year right after film school. He was a grad student in political theory at Columbia, and, like Hitler, had only one left testicle, something for which he compensated by specializing in lengthy and rather inventive foreplay—which was probably the reason I put up with him for nearly a month, given how otherwise mind-numbingly dull he had been. One of the prime topics he had bored me with, postcoitally, had been the science of homeopathy.

"If I remember it right," I went on, "they use very minute amounts of toxic substances, highly diluted in water. There's some theory about curing a disease by using substances that produce similar symptoms to the disease. They call it 'like curing like.'" But now that I thought about it, Richie Woodriff never seemed to get over his colds any faster than anybody else.

Denise smirked. "It's all a bunch of hooey."

"But what it means," I said impatiently, "is that Caitlin's not only very familiar with poisons, but probably also keeps a handy stock of them around the house."

Denise's jaw dropped. "Wow, that's right! So it all adds up then. Caitlin's got to be who murdered Jeremy! She must have, like, slipped Cheryl something poisoned and told her to give it to him."

"That's one scenario. But it's not necessarily the only one. For instance, she might just have supplied her very important movie star client Alison with a nice little vial of arsenic, no questions asked." I picked up a charcoal pencil and began absently doodling a face on the back cover of an old *Variety*. "Or for that matter," I added, "she might have supplied her other good client, Judie Levritz."

"Judie goes to Caitlin too?"

"I think so. I happened to notice that she had some VitalHerb bottles in her kitchen." I saw no reason to mention that I also happened to be illegally prowling at the time. "The bottles I saw had the peach logo on them and the names of some herbs, but not the company name. Am I right in assuming that those are the custom-made products for private clients?"

"I guess so. Alison's got a million of those little bottles and none of them have any company name on them. Just that peach."

"Three ex-wives. All they have in common is a loathing for their ex-husband and a belief in New Age medicine. It's not much to go on." I drew in features on my sketch and began to shade in hair, then stopped. I'd drawn an unmistakable caricature of Cheryl Wade—the clownish lips, the furious meringue of hair. . . . My guilt skyrocketed again: If only I'd taken her even half seriously, she might be up and around and visiting her astrologer instead of vegetating on a hospital bed. I ripped off the page and crumpled it.

"I think I'd like to have a chat with Caitlin Jones," I said.

"I'll set up a consultation for you. I've got her number programmed in my phone. I just talked to her a little while ago." Denise dug into her shoulder bag for a cellular phone, punched in several letters, assumed a professional purr: "Hello, this is Alison Wade's personal assistant. I'd like to arrange a private consultation for a close friend of Miss Wade's. Her name is Lucy Freers." A pause, then, "Marvelous, thank you so very much." She hung up. "That was Caitlin herself. She says come any time this afternoon. She's been expecting you."

"Expecting me?" I said uneasily. "Why?"

"I don't know, that's just what she said." Denise grabbed the charcoal pencil and scribbled an address on a drawing pad. "Here's where she lives, on the Venice canals. She sees everybody at home. She never sets foot in her offices."

Denise's beeper went off. She hit a speed-dialing button on the cell phone and said, "Yes, Alison?" Her face turned white; she listened for a half a minute, emitting only an occasional little *eep,* exactly the sound I'd once heard from a gopher cornered in a hibiscus bush by Furball the cat. "Yeah, okay, Alison, immediately," she quavered, then pocketed the phone and staggered to her feet. The color of her complexion had shifted to a kind of acid Kool-Aid blue, making me wonder if I'd finally be able to put to use those artificial respiration classes I'd taken at the downtown Y.

"I've gotta go right now!" she wheezed. "Alison has a photo session with *Mirabella* and I'm supposed to be there. She's going nuclear." With that, she charged out the door and clattered down the metal stairs. From the window, I watched her scamper toward a dark green Mercedes; French aristocrats had probably climbed into the tumbrels with greater insouciance.

The same Marvelettes tune spun into my mind again: "Too many fish in the sea . . ." I suddenly realized why. It wasn't the Marvelettes version that was haunting me. There was an ad that used it as a theme song, with some knock-off group performing it—a radio ad, probably, since I couldn't conjure up a visual to go with it. Somehow I seemed to have associated Denise with whatever product it was pushing. But what? Hairbands? Unlikely. Some Melrose boutique-of-the-moment specializing in cheesy vinyl? Or maybe mail-order self-flagellation kits?

With a shrug, I turned away from the window. Then I picked up the phone, called Kit at his office on the Fox lot, told his sun-dazed Native of Malibu secretary, Amber, that yes, I know he's on the other line, he's *always* on the other line, the other line is just about permanently grafted into his brain, but I need to talk to him right now! A short hold, then Kit picked up. "Hey, good thing you called. It turns out I have to go back to New Mexico tomorrow, I'm leaving at the crack of dawn. . . ."

"Listen!" I broke in. My voice assumed its finest Barbara-Stanwyck-as-Woman-Wronged tremolo. "Have you been telling people about my fertility treatments?"

"Of course not."

"Then how is it that it suddenly seems to be day-old news?"

"I have no idea. What's so top secret anyway? It's not like we're splitting the atom here."

"That's not the point. The point is we agreed we wouldn't talk about it. And anyway, I'm not Madonna, I don't particularly want my reproductive system to be a topic of general discussion."

"Don't worry, I don't think we're going to make the evening news. Listen, can we talk about this tonight? I've got six people on hold and a call list as long as my arm."

I muttered a grudging assent and hung up, knowing full well we wouldn't talk about it tonight: He wouldn't stagger home till after ten, there'd be a flurry of packing, spiked with frequent where-the-hell's-my-lined-khaki-jacket? crises, the phones wouldn't stop ringing till nearly one, after which he'd simply crash with exhaustion, and I'd toss and turn listening to the mockingbirds whoop it up till dawn. . . .

And then he'd be gone. The glamorous life of a producer's wife. It would make a great sob-in-your-Pilsner country song.

An aching sense of loneliness crashed through me. The empty floor, the deserted street outside . . . suddenly I felt abandoned by the entire world.

I picked up the address Denise had scrawled for Caitlin Jones. An appointment with a possibly modern-day Lucrezia Borgia in all the comfort and efficiency of her own home . . .

What the hell, I told myself. At the moment it seemed a more comforting prospect than staying here alone.

Sixteen

Normally—that is, when not on my way to call on a suspected poisoner—the Venice canals are one of my favorite places. They are the turn-of-the century relic of an Iowan named Abbott Kinney, who, after amassing a fortune peddling Sweet Caporal cigarettes to his fellow Americans, relocated in L.A.; here, in a city of orange trees and trolleys, he had a brainstorm—why not turn the marshlands that rimmed the ocean into a miniature replica of his favorite Italian city? In the entrepreneurial spirit of the day, he set immediately to work, digging sixteen miles of canals spanned by authentically Venetian arched stone bridges, importing gondolas and opera-singing gondoliers with ribbons fluttering from their caps, constructing a town center with palazzo-style buildings, the whole shebang linked by a winding Corinthian colonnade. It was the original theme park and, for a couple of decades, proved a hit: Crowds flocked to it, Caruso sang in the outdoor arena, and silent picture stars built second homes along the banks of the canals.

But by the end of the twenties, the neighborhood had fallen into seedy decline, the home of vagrants and bohemians. The palazzo architecture was torn down, the Grand Lagoon was paved over for a traffic circle, and most of the canals were filled in. Only a half dozen now remain, the gondolas and beribboned gondoliers having given way to families of rather messy ducks.

In recent times, though, the homes built by those long-dead celebs have once again become chic, the more grandiose selling for well over a million. Caitlin's was on Linnie Canal, a gingerbread mini-castle wedged between a redwood Sausalito-style villa and a Craftsman bungalow. It had little turrets from which I could imagine Rapunzel throwing down her golden hair, and the kind of fern-and-mushroom–themed stained glass that did brisk business for hippies in 1969. A suitable setting, I thought, for the fairy princess–like Caitlin.

I pressed the bell and waited, watching a rowboat knock desultorily against the brown-scummed banks of the canal. Caitlin answered the door. She looked more ethereal than ever in silver ballerina flats and a floaty, pale pink shift.

"Well, Lucy Freers," she murmured.

"Well, Caitlin Jones," I murmured back.

"I use the name Caitlin Lord actually," she said. She treated me to a not very subtle once-over, no doubt making mental notes: *We could certainly shave a good couple of pounds off those hips, and a potassium-zinc supplement would be just the ticket for that hair. . . .*

"Come in, please," she said at last.

I entered with trepidation, half expecting that someone would leap from a shadowy corner, throw a sack over my head, and drag me off to a horrific death. God knew, there were certainly enough shadowy corners: In fact, shadowy pretty much summed up the entire premises— eccentrically shaped shadowy rooms crammed with shadowy Victorian furniture, shadowy Oriental carpets, and satin brocade curtains that shaded out the sun. Caitlin drifted through this crepuscular atmosphere like a moonbeam, silvery and oddly incorporeal.

We appeared to be alone; there was no sound except for the *memento mori*–like ticking of a grandfather clock. No minions scurried in and out, no repairmen thwacked and sawed, no hangers-on burbled into phones. Caitlin, it seemed, had chosen to live the very opposite of her successor in wedlock, Alison.

"I hear you're looking for a puppy," she said abruptly. "My Lhasa apso just had a litter. They're mostly spoken for but I've got one left."

"We can't have a dog," I said. "My husband's allergic to them."

"I must have heard wrong." She shrugged.

An odd thought struck me: While Chloe was getting ready for school that morning, she was going through her usual cataloguing of

Things All Her Friends Had That She Didn't, which had wound down to the fact that Miri Pleischer had just acquired a black Labrador, and please, please couldn't we get a puppy, and finally after simple exasperation I'd said, "Maybe. We'll see." But even if Chloe had spread the glad tidings at school, how could it have leaked so quickly and obscurely to Caitlin Jones?

But before I could say anything further, footsteps clumped heavily down the front stairs. I'd been wrong—apparently we weren't alone.

Caitlin turned eagerly as her twin brother, Ralph, sloped into the hallway. "Baby, you're up!" she twittered.

He gave a noncommittal grunt, as if he could neither confirm nor deny that statement.

"Feeling any better?" she pursued.

"Fuck, no." He tottered closer. He was wearing nothing but a thigh-length Japanese *happi* coat tied loosely at the waist and rough leather sandals. His hair was dull and matted. Interestingly, so was his goatee. His skin had the color and consistency of day-old tapioca. The net effect was of a medieval villager in the kind of costume movie that strives for authenticity in depicting the true squalor of the period.

Caitlin fluttered up to him and tenderly lifted a lock of his hair. "How's your head?" she asked.

He winced and recoiled, as if she'd slugged him with a mallet. "It feels like a bomb's gone off in it." He glanced over at me and frowned. "Who the fuck's that?"

"A friend of Alison's. Just come for a consultation."

"I know you, don't I?" he demanded.

"We might have met before," I said evasively.

His bloodshot eyes continued to glare at me. I had the unsettling feeling they were about to glow, like in a horror film, when some heretofore mild-mannered character announces the fact that he's actually a demonic presence.

But instead he suddenly doubled over at the waist and began to produce a violent hawking sound, unloosing a gob of sputum which he deposited on the sleeve of the *happi* coat.

"Poor lovey," Caitlin crooned. "I'll go get your vitamin shake."

"Nah, I'll get it myself," Ralph said, shaking off her touch. He turned and slumped off to the back of the house.

They seemed, I thought, much more like a long-married couple than brother and sister. I remembered Lane Reisman's snide intimation of incest; suddenly it didn't seem completely far-fetched.

"He looks in pretty rotten shape," I remarked.

She exhaled a windy sigh. "It's that Wild Bunch crowd. After he's on one of their outings, Ralph always has to come to me to be detoxi-fied. Last weekend they went out to the desert for what they called "golf without gals." Hookers, I guess, don't count as gals. But I don't think there was too much golf involved, either." She floated over to the drapes and threw them back, revealing a pair of double French doors; the sudden flood of glaring sunlight made me wince. "Such a pretty day," she said, in a tinkly Ladies' Afternoon Tea voice. "Let's talk out in the garden."

I trailed her into a garden fit for a storybook, walled, of course, and with meandering paths and vegetation that climbed and spilled and flowered: All it lacked was a dwarf or two, shouldering a rake and sing-ing "hi ho, hi ho."

"Charming," I said, adopting the same tea party tone. "Did you plant it yourself?"

"Oh, yes, it's my own private little heaven. Are you a gardener?"

"I like to consider myself one. I've got a pretty good patch of roses. Though my blooms aren't nearly as glorious as these."

"The secret is to be totally ruthless with pruning and topping," Caitlin declared. In demonstration, she picked up a pair of rose shears and began vigorously assaulting a gaudy display of Myrna Loys.

I thought it expedient to keep a distance from this violence and rather casually backed toward a hobbit-sized bench. I crouched down on it, feeling like an overgrown kindergartner. "Why did you say you were expecting me?" I asked.

"I heard you'd already talked to Judie and Alison, so I figured you'd get around to me."

I was beginning to feel like my entire life was on *Candid Camera*. "How did you hear it?"

"God knows. People talk. Especially when it comes to things having to do with that filthy bastard." She attacked a bush of mauve floribundas with as much gusto as if ripping into the entrails of her former husband.

"Given that you had such warm affection for him," I said dryly, "I'm surprised you held on to his name."

"It's the only thing I ever got from the creep. It's how I launched my career, trading on his famous name."

"I guess it gave you access to the rich and famous."

"Correct. You see, I was always interested in diet and nutrition, even when I was a nanny. I was already an expert by the time I married Jeremy. I knew more about it than any of your high-priced Beverly Hills doctors. So after he dumped me, I started to do personal counseling. At first it was just the wives and other ex-wives, but then I started to get a reputation, and the celebrities started hiring me themselves. Actors, particularly. You know, they tend to be a little superstitious."

"Yeah, I've noticed," I said. "So?"

"They're oftentimes superstitious about starting a diet before a movie is completely set to go. I guess they think it's tempting fate. But it means at the last minute they've frantically got to crash off fifteen or twenty pounds."

"Which is where you come in."

She nodded. "Sometimes I'd actually move right in with them so I could control their entire diet, monitor every single thing they put in their mouth. And of course I'd also provide them with the right supplements, according to their physical and mental needs. To increase energy, cleanse the blood, control compulsive desires . . ."

"Kind of like still being a nanny," I observed.

"A lot of really big stars act like spoiled brats, so I guess that's true."

"And so there you were, no longer just Jeremy's rejected wife, but now diet guru to the stars."

"So to speak," she said coldly. *Thwack!* Off went the head of a stately Queen Elizabeth. "It was Ralph's idea to sell my products to a wider market. It was very helpful to have celebrity endorsements."

"And that's of course why you pursued Alison as a client."

She frowned. "Pursued Alison? What makes you think that? She came to me, practically begging on bended knee to take her on."

Exactly the opposite of what Denise was claiming. But I was inclined to believe Caitlin—Denise, the ultimate toady, would ultimately twist everything to cast Alison in the more favorable light.

"You didn't know, I'll bet," Caitlin went on, "that Alison is a former fatty."

"Alison Wade?" I repeated with astonishment. "I thought she was one of those depressing types who never put on an ounce."

"Guess again. Cheryl showed me a snapshot once of when they were both kids. Alison was the original Two-Ton Tessie. Her butt could've stopped a Mack truck if she'd had it parked in the street." Caitlin let out an incongruously crude guffaw. "That chick was big!"

"So what slimmed her down?"

"Basically, just Mother Nature. Most of the time, porky kids grow up to be porky adults, but Alison lucked out—she had the kind of baby fat that at sixteen or seventeen just melts away. But she still lives in constant terror that she's going to balloon back up any minute."

"Let me guess," I said. "Jeremy must have discovered this secret fear of hers and used it every chance he could to humiliate her."

"I see you've done your homework on the darling boy," Caitlin said acidly. "That's exactly what he did. They'd go out to Spago every night and Jeremy would order just about everything on the menu, starting off with the Jewish pizza, right through complete entrees and the most fattening desserts, with lots of wine and after-dinner drinks, naturally. He *was* one of those people who can eat anything and never gain weight. All through these enormous meals, he'd be urging her to try this, have some of that. . . . If she refused, he'd become nasty and mocking, calling her a spoilsport and a neurotic anorexic. But then when they got home, the minute she undressed, he'd instantly change his tune. All of a sudden, he's pointing out all her cellulite and criticizing her flabby thighs and fat tits. 'You disgust me,' he'd say and he'd refuse to have sex with her. That's when she came crawling to me, begging to help her get in shape."

"And so you very generously let bygones be bygones and helped her out."

Caitlin narrowed a suspicious look at me. "It's against my nature to turn away anyone who's in pain."

"And that's why you also smoked the peace pipe with Judie Levritz?"

She shrugged. "Judie was desperate for my help. She was terrified she was going to die. She'd had the operation and had started the chemotherapy, but she didn't trust it. And frankly, I don't put much stock in that stuff either."

"Meaning you trust herbs more."

"I put Judie on a homeopathic regimen," she said stiffly. "She's responded excellently."

"Did she stop the conventional treatments?"

A disgruntled look crossed Caitlin's face. "No, she continued with the chemo and radiation. And of course her doctors are claiming all the credit for her recovery."

High-priced Beverly Hills doctors, no doubt. My leg muscles were beginning to cramp from their unnaturally foreshortened position. I stood up and gave them a stretch. "What about Cheryl Wade?" I asked.

Caitlin set down her shears. "Poor old Cheryl. She came running to me for everything, anytime anything went wrong. A parking ticket, a bad hair day . . ."

"Or after a drag-out fight with Alison," I supplied.

"Especially after one of those," she said crisply. A snail oozed its way out from a herbaceous border. Caitlin stamped it unceremoniously with a ballet-slippered foot. I turned my eyes away from the little crushed mass of shell and slime.

"Did Cheryl and Alison fight a lot?" I asked.

"Please. It was their only form of communication. In fact, the last time I ever saw Cheryl was after one of their blow-outs."

"Yeah, so I heard. Did she tell you what it was about?"

"Of course. Cheryl's motto wasn't exactly 'Mum's the word.' Do you know about those Wild Bunch scavenger hunts?"

"I've heard about them. They get assigned tasks, usually getting some well-known woman to make a fool of herself. And they have to bring back Polaroids proving their success."

"Yeah, but sometimes what they're supposed to do is bring back actual items. On the last one they had, one of the items was a pair of Alison Wade's panties—worn and unwashed, of course. Apparently Cheryl supplied them. Then those jerks passed them all around town so all their other jerky friends could get a good whiff of them. They ended up being hung above the bed in Jeremy's trailer in New Mexico."

I swallowed a laugh. "No wonder Alison was just a bit pissed off," I said. "But it doesn't really make sense. Even ditzy Cheryl must have realized that if Alison found out, she'd go berserk. So why would she do it?"

Caitlin gave a rather superior smirk. "Because she was screwing Lane Reisman. And he sweet-talked her into it."

"Cheryl and Lane? I didn't think she was his type."

"Enough his type to bang her whenever it was convenient for him. She had a date with Lane that last night I saw her. It's why she needed something to cool her out—so she'd be in nice mellow shape for Mr. Reisman."

"Are you sure she kept the date?" I asked.

"Positive. Ralph was here at the time, and he very sweetly offered to drop her off at Lane's house."

I plucked a pink honeysuckle from an abundant vine and inhaled it, mulling over this new data. If it was true that both Lane and Ralph had been with Cheryl that Sunday, then I now had to add them both to the already populous lineup of suspects. It was exasperating that, instead of becoming more clear, things just seemed to get increasingly complicated.

"What *did* you give Cheryl to mellow her out?" I asked, in a casual tone. "Some homeopathic concoction?"

"Not exactly. It was a combination of Chinese herbs formulated to relieve stress."

"No minute traces of poison in it?"

"Of course not," she said brusquely.

"But I suppose you do grow poisonous plants here," I pursued. "For homeopathic purposes and all."

"You can find poisonous plants everywhere," she said. "See that white bush over there? That's oleander. It grows like a weed in this part of the world; they even plant it in the center strips of highways. But it's also a deadly poison. An entire family once got sick and died just from using oleander sticks to roast hot dogs."

"Somehow, I don't think a wiener roast was what did Jeremy in," I said.

Caitlin took a belligerent step toward me. "Look, I know you think Jeremy was murdered, and I figured you'd end up suspecting me. But you're totally wrong. I'm a healer. I don't kill things."

"Except for the occasional snail."

This took her back a moment. She shook her golden cap of hair. "I've got no choice. If I don't get rid of them, they'll wipe out all my herbs."

"So you have no problem killing things if there's no choice."

"What's that supposed to mean?" she snapped.

"I'm just trying to get things straight. After all, didn't you once even try to kill yourself? With some kind of poison, wasn't it?"

She flushed with fury. I suddenly became aware of the facts of my situation: I was standing in a secluded garden, enclosed by a wall too high to scale, provoking a woman who was not only possibly homicidal but also at the moment happened to be within a convenient range of a pair of razor-sharp shears. And just a shout away lurked a brother who was palsy-walsy with the kind of people who had an intimate acquaintance with the nonmusical uses of piano wire.

"Look," I said quickly, "I just heard these things. I don't know whether they're true or not."

"You know what I think?" she snarled, moving closer to me. "I think you hear too goddamned much."

"You're absolutely right," I said, backing away, "I've often been accused of being nosy. It's a lousy habit and I intend to immediately cut it out."

"I don't believe that for a damned second. I think you're gonna keep going around making trouble for me and my brother." She raised a menacing fist and started closer toward me.

I sprang at her suddenly and shoved her as hard as I could. She let out an *"Awp!"* then executed three or four steps of a sort of sideways polka before sprawling, knees bawdily up, in a bed of English lavender. The effect was so satisfying that for a split second I was tempted to hang around and enjoy it.

But self-preservation instincts prevailed. I raced back into the house, setting sprint records through the parlor, until I barked my shin on the clawfoot of one of the Victorian divans. "Ouch!" I yelled, hopping on my good leg, and nearly collided with Ralph Jones.

We stood goggling at one another, he with astonishment, I with the disconcerting observation that his right hand was dripping with blood. My God! I thought wildly, I've caught him fresh from the act of slitting someone's throat.

Then I realized that his ring finger was extended, as if in some kind of esoteric Italian curse; and that furthermore, this was the source of the blood—it was spurting freely from a deep gash across the pad.

"I sliced my finger on a grapefruit knife," he whimpered. "Right down to the fucking bone. Where's my sister?"

"You'll find her out in the lavender," I said and edged past him to the front door.

Outside I made tracks again, ignoring my throbbing shin, not letting up my pace till I reached the boardwalk and its strolling crowds. I insinuated myself gratefully among the multi-pierced guitarists and white Rastas, the tattooed panhandlers, oiled bodybuilders, and green-haired novelty hawkers: They looked like Beaver Cleaver's extended family compared to the spooky Bobbsey Twins I'd just left behind.

To catch my breath, I stood for a few moments watching a side-show on the scraggly lawn between beach and boardwalk. Two skinny black guys with platinum hair: One lay stretched out on the grass, while right above him, his partner juggled a Ping-Pong ball, a bowling ball, and a buzzing power saw. The juggler kept up a running patter: "You think this guy can get life insurance, you're outta your mind. . . . Hey, I also do circumcisions. . . ." *Bzzzzzzz* went the power saw, flipping in the air.

It seemed like a pretty good metaphor for my life at the moment. The Ping-Pong ball represented the current state of my career—lightweight, but fairly easy to keep up in the air. The bowling ball—that was obviously my marriage, much harder to juggle, always threatening to come down with a thud. And the buzz saw . . .

Well, that was my investigation of Jeremy Lord's death. Just one slip, and it could slice me right in two.

Part

3

SEVENTEEN

I frittered away the rest of the afternoon with a shopping spree, hitting the novelty stands that line the busiest part of the boardwalk, snapping up a Betty Boop Goes Hawaiian sweatshirt for myself and sunglasses shaped like pink smooching lips for Chloe. For Kit, I eyed a fine pair of chartreuse socks that, through some miracle of modern science, glowed in the dark. The pre-Virus Kit would have loved them. Post-Virus, however, he seemed to allow only charcoal cashmere to adorn his feet. Reluctantly, I passed the glowing wonders up.

The wallow in kitsch cheered me up, but only momentarily. Kit's departure was as frenetic and finally as abrupt as I'd predicted.

And in the morning, after he left, Chloe woke up feeling feverish and vomity. I put in a call to her pediatrician, a woman who, despite diplomas from Harvard, Princeton, and the Sorbonne, allowed—nay, encouraged—her patients to call her Dr. Bitsy. Dr. Bitsy was swamped, intoned her nurse, there was a bug going around, almost half The School had been laid low. "Expect temperatures up to a hundred and two, and incidents of vomiting," she added cheerfully. "Give plenty of fluids and check in with us in the morning."

The next couple of days I spent glamorously wiping off upchuck, fetching glasses of cranapple juice and ginger ale, watching *Harriet the Spy* for the umpteenth time, here and there letting Graciela take over a shift so that I could finish up with the libidinous Porter Penguin.

After three days, Chloe's temperature was down, but her stomach was still performing loop-de-loops. After much messy experimentation, I'd discovered that Baxter's All Natural Chicken Broth was one of the few foods I could feed her without having it immediately revisit her bed comforter. The only store in the vicinity that stocked the brand was a shop on Montana called the Gourmet Hut. It was kind of a 7-Eleven for the rich, opened early, closed late: Among the items you could *not* buy at the Gourmet Hut were iceberg lettuce, sliced bread of any kind, Oreos, Cheese Doodles, or Kellogg's Rice Krispies; what you could purchase, had you the inclination and deep-as-Lake-Tahoe pockets to pay for it, was tins of stuffed baby octopus in oil and pots of pomegranate glaze imported from Athens, cunning little boxes of dried lentil curry, and festive cellophane packets of Chinese pilaf. There were about ninety different kinds of olives from Atalánti to Santa Barbara grown; ditto for olive oils, with the going rate of fifty bucks for a miniature bottle of the palest green extra virgin from Umbria.

I now made a quick consommé run to the Gourmet Hut; I grabbed a basket, threw in three or four cans of soup, and was negotiating the tiny aisles to the register when I heard a *"Pssst!"* It was a sound you often saw written but rarely heard spoken, "Hey, you!" being the more contemporary choice of attention-getter. I glanced around, but saw no one. It came again, "Psst," followed by a "Lucy, over here!" I peered through a loosely stacked pyramid of jarred fancy fruit; a tiny face peered apprehensively back at me.

It was Judie Levritz. "I want to talk to you," she hissed in a stage whisper.

I felt a twinge of alarm—she was going to tell me she was pressing charges for my Halloween prowl. It was followed by an even stronger twinge of paranoia. What was the wife of a gazillionaire who had hot and cold running servants doing pushing a minicart through a gourmet convenience store? In particular, how was it that she happened to be here in the rare and brief instance that I was as well?

But then again, why shouldn't she be here? In these egalitarian days, plenty of the rich and even the famous are not above doing the occasional grocery run. Once I'd seen Tom Hanks here, buying a package of sun-dried tomato croutons. He'd even counted his change.

It seemed ridiculous to continue our conversation through a lattice of crabapples in their own syrup. "I'll come around," I told her and quickly rounded the shelves to her side of the aisle. "Hi," I said awkwardly. "How was Hawaii?"

"We had to leave," she said. "There was a cyclone coming through. We got out just before they closed the airport."

"Sorry to hear it," I said.

She agitatedly patted her hair. I suddenly realized it was a wig, a superbly fitted and styled wig made of natural human hair.

"I'm the one who wants to say I'm sorry." She still spoke in a dramatically lowered voice, as if she thought these shelves of specialty items had ears. "I was horrified when I heard that Mr. Trinh had called the police on you! I'm so embarrassed I don't know how to begin to apologize. He's not that familiar, you know, with the idea of trick-or-treat."

I breathed a sigh of relief—it seemed there would be no sticky questions about my foray through her private quarters. "There was no real harm done," I said with a gracious shrug. "Let's just forget the whole thing."

She directed a few darting little glances around the shop, then edged closer to me. "The problem is our entire household is on a kind of alert," she whispered. "We think we might have had an intruder."

"Why?" I asked quickly.

"It's hard to say exactly. We'd get up in the morning and it would seem like things were different, not in the places they were left. Of course, we have quite a few people on staff so it's not that simple to keep track of everything. But I'm positive I've noticed things that were moved."

"I've had the same feeling," I told her. I dropped my voice to the same conspiratorial level. "Cheryl Wade thought it too, and look what's happened to her."

"My God!" Judie gasped.

"Remember the story about Charles Manson? How, to begin with, he and his followers would break into households at night and move some furniture around? It was just so the people would get up the next morning and know they'd had someone in their home. They called it 'creepy-crawlies.' Of course," I added, "that was before they moved on to disembowelment."

Judie seemed to teeter a bit on her Bottega Veneta heels. "We had state of the art security," she said. "Only a top professional could have defeated the system, according to the law enforcement people we've talked to. Morty's beefed it up even more since then, and we've now got round-the-clock armed guards. German shepherds as well. I'd strongly advise you to do the same."

"Yeah, thanks," I said dryly.

"Anyway," she went on, "it's why poor Mr. Trinh panicked when he saw you. I just wanted you to understand."

"Perfectly."

We basked for a moment in a good vibe of mutual relief: me at no longer having to entertain the prospect of becoming an inmate of the county holding tank; Judie, no doubt, at not having herself and her housing-baron hubby sued for false arrest and causing a stir in the popular press.

"By the way," she said abruptly, "did you get rid of all the nits?"

I blinked, baffled a second. "Oh, you mean the lice. Yes, I think we managed to defeat their system."

"I hope you followed Ms. Baljur's instructions to the letter. We certainly don't want *that* kind of thing recurring at The School." She shuddered at the thought: Apparently even disembowelment at the hands of delusional maniacs was preferable to such a low-rent indignity as head lice.

"We certainly don't," I agreed.

She made a show of consulting a diamond-studded watch, raising her brows to her wigline, gurgling about how surprisingly late it was. "I've got to get to The School," she announced. "I'm leading an origami workshop for the Second Form. It was marvelous to see you again, Lucy."

Yeah, nice chatting among the tinned squid, I thought as she sauntered out to a car and driver hovering right outside the entrance.

I proceeded on to the register with my broth. Feeling the need for

some quick sustenance, I grabbed a box of Snyder's of Hanover sour-
dough pretzels. "INDIVIDUALLY TWISTED," claimed the box copy. . . .

Which, on reflection, pretty much summed up everyone I'd met
so far, vis-à-vis the late, great Jeremy Lord.

✳

Even with Chloe out of commission, I still had car pool duty. My
impromptu meeting with Judie had set me behind schedule: my contingent would be getting out in twenty minutes, and my being even
a few minutes late would mean a barrage of phone calls from moms
frantic that their children would forevermore suffer from an aban-
donment complex. I rushed home, dragged Graciela away from a
flirtation with a shirtless Mexican carpenter, and gave her the soup
to prepare, then headed to the stairs to make a quick check on
Chloe.

"No in bed," Graciela informed me rather grumpily.

"She's up?"

"She do computering."

This was good news: If Chloe felt well enough to be back cruising
the Internet, she must be definitely on the mend. I found her in the
den, wearing one of my terry-cloth robes over her pajamas, and hun-
kered in front of the Mac, engrossed in what was on the monitor. "Feeling better?" I said.

She gave a suspiciously guilty start and whirled to face me.

"What are you looking at?"

"Nothing," she said a shade too quickly. "Just a chat room."

"What chat room?"

"I don't know." She moved to click it off.

"No, wait, I want to see."

Reluctantly, she shifted so that I could get a glimpse of the screen.
This particular chat room, I was fascinated to note, was entitled "Hunks
'n' Holes." The participants, the majority of whom seemed to fall under
the rubric of "Hunks" rather than "Holes," sported such *noms de* chat
room as "HOT2TROT," "STUDMAN," and "STEEL ROD"; the discus-

sion at hand appeared to revolve around the female cast members of the sitcom *Friends;* more precisely, a running critique of their physical attributes, interspersed with commentary on how said attributes could best be employed. Old STUDMAN seemed a particular connoisseur of the culinary double entendre, weighing in with such memorable lines as "I'd like to lick those lollipops" and "I sure could stuff that muffin."

"Very educational," I said, in a strained voice. "How long have you been looking at this?"

"Just a couple of minutes."

"Where did you find it? This kind of stuff is not supposed to be on your line." We had what we thought was a pretty stringent "filth filter" on her AOL account.

"I kind of logged in using your name," she mumbled.

"Oh yeah? How did you get my password?"

She shrugged. "I tried my name and my birthday, and then I tried 'Amerinda' and that worked."

Duh.

On screen, the chat room gang, having exhausted the subject of Jennifer Aniston's nipples, had moved on to the ladies of *Melrose Place.* I clicked it off. "From now on," I told Chloe, "you're not to use my line or Daddy's even if you do figure out the password. Is that clear?"

"Miri Pleischer's got her own Internet in her own room, and she's got no restrictions on it, and her parents never ever check up on her."

"Miri Pleischer's parents might let her go out and pick up sailors on Hollywood Boulevard, but that's not my concern," I countered. "That's the rule. And now I think it's time for you to go back to bed." She began to protest. "Come on, scoot," I said firmly.

She trudged sulkily toward the stairs. "You've got E-mail," she informed me over her shoulder. "And it's not from me."

"Who's it from then? Nobody else knows my E-mail address."

"*I* don't know, I didn't read it."

I was getting dangerously late for car pool, but curiosity made me pull up the menu. A message had been sent at 3:43 A.M. Under the SUBJECT heading, it was blank. The sender was listed as 113x4@anon.stealth.fi.

Gibberish to me. Probably junk mail, I thought, calling it up.
A single sentence appeared on the screen:

DON'T GO STICKING YOUR GODDAM NOSE WHERE IT DOESN'T BELONG

I stood staring at this communiqué for some moments as if it
couldn't possibly exist—as if at any moment the letters would rearrange
themselves into an ad for cut-rate office supplies or a new All Nude
Dancing joint in Silverlake. But no, it stubbornly stayed as it was.

I printed it out and stuffed the printed page in my purse; then I
stabbed DELETE and rushed back out to my car, with barely minutes
to spare to get to Windermere on time.

✳

I was back driving the Cherokee, which had had two five-inch nails
excised from its tires and which, after the Corvette, felt like hauling
around a tractor-trailer.

Even without Chloe, I had a full Jeep-load, having acquired an
additional passenger, an eight-year-old named Dana Rich with red Shir-
ley Temple ringlets and perpetual hay fever. Both Dana and Skye Castaneda were transporting frogs in takeout Chinese-style waxed
cardboard boxes, the end products of a Third Form science project on
polliwogs; the amphibious croaking added a kind of samba backbeat to
the two Seiglers' bickering and Dana's snuffles.

Skye, who had chosen the apt name of Mr. Slime for his new pet,
began tapping on its container. "Hey, Mr. Slime, chill out."

Dana, who occupied the front seat beside me, swiveled primly.
"You keep on hitting his box, no wonder he's upset." She sniffled and
daintily swiped her nose with the back of her hand.

"I think he might be sick or something," Skye said. I heard him
pulling at the top flaps of the container.

"Don't open that," I warned, merging into a clot of traffic on Santa
Monica. "He might jump out."

"No, he won't," Skye replied and gave another yank of a flap.

"Oh, gross, Mr. Slime jumped out!" squealed Tracy Seigler.

"Put him back, Skye," I ordered.

"I can't find him, he went under the seat."

"You'd jolly well better find him," I said in an I-mean-business-tone. I already had an assortment of cold-blooded creatures inhabiting the nether regions of my house; I was damned if I was going to have them set up housekeeping in my car as well.

Sky unbuckled his seat belt and squinched himself down to peer beneath the front seat.

"Not now," I said with exasperation. "When we get to your house. Sit back up and put your seat belt back on."

"Hey, look what I found," he announced.

Through the rearview mirror, I saw him wave a cigar like a phallic wand. I knew immediately where it had come from: Ever since Cheryl had spilled the contents of her purse, I'd been finding odd objects on the floor of the car—only the day before, a tube of flesh-colored lipstick had rolled beneath the brake pedal.

"My daddy smokes cigars," piped up Dana.

"Big deal, my dad does too, and he has them made specially for him by Dunhills," said Tristan Seigler.

"You don't really have a dad," Tracy Seigler put in. "You were *in vitro*. You got made in a test tube."

"Shut up, you meat ass." *Whap!* on the shoulder.

"You shut up, dog dip." *Counter-whap!* on the thigh.

"Hey, can I keep this?" asked Skye.

I glanced again in the mirror and watched him begin to put the cigar in his mouth.

"No!" I shrieked suddenly and, letting go the wheel, twisted violently to slam the cigar out of his hand. The Cherokee veered into oncoming traffic: I grabbed back the wheel and wrenched it to the right, zigzagged between a Honda, a Mustang, and a delivery vehicle shaped like a pink hot dog on a bun. The car jumped the curb as I smashed the brake pedal and came to a jolting stop on the sidewalk, which—this being L.A.—was fortunately devoid of pedestrians.

The two Seiglers were stunned for once into an uncharacteristic silence; the frogs had also seemed to find it prudent to shut up. Little Dana, however, had burst into snuffling tears, and Skye was bleating, "I'm telling my mom you hit me." The proprietor of the Armenian restaurant, whose doorstop we now occupied, peered bug-eyed from behind the MasterCard logo on his shop window.

I was only dimly aware of any of this, or of my teeth chattering like castanets, or the Niagara of blood roaring in my ears. All I could think about was my memory of Jeremy Lord's body atilt on the toilet in Cheryl Wade's hotel room john. . . .

And that faint, pungent odor, which I suddenly realized was cigar smoke.

EIGHTEEN

Terry Shoe's table, located under a floating white sign marked HOMI-
CIDE in the bull's-eye center of the West L.A. Station Detectives'
Room, seemed to defy a basic law of physics—two objects cannot oc-
cupy the same space at the same time—since it seemed otherwise impossible that the small surface could embrace such a sheer quantity of
stuff. Files and forms slopped over clipboards and notebooks and en-
gulfed a computer monitor like layers of geologic sediment. There were
two coffee mugs (a Dilbert and a Snoopy), an array of dusty birthday
cards, an anthropophagic-looking philodendron clawing the air as if for
means of busting out from its cracked plastic pot, pencils, erasers, a
silver pierced earring in the shape of a shamrock, a turquoise leather
pet collar and—most mystifyingly—a mitten.

I sat in a hard metal chair obliquely facing this maelstrom while
Terry finished a convoluted phone conversation about the disposition
of a body just fished from Santa Monica Bay. I had raced directly here
after discharging my last passenger, little Dana Rich, who'd stopped
crying, but whose runny nose had become an epic discharge. I had
deposited the cigar in a Poquito Mas takeout bag I'd found crumpled
in the glove compartment and which I now clutched as gingerly as if
it contained a ticking bomb.

Terry finally hung up and turned to me. "To what do I owe the
honor?"

"I think I've discovered a murder weapon," I said dramatically and
handed the fast-food bag her.

She regarded me a moment with eyes the amber of a traffic signal;
then she pried the paper edges apart and peered in. "What's this?"

"It's a cigar. And I think it's what killed Jeremy Lord."

She shook it from the bag. It plopped out onto the mitten. For the first time, I looked at it closely. It was a slender stogie, the color of rich earth, with a plain red-and-gold band, and it had been smoked about a quarter of its length.

"And you obtained this from . . . ?" Terry queried.

"My car."

"Why didn't I guess that?"

"Let me explain," I said impatiently. "Remember how I told you that Cheryl Wade had hidden in the back of my Jeep? It was the night before she was found in a coma."

"Yeah, I remember. So?"

"It was when she told me she had unknowingly poisoned Jeremy and that she had something that could prove it. She also had overturned her bag in my car, and everything in it had spilled out."

"So you figure the cigar came from Wade's spilled-out bag and it's the evidence that could prove her statement."

"Exactly!" I said, leaning back in my chair.

"You really ought to try out for the Olympics. When it comes to jumping to conclusions, you're world-class material."

"I am absolutely not just jumping to conclusions!" I burst out.

Two detectives sitting under the ROBBERY marker turned to stare with interest in my direction—both paunchy guys in short-sleeved shirts and jazzy medium-wide ties. I had the horrible sensation that they recognized me from my recent sojourn in the slammer. I fervently wished I was wearing something less conspicuous than my vintage tangerine rayon blouse with hula girl pattern and clattering Bakelite bangles.

I scrunched down a bit in my chair and lowered my voice to a more discreet level. "It all fits perfectly," I went on. "Say you're somebody who wants to knock off Jeremy Lord. You hit on a plan to have Cheryl Wade unwittingly slip him something lethal. The first thing you'd have to be sure of is making it something Jeremy couldn't resist. You might think of drugs, top-grade cocaine, or one of those designer psychedelics. But if it had been something like that, it would have turned up in the autopsy. And besides, no one in their right mind would trust Cheryl Wade to pass along a controlled substance without being tempted to try just a taste herself." I tried to lighten the atmosphere with a chuckle. No reciprocation from the Doyenne of Deadpan.

"A really fine cigar would fit the bill," I plunged on. "It would be right up Jeremy's alley, and Cheryl wouldn't want to cop it for herself. She gave it to him when she got back to New Mexico and that night, in her hotel room, he went into the bathroom to smoke it. The poison hit, he dropped dead. And Cheryl, in her panic, removed the half-smoked cigar from the scene."

Terry gave a noncommittal grunt.

"An hour later, when I went into the bathroom and found the body, I noticed a faint odor that I couldn't identify. It was only after finding this in my car that I realized what that smell was. I'm positive it was from cigar smoke." I saw little benefit in mentioning that I had arrived at this sudden revelation after watching the cigar being conveyed to an eight-year-old boy's mouth. "I think if you test this out, you'll find it's loaded with a deadly poison," I concluded.

Terry peered at it dubiously. Then she waved at Armand Downsey, who was two desks over, cradling a phone. "Downsey, come and take a look at this, will you?"

He held up a "one-second" finger, wrapped up his call, and sauntered over.

"What do you think?" Terry asked. "Would you call this a fine cigar?'"

He picked it up with tweezerlike fingers and examined the band. "Cuban, with a Partagas band. Off the top of my head, I'd say it's pre-Castro."

"That's good, isn't it?" I asked.

"Put it this way—I just heard of a box of a hundred and fifty going at auction for seventy-five thousand dollars." He set it reverently back on the desk. "This baby is worth about five hundred bucks. So yes, I'd call that rather an outstanding cigar."

I couldn't help shooting a quick I-told-you-so look at Terry Shoe.

Downsey propped a chalk stripe–tailored hip against the edge of her table. "So what's this all about?"

I ran through an encapsulated version of what I'd told Terry.

"Interesting," he said. In his purring voice, the word sounded like extravagant praise. "One thing I don't quite follow," he said. "Why would he have gone into the bathroom to smoke?"

"Maybe he was being polite," I suggested. "Sparing Cheryl second-hand smoke . . ."

"From what I've heard, he wasn't the type to be so considerate."

This was true: Jeremy Lord had been the type to blow smoke rings in an asthmatic's face. "The autopsy showed he was pretty drunk," I said. "He probably wasn't thinking too clearly. He could've stumbled into the bathroom to take a pee, then while he was there, remembered he had the cigar and decided to light up."

Neither detective stood up and saluted this dim theory.

"Your husband, Kit," Terry said, "does he ever smoke Cuban cigars?"

"Yeah, occasionally, but—"

"Does he ever borrow your car?"

I drew an impatient breath. "Well, sure, sometimes he takes my car—"

"Recently?"

I paused. Over the weekend, he'd grabbed my keys for a quick run to a deli. It *was* possible that he'd been given a five-hundred-dollar cigar, it was just the kind of thing Lane Reisman would blow his studio expense account on. . . .

"Look," I burst out, "if I'm so entirely off base, then why the hell am I getting threats?"

The detectives glanced at me, eyebrows raised skeptically.

I dug into my purse for the printed E-mail message and presented it with a theatrical flourish.

"This was E-mailed to me at three A.M. this morning. I don't recognize the address of the sender. It just looks like technical gobbledygook to me."

Terry scrutinized the sheet, then handed it to Downsey. "Can we trace this through America Online?"

He frowned. "Doubt it. It looks like a remailer."

"What's that?" I asked.

"It's a service you can use if you want to send E-mail and have it masked. You open an account with a remailer, and they resend all your mail anonymously."

"It's kind of like having a Swiss bank account," Terry added. "All you are to them is an account number."

"But isn't sending out threats illegal?"

"You bet," said Downsey.

"So can't you get a warrant to find out who opened the account?"

Terry Shoe produced the standard disgruntled moue of a cop thwarted in the line of duty by a technicality. "Remailers are usually fly-by-night operations out of little countries like New Zealand or Liechtenstein. Even if we had the resources, which we don't, it'd be pretty hard to trace."

"Yours appears to have been sent from Finland," Downsey said. He smiled dryly. "Welcome to the global village."

"And anyway, we can't even say for sure this is a threat," Terry added. "It's a piece of advice. Some might even say good advice. Nothing says they intend to harm you if you don't follow it."

"That's all you're going to do?" I burst out. "Just tell me I'm getting anonymous advice from Finland and wish me lots of luck?"

"We can still attempt to check it out," Downsey said smoothly. "It's just a forewarning that we probably won't get very far."

"What about the cigar?"

He glanced at Terry with a what've-we-got-to-lose shrug.

"Okay, I'll take it to SID," she allowed. "With no case number, they'll give me a lot of grief, but what the hell. . . . They owe me a couple of favors."

"Thanks," I said warmly. I stood up, surprised to discover that my knees felt made of chewing gum: for equilibrium, I grasped the back of the chair. "What should I do in the meantime?"

"Offhand, I'd say you ought to follow their advice," Terry said. "Don't go sticking your nose where it doesn't belong."

*

Chloe was sound asleep when I returned home, so I used the momentary peace and quiet to catch up with the mail. There was a postcard from my best friend, Valerie Jane Ramirez, a costume designer on location with a Kevin Costner movie in Puerto Vallarta, reporting that the entire cast had come down with *turista*; an onslaught of bills, including a whopper from the joke-cracking fertility expert, Dr. Kelshok; a flyer from The School announcing that the tennis courts would be resurfaced the last week of November. . . .

And a large embossed envelope of heavyweight cream-colored paper addressed to Kit. Probably a benefit invitation, Help End the Tragedy of Myasthenia Gravis, guest of honor, Mary Tyler Moore, two hundred fifty bucks a head donation—since his comeback to the Big League, Kit's name had popped up on every charity list in town. I felt no compunction about opening it.

The New Cubana Room takes pleasure in welcoming Mr. Christopher J. Freers as an honored member. . . .

This'll make Kit's day, I thought wryly—accepted into the most exclusive club in town, "the one with all the movie stars." I examined the enclosed membership roster. Movie stars galore, as well as a hefty contingent of satellite fish: agents, publicists, studio execs. Some heavyweight lawyers for ballast, a sprinkling of top directors to give extra sail. Jeremy Lord remained on the rolls, presumably a member still, in spirit if not in corporeality. Lane Reisman's name appeared, of course, as did Ralph Jones's, asterisked as cofounder. And housing baron Morton Levritz, ironically listed right above Jeremy Lord.

The envelope also yielded a card on which was fastened a polished brass key—the key to the club's humidor room, in which Christopher J. Freers now possessed a private cigar locker.

And there was a third communiqué, this soliciting the prompt remittance of a membership fee of ten thousand dollars.

I was reeling from this sum, vaguely calculating how many Brazilian orphans it could clothe and feed for a year, when the phone rang. I absently snatched it up.

There was a shriek of a small animal in indescribable pain.

"Stop that!" I yelled into the receiver. "Whoever you are, whatever you're doing, stop it immediately!"

The tortured shriek coalesced into a voice—an electronically distorted voice. This was what I had mistaken for someone mutilating a bunny—it was nothing more than the feedback of some voice-distortion device. The words it produced now came out with a terrifyingly inhuman pitch and cadence that I could barely decipher: "Don't go snooping around in what doesn't concern you."

Another agonized electronic squeal, and once again the line went dead.

Nineteen

Once upon a time, if you made it big in Hollywood, you'd flaunt your success with the suitable trappings: Bugatti roadsters with monogrammed doors, swimming pools in the shape of bee-stung lips or grand pianos, sable and silver-fox coats of a luxuriance to beggar the imagination. But nowadays, when wearing a fur means to risk being splattered with ketchup by incensed animal-rights defenders, when swimming pools are as common as built-in barbecues, and even the mailroom boys drive dazzling cars, the *au courant* way to announce your arrival is to start up your own production company.

Alison Wade announced hers, called Leading Lady Productions, scarcely minutes after her second box-office smash had established her as a bona fide star. Only the initiated could identify the building that housed her offices, a horizontal slab of fawn-colored brick with a windowless street facade tucked blandly among the neon-signed coffee shops and Art Deco emporia of Beverly Boulevard. For the sake of security, no sign of any sort graced the exterior. Also for security's sake, visitors were buzzed through not one, but two metal doors and subjected in between to the scrutiny of an armed guard in powder blue uniform. For security's sake as well, video cameras immortalized every step of the visitor's way.

At two minutes to eleven on Wednesday morning, I found myself running this gauntlet, clutching a portfolio containing the storyboard I had sketched for Alison's schizophrenia festival. I passed muster with the guard and was admitted into a cozy reception room. "Hi, Lucy," trilled the receptionist, as if we weren't complete strangers but rather bosom friends since the cradle. "Go ahead and have a seat, and I'll let Richard know you're here."

I took a chair. It had been three days since the inhuman voice on the phone had warned me to stop snooping around. Three days without further incident. No threats or unusual messages of any kind by phone, fax, computer, or U.S. mail. No creepy rearrangement of household goods, no unexplained mechanical failures, no things that went bump in the night. It seemed that Terry Shoe was right: As long as I kept my goddamned nose out of other people's business, I'd be scratched off the threats list.

Which didn't keep me from obsessing over who was perpetrating said threats. The possibilities were many. There was Judie, who had been ready to kill at even the remote possibility her kids would end up with her loathed ex-husband, and who'd no doubt go to equal lengths to cover up anything she had done. The rejected Caitlin, who had practically a Ph.D. in toxic substances, and her cutthroat-cherub brother, Ralph, who had been double-crossed by Jeremy in a movie deal. And Lane, desperate not to have his first major production head for Flopsville. And of course Alison, exquisitely humiliated by Jeremy time and again.

I could even add Denise, the consummate toady, who might have acted in the service of any of the above.

Or it might be someone I didn't even suspect yet, one of the legions the fun-loving director had managed to piss off in the course of his abbreviated career.

My musings were interrupted by a young man bounding into the room. Dope-fiend thin, dandyishly tailored, in the manner of David Niven playing a gentleman's gentleman. "Richard Landrotti, I do Alison's development," he said, warmly squeezing my hand. He pronounced my work to be brilliant, though allowing he actually hadn't seen any of it himself. "Alison's terrifically enthused about your involvement in this project," he added hastily. "I don't think I've ever known her to be so excited."

This I understood was standard premeeting stroking, rather the way a nurse might exclaim, "What lovely veins you have" before jabbing in the needle. I murmured something along the lines of "I'm hugely excited too" and followed his lead into Alison's office. It was a disorienting simulation of Alison's boudoir—same gauzy fabrics, same cushion madness, same pale shades of bubbly: All it lacked was the Arabian Nights bed. I sank onto a Dom Pérignon-colored sofa and waited rather nervously with my portfolio straddled between my legs.

We were quickly joined by others, their order of appearance dictated it seemed by their order of importance. First, a duck-mouthed girl who was evidently too lowly to be introduced and whose function seemed to be to fetch coffee, tea, and sparkling water. Then Denise, who promptly busied herself setting out pencils and Leading Lady scratch pads. She was followed by two of Alison's agents, both in Armani sport coats, faded jeans and loafers, no socks, with the difference being that one wore Replay jeans and the other, Big Star; both immediately flipped open cell phones and began tapping in numbers with the staccato virtuosity of old-time telegraph operators. Then a contingent of three lower-level executives from the studio, whose function, it appeared, was to fill the air with social chitchat until the mainframe players arrived.

Lane Reisman swaggered in at 11:14. "Howdy, folks," he drawled. He was in peak Bruce Willis mode, bleary-eyed, stubble-chinned, Dodger-capped. The agents flipped shut their phones and competed with each other through an aggressive jostling of elbows to be the first to pump his hand. The studio underlings popped smartly to their feet, like English schoolboys at the entrance of Mr. Chips. Denise looked as if she couldn't decide whether to salaam or curtsy.

Lane cruised the room, democratically greeting everyone, even the anonymous duck-mouthed girl. He concluded his rounds by plumping onto the sofa next to me, so close our thighs touched. "Ready to strut your stuff?" he asked. The ham of his thigh pressed insinuatingly against mine and he got in a sneaky frottage. "I've been looking forward to seeing you put out for a long time."

"I'm flattered," I said icily. I wriggled my own butt a discreet half inch to the right.

"Heard from your old man recently?" he pursued.

This was a sore point: I hadn't had a call from Kit in two days. "I don't expect to talk to him every day," I said airily. "I know what it's like for him on the set, so busy he can hardly think."

"Busy as a little bee, day and night. Especially those nights. You know what I call a location set?" Lane gave a lubricious smirk. "Summer camp with sex."

My face grew hot. Lane, either knowingly or inadvertently, had touched an even sorer point: Kit had once confessed to me that some years ago, while on location in Canada, he had indulged in a one-night stand with a reporter from *Vanity Fair*.

Lane pounced on my momentary confusion. His thigh squeezed back against mine, and his mouth inclined close to my ear. "And when the cat's away," he crooned, "the mouse should lay."

I turned an innocent gaze on him. "Let me get this straight, Lane," I said. "Are you suggesting that I go to bed with you?"

He looked a bit disconcerted by the plain question. "Well, I . . ."

"Like Cheryl Wade?" I persisted.

"Huh?" His thigh muscles, still pressed against mine, went rigid.

"Weren't you having an affair with Cheryl Wade just before she died? Or was I misinformed?"

Lane shot a quick glance around the room to assure himself we weren't being overheard. "We might've fooled around a couple of times. Big fucking deal. Who didn't nail Cheryl Wade?" He recovered his smirk. "In case you hadn't heard, she was public property."

"That's not the way Cheryl saw it. I think she was crazy about you. She must have been, considering what she did for you."

"What are you talking about?" he shot back.

"I mean the panties. Didn't she swipe a pair of Alison's undies for you, just so you could win a scavenger hunt? That was a pretty risky thing for her to do, considering how much she depended on Alison." I nonchalantly bit a fingernail. "It kind of makes me wonder what else she was willing to do for you."

"What's that supposed to mean?" he said warily.

"Oh, I don't know. . . . Maybe, for instance, help you get rid of a director who was turning your first major production into a flop?"

Lane shot up from his seat as if he'd been spring-loaded. "You don't know what the hell you're talking about!" he snarled.

Every face in the room now turned our way, every set of brows shot up with startled interest.

Well done, Lucy, I told myself: You've just as good as accused the head of Keystone Studios of having sent a world-famous director to his heavenly reward, manifestly a Bad Career Move. I glanced at Lane, who was quivering with rage, and waited for him to pronounce this meeting null and void and have me summarily booted from the room.

But before anything else could happen, the door opened and Alison Wade blew in.

"It's simply criminal how they put these beastly people in charge of this stuff," she announced, as if we were all in the middle of an ongoing conversation. It was something I'd long noticed about the superfamous—they generally expect everyone in their immediate vicinity to understand intrinsically whatever they happen to be talking about, no matter how obscure or personal the reference.

Escorting Alison, with a proprietary hand on her arm, was a silver-haired man; he had a hint of a paunch and sported the sort of chunky gold accessories I thought had gone out with the breakup of the Rat Pack; this was unquestionably the dermatologist fiancé. The two were trailed by Alison's bodyguard, Laraine; she did a quick visual sweep of the room, making hard and prolific eye contact, as if daring someone to make a sudden move so she could wrassle him to the ground. The room was starting to have the feel of one of those Eisenhower-era college pranks, the kind where they'd see how many sophomores could be crammed into a phone booth or the back seat of a Studebaker.

Alison toured the room, though not as democratically as Lane: Only Lane, the agents, and two of the studio personnel received her throaty "Hello, dearest" and a fluttery air kiss beside the face. She also concluded her rounds with me. Her flawless face loomed in mine. "I can't wait to see what wonderful things you've come up with for me," she crooned. No air kiss. I wondered if that was a bad sign.

She turned toward the couch occupied by the studio menials, who instantly vacated it and scattered to opposite corners. Then she and her fiancé settled grandly on it, Lane straddled one of the arms, and for the next ten minutes we talked about Alison. Or more precisely, we listened while Alison talked about herself, a rambling disquisition on how staggeringly difficult it was to be the rich and celebrated Alison Wade. Topic A was The Help, from the stupid maids who failed to notice hairs in the bathtub to the masseuse who waltzed in seven minutes late this morning. Topic B was People Who Tried to Take Advantage, and their numbers were apparently legion. Somewhere between the antique dealers who doubled their prices the second Alison walked in and the "charity creeps" who were forever conniving to get her to lend her name, I tuned out.

Then my own name was spoken and I looked up with a start. All attention was now on me. "We're all looking forward to your take on this project," the aide de camp Richard was saying. "Are you ready?"

"Absolutely," I said, rather more confidently than I felt.

Pitching my work has never been my strongest point: My voice wobbles and cracks, and I become fumble-thumbed while displaying the sketches. But somehow I made it through my rehearsed spiel— how in the first act of the movie, when the character, Cecile, was just beginning to slide into schizophrenia, the hallucinations would be amusing, even charming, becoming increasingly nightmarish as the disease progressed. As a finale, I produced the screaming bunny, the bug-infested wedding cake, and a few nifty semi-human, semi-industrial machine monsters.

I sat back down, feeling I'd succeeded in at least grabbing their attention. All eyes now swung expectantly to Alison, whose face wore an expression of pure and intense concentration. A hush fell over the room.

"My foot's asleep," she announced.

The air became suddenly abuzz with yelps and murmurs of consternation. Alison daintily kicked off a kidskin pump and rotated her slender ankle, grimacing with the insupportable agony of pins and needles. The agent in Big Star jeans advanced the theory that potassium was just the ticket for a muscle cramp. Denise chimed in that bananas were a terrific source of potassium and offered to rush out and procure a bunch. The dermatologist weighed in with a medical opinion: This wasn't a muscle cramp, but the result of restricted blood flow. "Massage would be good," declared Lane and flexed his fingers, clearly ready and willing to be tapped for the duty.

Alison prettily stamped her nyloned foot. "Better. There, that's better, it's coming back now."

This news was received with the kind of jubilation generally displayed by courtiers at the birth of a royal heir. She slipped her foot back into her shoe and resettled in her seat.

Richard loudly cleared his throat. "So, what do we think of, ah, Lucy's presentation?" His eyes sidled to Lane. Lane's eyes shifted to Alison.

Alison cast a fluttery glance at her fiancé. "Jack, what do you think?"

Jack pinned his elbows to his chair in a take-charge attitude. I don't believe this, I thought—my future in feature films is about to be decided by an acne doctor. And apparently it was to be a dim future: Dr. Jack was eyeing my drawings with the dyspeptic aversion of a vegetarian contemplating a richly marbled slab of prime rib.

"The imagery is quite inventive," he pronounced at last. "But it's a little rough-edged in technique. I'd like to see a little more fluidity of action, on the lines of the Toontown sequences in *Roger Rabbit.* But I suppose we can work on that."

"Exactly what I was thinking!" Alison cried.

And remarkably, everybody else seemed to be thinking the exact same thing; there was a vigorous nodding of heads, while the words *fluidity* and *Toontown* sputtered in the air like popping corn.

It appeared I'd got the job. A thrill of excitement shot through me.

Alison rose to her feet, tripped over to me, and this time smacked the air beside both my cheeks. "Jack and I are delighted you'll be working with us," she cooed. "And of course I'll be seeing you at my shower. Lane," she added, swiveling, "join us for lunch?"

"Love to," he said promptly. The two agents positioned themselves strategically by the door, angling to be included in the invitation. The junior execs followed suit. Alison and her hubby-to-be sashayed out amid a roiling cluster of sycophants. Richard paused long enough to assure me I'd been brilliant and a deal memo would be forthcoming; then he too vanished, the duck-mouthed girl disappearing with him.

Denise, the last of the remaining personnel, trotted up to me. "I had no idea you were supposed to be invited to the shower," she gasped. "I feel like shit. I'll send you an invitation immediately."

"Don't worry," I said quickly. "I've got a strong feeling I wouldn't have been invited if Alison had hated my drawings. Or I suppose I should say if Jack hated them."

Denise's face contorted in a sneer. "She's made him coproducer, can you believe it? He's calling all the shots with everything she does now—it makes me just about puke. She won't do a thing without getting his approval first. She's, like, 'Jack, do you think I should say yes to this script?' and 'Jack, baby, should I change agents?' and 'Jackie-poo, should I go to the bathroom now or wait till later?' " She shuddered with revulsion. "God, I think it's disgusting when women let themselves be used like doormats."

This coming from someone who was ostensibly the *ne plus ultra* of doormats was somewhat startling. I gave a perfunctory smile.

Denise dropped her voice and glanced at the outer door. "I guess it'll be kind of weird, you working for Alison. I mean, considering the fact you suspect her of murder."

In my elation over landing the job, I'd temporarily managed to forget this little complication. The reality now came back to me like a slap. "Maybe I won't have to just suspect her much longer," I said. "I might be able to prove it one way or another."

Denise went rigid with attention. "You've found something out?"

"Maybe. I'm not sure yet."

"What? Maybe I can help out."

I hesitated. Denise was gazing at me with the bated expectation of a terrier watching a tin of Alpo travel to a can opener. "Do you know if Alison ever had any rare Cuban cigars in her possession?" I asked her.

Denise's pale, broad forehead scrunched in thought. "I don't know. I mean, Jack smokes cigars like a fiend. And Alison, ever since she saw Demi Moore on the cover of that cigar magazine, now she thinks it's the cool thing to do too. But I wouldn't know if they were Cuban or not. Is that important?" she added eagerly. "Do you want me to try to find out?"

I picked up a Leading Lady scratch pad and printed the word Partagas. "This is the name that would be on the band of the kind of cigar I mean. If you see one, let me know."

"Cool." Denise pocketed the paper, then began gathering up the used coffee cups and empty Perrier bottles; apparently another of the perks of her job was the privilege of cleaning up. "I'll let you know immediately."

I finished packing my drawings and headed out. As I passed the reception desk, I had a jolt of guilt—what if by making Denise a spy I was throwing her into danger? I didn't relish the thought of another coma patient on my conscience. I darted back into Alison's office.

Denise was no longer there. I'd call her from the car and warn her, I decided. I turned and retraced my steps out.

*

To celebrate my new employment, I treated myself to one of my favorite Goodwill shops, a storefront on the next block of Beverly—a musty-smelling place with curling linoleum floors and harsh crematorium lighting in which I could always spend many a happy hour. But I only had time for a pit stop. With well-practiced pace, I cruised by the lava lamps and cheesy aluminum cookware, idly sifted through a toppled stack of *Life* magazines from the boom years of Ronald Reagan and, just when I'd resigned myself to leaving empty-handed, came upon a genuine find: a Howdy Doody penny bank, vintage circa 1954—an excellent addition to my collection of old toys. In great condition, too—just the slightest wearing of carrot-colored paint on Howdy's cowlick. I coughed up the seven-fifty sticker price without haggling and jubilantly returned to my car.

I had parked off an alley parallel to Beverly Boulevard, in the spaces behind a gone-out-of-business waterbed store. A hand-lettered sign on the filthy back window screamed WE QUIT! No great surprise, I thought, fishing out my keys; they were about twenty years out of date.

Then I suddenly flashed on a memory: The first time Kit and I made love had been on a waterbed. It was in the grungy Bleecker Street walk-up above an Italian deli he'd lived in our first year at NYU, a sunless apartment that always smelled faintly of provolone and proscuitto; in the heat of our passion, we hadn't noticed the bed had sprung a leak until afterward, when we discovered we were drenched with more than just sweat—and that the sheets were sopping, the floor was flooded, and the Neapolitan proprietor from downstairs was pounding irately at the door.

Still smiling at the remembrance, I unlocked the Cherokee. I was about to climb in when I heard the sound of padded footsteps behind me.

I took sudden stock of my situation: alone in an alley behind a boarded-up store, screened from all sight of boulevard traffic. . . . With a tingle of alarm, I swung around and found myself almost nose to nose with a kid in basketball sneakers.

"Gimme the keys," he said. His voice was at once reedy and hoarse, the way Mickey Mouse might sound if Mickey were in the regular habit of bellying up to smoky bars. He wasn't a kid, I realized, even though he was scarcely five foot one. I registered a blond buzz cut, heavy black-rimmed shades in the style of the late Roy Orbison, and a grainy chin stubble that would have made Lane Reisman gnash his teeth with envy.

"The keys," he repeated in his dissolute Mickey voice.

"You don't really want to do this," I said condescendingly. Considering that I had a good four inches on him, it was hard to feel intensely threatened.

"Shut your trap," he piped.

"It's not worth it," I persisted. "Look, if you're short of money, I'll give you some. Tell me what you need."

In response, he lunged closer, and from beneath his jacket produced what appeared to be a stapler—the basic gray Swingline model. "Gimme those fuckin'-ass keys or I'll blow your guts out," he said.

I had the urge to laugh. The stapler suddenly metamorphosed into a gun, and the gun suddenly jabbed into my midriff. I inhaled sharply and dropped the penny bank that I'd been carrying in my left hand.

"What the fuck is that?" the mugger said.

"Howdy Doody," I replied.

"Jeez," he exclaimed with disgust and pressed the gun harder into my stomach.

The sounds of Beverly Boulevard sounded so close—the whoosh of traffic, sporadic horns, the high laughter of a passing pedestrian— but the alley was as deserted as Mars. Was this it? I wondered—was I about to be gunned down behind a failed waterbed store by the world's shortest mugger? I jingled the keys in my other hand. "Please, just take the keys and don't hurt me," I said.

He snatched them and then, as if in an afterthought, wrenched my purse off my shoulder. Then, almost jauntily, he flung himself into the Cherokee and started the engine. I expected to see the car peel out; astonishingly, it didn't budge. The mugger instead seemed to be playing with the various electric controls. *Whrrrrr:* His seat rose up. *Whrrrrr:* The seat descended. *Whrrrrr:* The back window rolled down.

I stood, mesmerized by this Fun with Controls. Then it struck me—his little legs couldn't reach the pedals, and he was trying to read- just the seat. *Whrrrr:* The seat traveled forward, a maneuver that seemed to do the trick; the car skidded into reverse, then jumped for- ward and roared off.

I picked up the Howdy penny bank, feeling absurdly grateful that he hadn't taken it as well. Then I staggered back around to Beverly. I had no car, no money nor credit cards—the city now seemed to stretch in an unbreachable vastness, the traffic whizzing by faster than, and as indifferent as, a speeding bullet. There was a bar on the next block with a spluttering Michelob sign in the window. I ran to it, pushed open the door, and burst into a whiskey-reeking gloom.

"Call nine-one-one," I gasped. "I've been carjacked."

TWENTY

"You were smart not to resist," said one of the half a dozen cops milling on the sidewalk—a stocky, pucker-browed officer who, having been the first on the scene, was now the de facto leader of the pack. "A lot of these carjackers, they'll kill ya as soon as blink. A lot of times, they kill ya anyway, even if you do everything they say."

"The young kids especially," interjected his partner, a woman with Florence Henderson hair. "The younger they are, the more vicious. You get a wired-up fifteen-year-old, he's got no respect for human life. He'll blow you away and not feel a speck of remorse."

"My guy was a lot older than fifteen," I said, rather redundantly. I had already sketched him on the back of a cocktail napkin from the bar, one that featured a cartoon of a mooning fat lady on the front. The Florence Henderson cop had radioed an immediate APB for both him and my Cherokee, though the general cop consensus was that if they didn't pick them up within the next fifteen minutes, I could abandon all hope of ever laying eyes on the car again. "It's probably already in a chop shop," said an officer with hound-dog bags under his eyes. "What they do is exchange the serial numbers with the ones from a junked car and then ship it off to the black market in South America." This prompted a brief sidebar on the current make and model preferences of car thieves, sports utility vehicles weighing in as the current fave, displacing a previous vogue for Honda Preludes and LeBaron convertibles. One rather grizzled officer nostalgically reminisced about the days when Cadillac Sevilles were in style—a conversation that gradually evolved to the fact that among sports utility vehicles, a Jeep Grand Cherokee Laredo was the carjacker's crème de la crème—indeed, that to drive a Jeep Grand Cherokee Laredo was practically to wave a banner that said STEAL THIS CAR. All of which led to the stocky cop congratulating me on having preserved life and limb by Offering No Resistance.

I had been advised to call someone to pick me up; taxiing crime victims back to their homes didn't seem to be among the duties of the LAPD. I'd rung up Patrice Castaneda, figuring she'd come if for no other reason than to get the scoop on the sordid details. Now I saw her green Mercedes nudge through the little traffic jam of rubbernecking motorists. "Am I done here?" I asked the stocky cop.

"Yeah. We'll call if we got any news." Don't hold your breath was the subtext.

I trotted up to Patrice's car and with relief slid in beside her. "So what exactly happened?" she panted.

"Oh, Patrice, it was awful!" I exclaimed and awarded her a luridly enhanced account of a wild-eyed—and enormous—assailant, possibly an escapee from a maximum security prison or home for the criminally insane.

"Did he . . . touch you?"

"Thank God he didn't seem interested in that. He just wanted my money and the car."

"Oh, well, that's good," she said, with flat disappointment. For the rest of the drive she regaled me with an account of a friend of a friend who was followed back to Brentwood one night by a car packed full of Crips gang members and gang-raped right on her *very own* priceless Bessarabian carpet.

She dropped me off at the gates of my driveway and zoomed off. At the curb, tucked among the construction crew pickups, was a familiar tan Caprice. I gave a grunt of exasperation as Terry Shoe hopped out.

"You don't waste any time, do you?" I said. "Did you come here to gloat?"

"About what?" she asked.

"You mean you haven't heard on the cop grapevine? I was carjacked."

Her tawny eyes glittered with wonderment. "Boy, it's never a dull moment with you, is it?"

"If I had my way, from now on, I'd have nothing but dull moments. I'd happily lead the most boring, stupefyingly uneventful life in the world." I started into the house, Terry following. "What are you here for then?"

"I need to talk to you."

"Can it wait? I've got to cancel all my credit cards and stuff." My little mugger was probably already having an early Christmas, charging up little suits at Barneys, chatting with pals in Riyadh, Adelaide, and Ho Chi Minh City. . . .

"It'll only take a second," Terry said.

We entered the kitchen. The sight of my novelty cookie jars made me realize I'd left my Howdy bank back at the Shamrock Tavern, and I muttered a low epithet. It also made me realize I'd had no lunch. I grabbed the stepstool, pulled it to the refrigerator, and climbed up to reach Chloe's Halloween bag.

"What're you doing?" Terry asked.

"Getting a candy bar. I'm starving. You want one?"

"Sure."

I rummaged for peanut candy, and came up with a Mr. Goodbar and a Cadbury Picnic. Snobbishly concluding that Terry would prefer the more plebeian of the two, I tossed her the Mr. Goodbar. Then I climbed down from the stepstool and settled at the table. "So what's so important," I said, ripping the Cadbury wrapper open with my teeth.

"Turns out you were right about that cigar," she said.

I froze, a strip of the wrapper still clenched in my teeth. I plucked it off and said, "It was poisoned?"

"Yep. Loaded with a substance called ricinase. It's a newly developed compound related to ricin."

"What's ricin?"

"A pretty nice little toxin," she said, with rather undue relish. "It's a white powder derived from castor beans. One of the deadliest and hardest of poisons to detect. About six times more poisonous than cyanide, just to give you an example. The KGB loved it."

"KGB?" My head was spinning. To hear the almost fanatically sensible Detective Shoe suddenly spouting off like James Bond just didn't compute.

She took an exuberant bite of her Mr. Goodbar. "Yeah. There was the famous case back in the seventies concerning a defector from Albania . . . or maybe it was Bulgaria. Anyway, one of those. This defector was waiting at a bus stop in London and suddenly felt a little sharp stab in the back of his leg. Turned and saw a guy with an umbrella who jumped into a taxi and drove away. Four days later, after suffering like a dog, the defector was dead. At first the pathologists were stumped, couldn't figure out what he died of. Then finally they discovered the minuscule pellet embedded in his leg. It had two hollow chambers, kind of like the ball point of a pen."

"Let me guess," I said. "The chambers were loaded with this ricin."

"Loaded meaning just a couple of hundred *millionths* of a gram. That's all it took to get the job done."

The old Brylcreem jingle stupidly popped into my mind: *A little dab'll do ya.* I let out a feeble laugh.

Terry narrowed her eyes at me. "You got a singular sense of humor."

"It's not funny," I said quickly, "it's just all so incredible. But didn't you say it wasn't ricin in the cigar?"

She nodded. "The drawback of ricin is that though it's always fatal, it generally takes several days to finally kill. The form of it that was used in the cigar, ricinase, has got the advantage of working faster and with subtler symptoms. On the other hand, it's not as deadly. It's got a toxicity rating of only four as compared to ricin's six."

"So that would explain why Jeremy, being in pretty lousy shape, dropped dead pretty quickly," I said. "But Cheryl, who was going through a health food and vitamin kick, was only put into a coma."

"It's a speculation," allowed Terry the Cautious. She wolfed the last of the Mr. Goodbar, balled up the wrapper, and set it on the table.

I took a more contemplative bite of the Cadbury bar. "You said it was made from castor beans. You mean like in castor oil?"

"Yeah, except that they're distilled by totally different processes. Castor oil does not possess the toxic properties of ricin or ricinase. Obviously," she added with a quick grin.

"The castor plant's pretty common, isn't it?"

"A weed. I pull it up in my backyard and another sprouts up overnight to take its place."

Poisonous plants are everywhere, they grow like weeds—precisely the words of that talented horticulturist Caitlin Jones.

"But you gotta keep in mind," Terry went on, "that getting ricin or one of its derivatives out of the castor bean is a pretty sophisticated process. You don't just bake it up like brownies on your kitchen stove."

"So where could you get it?" I asked.

She shrugged. "Ricin's used in cancer research, so maybe you get it stolen out of a research facility. Or smuggled out from Russia where they've still got stockpiles. If you've got the juice, if you're rich enough or got the right connections, you can get access to anything." She chuckled grimly. "Or even if you're just smart enough."

I licked some chocolate off my fingers. "What about the cigar itself? Were you able to trace it?"

"It was just as Downsey called it, a Partagas cigar that was made pre-Castro. We know a box was sold privately in Havana about three months ago. The buying party was from New York. The Feds think it was a member of one of the organized crime families." She pulled a sour face. "Beyond that, we've got nothing."

"You mean the Mafia?" I asked excitedly. "It all makes perfect sense then! It all points to Ralph and Caitlin Jones. I mean, Ralph practically wears T-shirts advertising his connections with the mob, plus he's the cofounder of a club that's dedicated to cigar smoking. And it's Caitlin's specialty to know how to derive substances from common plants. Both had extreme motivation to kill Jeremy, and both had contact with Cheryl Wade just before she went back to New Mexico."

"None of which is enough to convince a judge to even issue a search warrant," Terry said. "We're still entirely at sea here."

"So what does happen?"

"It's all going to be a phenomenal pain in the butt. We're gonna have to get hold of New Mexico, tell them we've got new evidence regarding Jeremy Lord that might interest them—meaning we're gonna have a bumpkin homicide team on our hands, getting in everybody's way." She gave a grimace, as if already experiencing the projected derrière discomfort.

I thought of my cutie-pie Young Sergeant Hallock of the San Miguel County homicide squad; I wondered with a brief tingle of interest if he'd be sent with the team.

"There'll be Feds barging in as well," Terry went on. "Guys from poison control, maybe even chemical warfare." She belched loudly. "Aah, shoot, I've got a real case of heartburn just thinking about it. Mind if I use the facilities?"

"Of course not." I noticed she was chalk pale. "Are you okay?"

"Oh, sure. Just a touch of indisposition. Goes with the job."

She headed toward the bathroom. There was suddenly a crash and the sound of shattering glass from outside, followed by a commotion of angry, yelling voices. I darted out to see what had happened.

A sea of jagged glass shards covered the patio, and a wooden double window frame lay splintered nearby. Harold Green came jogging up just as I reached the scene; for once he had lost his preternatural serenity. He shuffled his feet. He ran a hand through his hippie hair. He even blinked.

"Oh, man," he muttered, then followed it up with a relatively expansive "Oh, shit, man!"

"Is this bad?" I asked.

"You bet it's bad. This was the special order double-glazed for the bay. Even if we put a rush on the reorder, it's gonna set us back a good couple of weeks."

"What's it going to cost?"

"*Nada* to you, Lucy. It's out fault, my bond will cover it." He shook his head. "I just feel like ultra-bummed out about the setback." He fired off something in his rapid Spanish at the gathered crew; a quick, intense dialogue ensued. "The guys admit it was their fault, and they feel real bad."

"Accidents happen," I declared.

He nodded sagaciously. "That's the truth, Lucy. You just can't control everything in life."

I wondered how long we'd have to stand here swapping platitudes. Then Harold added, "Rigoberto wants you to know that though he apologizes for the window, he didn't like being treated rudely by your sister."

"My sister?" For a moment I wondered if one of my two stepsisters, Jilly or Kyra, had popped in unexpectedly from Minnesota; I looked around, half expecting to see a high-boned, wind-chafed face beaming at me. "What's he talking about?" I asked.

Harold posed the question to a barrel-chested young man in white overalls. "Rigo says he was carrying a board around to the front just as she was locking up the front door. He must have surprised her, but he doesn't think that was a good enough reason for her to call him a filthy name."

My blood ran cold. "When was this?"

"A couple of hours ago, he said."

Just about the time I was wrapping things up outside the old Shamrock Tavern. "What makes him think she was my sister?"

The man, Rigoberto, shrugged and gave one of those sweetly enigmatic Mexican smiles.

"She had the key to your house," Harold supplied.

I was starting to feel truly frightened. "What did she look like?"

Harold translated. "Rigo said she was wearing a hat. That's all he remembers."

Another of the men spoke up. A rather raucous burst of laughter followed his remarks.

"Victor says he was up on the roof and saw her leave," Harold translated. "He said she had a good ass." He grinned.

Victor added another rapid statement.

"He said the man who was driving had light hair and a barbita. A little bit of a beard."

"Oh, my God!" I gasped. Ralph and Caitlin! Who else could it be but Caitlin with her aerobically toned buns, Ralph with his goatee. I turned abruptly and raced to the driveway, glad to see Terry's car still parked at the curb. Terry was just emerging from the house.

"Terry, wait, listen!" I yelled. "I just found out that Ralph and Caitlin Jones were here, they've got access to my house, somehow they got a key! I've got witnesses that can identify them!"

Terry greeted this news in a startling manner. Her face contorted in an expression of utter horror, as if I'd just informed her it was Satan and a few of his select friends who had invaded the premises.

As I watched, her features continued to distort until they seemed as skewed as a Picasso. A harsh racking sound escaped from her throat. She opened her mouth and bloody vomit spewed out; then her entire body began to convulse and she dropped violently to the asphalt.

P a r t

4

TWENTY-ONE

The response to my 911 call was breathtaking once I got across the fact
that the victim was an LAPD cop on duty. An ambulance screeched up
so fast, it was as if it had been cruising the neighborhood in the likelihood of just such an exigency. In a twinkling there materialized a fleet
of black-and-whites and unmarked detective cars; almost simultaneously, a chopper began to circle overhead, blowing up dervishes of dust
and eucalyptus leaves. Cops of all sizes, shapes, and functions rapidly
swarmed over the house and yard.

Harold Green and his terrified crew were herded off to the station
for questioning. I refused to go, having had enough of precinct houses
lately. "If there's any questioning to be done, you can do it right here,"
I pronounced, amazing myself with such assertiveness.

Now I sat huddled on the sofa of my living room surrounded by a
cadre of L.A.'s finest, the tune "Seems Like Old Times" revolving in
my head. The ringleader was an egg-faced detective named Kretchmer
who indicated by his disgruntled manner that the absence of such standard interrogation paraphernalia as hot blinding lights, rubber hoses,
and wall-sized one-way mirrors was sincerely regrettable.

"You knew the candy was poisoned?" He posed it as a question,
but his tone was pure *"j'accuse!"*

I shook my head impatiently. "No, not until I saw Detective Shoe
go into convulsions. Then I immediately figured she'd eaten poison that
was meant for me."

"How do you know it was meant for you?"

I gave a long-suffering sigh. "I've already explained all this. Because I was sort of investigating the death of somebody who turned out

to have been poisoned. Jeremy Lord. That's why Detective Shoe was here, to tell me the cigar I'd found contained this toxic ricinase. Add to that the fact that I've been receiving threats lately, and it's more than obvious that it was meant for me."

"So how was it that you gave Detective Shoe the Mr. Goodbar instead of taking it yourself?"

I suddenly remembered exactly how it was. Due to my little flicker of elitism, Terry Shoe was now fighting for her life instead of me. "Just luck of the draw," I mumbled.

The egg face cracked with suspicion.

"I might have eaten the Mr. Goodbar," I burst out. "I was certainly willing and able to eat the Mr. Goodbar. But it just so happened that I took the Picnic bar instead."

This drew fishy stares all around from the assembled officers. I had the intense urge to stagger to the wet bar and pour myself a stiff finger or two of Cuervo. Then I remembered that ingesting anything in the house at the moment could be severely detrimental to my health. Besides, every scrap of foodstuff was in the process of being bagged, tagged, and taken away, including a dusty jaw-breaker found moldering under Chloe's bed and the packet of Ratty the vanished rat snake's frozen baby rats from the freezer. The young officer who had removed the rats had looked aghast. I wondered what he thought they actually were—some outré delicacy to tingle the jaded palates of us decadent movie folk?

A piteous mewling came from the front hall, where the two cats had been shut up in the coat closet so as "not to impede the investigation." I know what you're going through, guys, I telepathically assured them; I feel pretty damned hemmed in myself.

The thought of cats stirred something in my brain. Something to do with pets in general. . . . It was when I had gone to see Caitlin Jones, how she'd said she heard we were thinking of getting a puppy, and how I'd wondered how she could've known I'd just been talking to Chloe about it. . . .

I leaped up from the sofa. "This house is bugged!" I cried.

"Huh?" Kretchmer edged back from me, obviously not entirely convinced of my complete compos mentis.

"Somebody's been listening in to everything I've been saying, maybe for a long time."

"That's highly unlikely, Mrs. Freers," another officer said in a soothe-the-hysterical-woman tone. "It takes quite a bit of technical expertise to plant bugs."

"But listen. Somebody knew exactly where to put the poison so only I'd get it and not my daughter. You see, Chloe is highly allergic to peanuts and won't touch anything with them. On Halloween night, we were talking about the candy in her bag, and I promised I'd only take things that contained peanuts. That's how they knew."

"It's no secret, is it, that your daughter's allergic?" Kretchmer pointed out. "There's gotta be a lot of people who know it. Your husband, for starters. Her friends, teachers . . ."

"But none of them would have known where I'd stashed the Halloween bag unless they were also listening when I told Chloe where I was putting it."

"You wouldn't exactly need a treasure map to find it," said the soothing-toned cop. "All it probably took was a quick look through the kitchen. This ain't no Fort Knox." His comrades sniggered.

I shook my head impatiently. "It's not just the candy. It's other things. Lately it seems that people know things about me—private things I've done or said. It's like I've been on the world's longest *Candid Camera* episode."

"Your husband—" began Kretchmer.

"No," I snapped, "not even my husband could have known some of the things that have got back to me." I confronted a hard frieze of dubious faces. "Look, I can't quite explain it, but I know I'm right. Don't you have people who check this kind of stuff out?"

Kretchmer grudgingly turned to a confederate. "Call the lieutenant. See if he'll send a tech to do a sweep."

✳

The cops broke rank. Temporarily relieved from the hot seat, I hit the phone, putting in my third call to Kit and for the third time getting a prepubescent-sounding PA's voice on an answering machine. Then I busied myself with canceling my credit cards and license. The theft of my Jeep and pocketbook now seemed like pretty small potatoes compared to deadly toxins in a Mr. Goodbar.

Over the next hour, a steady parade of new recruits marched in. Guys with arcane technical equipment, no doubt for the detection of spying devices. Guys in suits from various federal agencies, their clenched jaws signaling their intent to boss everybody around—which caused the LAPD contingent to square their shoulders in manifest declaration that they weren't about to be bossed around. A dog from a K-9 unit bounded upstairs and yapped excitedly. His policewoman handler came hurrying into the living room. "There's some sort of animal under the bed upstairs," she reported.

"Snake or lizard?" I asked.

"It looks like some kind of lizard."

"Gordon the gecko. He belongs there. If you come across a spangled red snake, let me know."

The policewoman gazed at me long and intently, then withdrew.

✳

I heard Armand Downsey's voice in the next room. I leapt up, pushed past my interrogation squad, and bounded toward him. He was wearing green cotton scrub pants beneath his houndstooth jacket.

"Downsey!" I yelled. "How's Terry? Is there any news?"

"She's going to make it," he said softly. "They got her just in time."

"Thank God!" I said, nearly sobbing in relief. "When can I see her?"

"Not for a while. She's in pretty rough shape: she must have got a much stronger dose than Jeremy or Cheryl—only the timing factor saved her. But it's quite a mess. She expelled most of the lining of her esophagus. It's going to be a week before she gets much of her voice back." He grinned. "So maybe for once one of us'll be able to get in the last word."

I returned a weak smile.

"I've got some other news," he said. "Ralph and Caitlin Jones have gone on the lam. They've relocated to Argentina."

I caught a breath. "When?"

"Last night. We just found out now."

"Are you positive?"

"Pretty much."

It was as if he'd yelled out *alley alley oxen free:* I suddenly felt five hundred pounds lighter.

"A couple of detectives went to the VitalHerb offices to question Caitlin," he went on. "Her assistant said she left for Bangkok to attend some sort of homeopathic conference. There's no record of her on any flight to Thailand. What did check out was that a couple named Robert and Marylee Grimes caught a six-oh-five P.M. Aerolineas Argentinas flight to Buenos Aires. The ticket agent positively ID'd their photos." He cracked a grim smile. "I don't think they're on vacation."

"So they used aliases to skip the country?"

"Nope. They used their real names. Little Bobby and Marylee. They originally came from a hardscrabble town up in northeast Oregon. Dropped out of school together at sixteen. Ralph, or rather Robert, already had quite a little record of car theft, shoplifting, petty burglary. At seventeen he was shipped off to a juvenile facility for six months. His sister headed south and got hooked up with some New Age-y commune near Eureka. That's where she started picking up all her herbs and New Age healing goobledygook. Then after her brother was sprung, they hit L.A. With new names, of course, and a batch of well-forged references."

"And that's when Caitlin started her nanny career," I supplied. "With a nice little fencing operation on the side."

Downsey shook his head. "It flabbergasts me that wealthy people would take a total stranger into their homes without making the most exhaustive checks."

I gave a mirthless laugh. "You don't understand. A nanny like Caitlin Jones is a dream come true. An American citizen who speaks English and drives a car. She's got a dazzling line about organic nutrition, so you figure she's not going to stuff your kids with Fritos. Throw in a good rap about holistic healing and New Age values and she sounds like a regular Mother Teresa in training. If her references seemed even halfway on the level, there are zillions of women in this town who'd kill to hire her."

Downsey's dark eyes narrowed with disgust. We were interrupted by a guy bursting into the room. He looked like an eleventh grader, specifically the kind who's forever getting busted for hacking his way into General Electric or the U.S. Strategic Air Command—junk food–pumped complexion, wiry hair bunched in weird clumps like topiary gone bad.

"Whoo boy!" he cackled. "This place was wired for sound! It's got more bugs than an ant hill."

"I was right?" I gasped.

"Oh, yeah, you've been the star attraction of somebody's movie for however long these babies have been in place. You sneezed, they could've said *gesundheit*. You went to the john, they heard you tinkle."

"In the bedroom too?"

"You bet."

I flashed on Kit and me making extremely vocal love several nights before. The idea of Ralph Jones listening to our whoops and hollers and oh-god-yeses made me almost physically sick. This had to be what rape felt like, at once violated, dirtied, and scared out of your wits.

The hacker dangled a black metallic device no bigger than a Triscuit. "See this sucker?"

"Is that one of the bugs?"

"Yup. Works on remote control. You hide it in the wall plugs so it can draw juice from the line. When you want to listen in, you just activate it, jiggety-boo, with a simple little gadget, kind of like a garage-door opener. The beauty of it is in the simplicity."

"How far away can they be? To listen in, I mean."

"It's not a huge range, that's the downside. Maybe two hundred feet, two fifty max. Have you noticed any suspicious-looking vans parked on your road lately?"

I made an amused sound. "With all the construction we've had going on, the entire street's looked like a used van lot. I wouldn't have noticed one more or less."

"The perfect cover! They could park in plain sight, switch on the bugs and listen up." He gave an admiring chuckle. "Simplicity itself."

The phones had been jangling nonstop for the past hour, so reminiscent of when Kit worked at home that it was oddly comforting. An unidentified suit was on answer duty; from what I could hear, it appeared the media had gotten wind of the fact that a cop had been felled by, variously, terrorist activity, cult revenge, or—in the most overheated of reports—the Ebola virus, all of which the suit flat-voicedly denied. But now he was calling my name: "Mrs. Freers? Your husband's on the line."

Reluctantly, I picked up.

"Who was that?" Kit said.

"I'm not sure. I think he's got something to do with chemical warfare."

"I'm on the set. I don't have time to joke around." In the background, I could hear elfin voices singing, "Christmas comes but once a year, *now* it's here. . . ."

"I'm not actually joking," I said. As succinctly as possible, I summed up the day's interesting events. Kit listened, breathing laboriously, not saying a word.

"Jesus!" he finally breathed. "I can't believe it. I told you if you continued to stick your nose into this crap all hell would break loose. And now you've not only put yourself in danger but Chloe as well. And me too, for all I know. Christ, this is a disaster!"

"It's over," I said firmly. "The Joneses have fled the country and the cops have combed every inch of this house for any traces of poison left."

"How do we know for sure it's over?"

I hesitated. "Armand Downsey is pretty confident about it, and you know how supercautious he is. But I'm going to come up there with Chloe for a few days. The media's already heating up, it's going to be a zoo. I've got a seven o'clock flight. You don't have to send anybody, I've reserved a car."

He gave a resigned sigh. "Yeah, I guess you're right, it's the best thing to do. But Jesus H. Christ, this is not a good time. We've got night shoots coming up, I've got a shitload of things to deal with. You know what it's like here."

"Yeah, summer camp with sex," I said.

"What?"

"Nothing. I'll see you tonight."

TWENTY·TWO

It had been incredibly strange to be back in New Mexico, where it seemed almost a lifetime ago, rather than weeks, since I'd barged into Jeremy Lord slumped on the porcelain throne. Chloe had fallen instantly in love with the reindeer and spent most of her time happily pestering the wrangler. Kit, as he had warned, was constantly on the run; I'd be aware of him slipping into bed at 2:00 or 3:00 A.M and I'd watch him dash out the door five hours later. There was no mention this time around of trying for little Hepzibah or Thaddeus Thor; neither of us had the least inclination for sex.

And everywhere I went, I kept expecting Cheryl Wade to materialize beside me, arms and legs akimbo, tossing her furious cumulonimbus of hair and offering me free advice on how to spiff up my aura.

After five days it seemed safe to come back home. Home to what seemed like deafening quiet. All construction had stopped due to the crew's refusing to return to the scene of the crime. "I'm real sorry, Lucy," Harold told me via the telephone. "But the guys were considerably upset about being arrested."

"But they weren't arrested, they were only taken to the station for questioning," I protested.

"Don't matter, they get real uncomfortable around cops. Maybe you didn't know this, but most of them don't have their green cards." He promised that a buddy of his would take over the job as soon as he'd finished work on Tim Allen's pool house. "Shouldn't be more than another four or five weeks," he said and before I could get in any further complaints hung up.

The following morning, I paid a visit to Terry, lugging a guilt offering of a massive bouquet.

Her semiprivate hospital room was filled with so many balloons it looked like an election headquarters; they were mostly of that shiny silver substance that looks as if it had been originally developed for walking on the moons of Jupiter and sported copy on the lines of "We Miss Your Sunny Smile." It was so un-Terry Shoe–like that I'd have assumed they were meant for her roommate if it weren't for the fact that the second bed was unoccupied.

The last time I'd been in a hospital was when Chloe was born, and that peculiar hospital smell, a melange of antiseptics, latex, and Salisbury steak, sparked a kind of excitement in me, as if I'd be collecting another baby on my way out; as such, I was grinning somewhat inappropriately as I entered the room. But one look at Terry was enough to sober me up. She was skeletally thin, her complexion the shade of Cream of Wheat; her amber eyes now looked eerily large, like those of some nocturnal animal, a lemur or a potto, and her short mousy hair lay matted to her head like a skullcap.

I wasn't the only visitor. Two paunchy men in jazzy ties that marked them as fellow detectives roosted on the edge of the second bed. An elderly Korean couple whose neat clothes seemed to overwhelm their slight bodies sat almost motionless in chairs—these I presumed to be Terry's in-laws. And the rather good-looking man with Korean features hovering at her side had to be her husband, Frank. The clerical collar peeking through his open-necked flannel shirt confirmed the hypothesis.

Terry eyed my floral tribute. "What did you do, rob a mortuary?" she said. Her voice was little more than a hoarse croak.

"I thought some flowers might cheer up the room," I said brightly: Little Mary Sunshine Freers.

"All those lilies, makes me feel like I'm already six feet under."

I wondered what I should have brought—perhaps a balloon with the message "We Miss Your Acerbic Wisecracks." I set the bouquet on the spare bedside table and stood uncomfortably next to it.

The two detectives shuffled to their feet. "Guess we better get back to the grind," said one. There was some standard cop persiflage about laying down on the job and vacations courtesy of the taxpayer, then they nodded to the rest of the room and headed out.

Terry introduced me to the others. Her mother- and father-in-law bobbed in a sitting bow, which I awkwardly returned. Frank Shoe eyed me with the wary apprehension of, say, a medieval German burgher being introduced to Attila the Hun. "So you're Lucy," he grunted.

"Yeah," I admitted. "And I can't tell you how sorry I am about what happened. I feel like it should have been me."

He gave another grunt, as if in corroboration.

"Come on, Frank, Lucy didn't personally put the poison in the candy," Terry said. "It was a total accident I got it. So don't beat her up, okay?"

The black eyes softened. "Yeah, I'm sorry," he said to me. "It's just that this has scared us out of our wits. We couldn't even let the kids see her until yesterday. So you can imagine."

"I can definitely imagine," I said. "You certainly don't have to apologize."

Frank turned to his parents, spoke briefly in Korean. "I'm gonna take my folks down to the cafeteria for a bite to eat," he told Terry. "You can visit with Lucy." He stroked her matted hair. "I won't be long."

"Better not be," she whispered.

He fussed over her a few more moments, making sure she had everything she needed, exchanging more endearments. I wondered, if it had been me—if I were the one now attached to the IV looking like a rejected extra from a zombie flick—whether Kit would be fussing over me this way. Of course he would, I told myself—as long as he had no pending deal about to close or there was no immediate crisis on the set.

Frank led his parents out. I perched gingerly on one of the vacated chairs.

"How do you feel?" I asked.

"How do you think? Like a hydrogen bomb's gone off in my insides." She gave a disgusted shake of her head. "It's my own stupidity to blame. I come waltzing over to tell you a toxic substance is on the loose, and scarf down a candy bar from your house while I'm doing it. Dumb or what?"

"I was the one receiving threats. That didn't stop me from pigging out either."

Terry reached for a water glass and took a pull of the straw. "Shit, that hurts," she grimaced. "I've been wanting to drop a few pounds. But this is a hell of a crash diet."

I grinned sympathetically. "Speaking of crash diets," I added, "I guess you've heard the news about VitalHerb."

Terry nodded at the overhead TV. "Can't turn that thing on without hearing about it. Caitlin Jones was pushing speed."

"Apparently." Armand Downsey had filled me in that morning: In the course of investigating the source of the poison, ricinase, all the VitalHerb products had been extensively analyzed. It was discovered that certain of Caitlin's all-natural Chinese herbs duplicated rather efficiently the properties of methamphetamine. "No wonder all her clients lost weight like mad," I said, with a wry chuckle. "They must have been speeding so fast they were ricocheting off the walls."

"She knew it was just a matter of time before she was busted. She and Ralph had been skimming their companies dry. They'd scooped out the cash before their investors or the IRS got wind of it and stashed it in a Swiss bank account. They'd been planning to go on the lam for months." Terry took another pull of water and winced.

"They were?" An unnerving thought hit me. I shifted uneasily in my chair. "Doesn't that strike you as being peculiar? I mean, if Caitlin and Ralph had been planning a getaway for so long, why didn't they take off right after killing Jeremy? Why did they bother sticking around trying to kill Cheryl and then me?"

"Greed," Terry shrugged. "There was still more money to be made. I see it happen, guys can't stand to leave one last nickel on the table and end up sticking their heads in a noose."

"Maybe," I conceded. "And I suppose Argentina's got a hell of a cost of living."

Terry was silent a moment, giving her throat a rest. Then she said, "There's something that bothers me a lot more."

"Yeah, what?" I asked, tensing.

"There's no evidence. Not one shred to link either of them to the cigar or that kind of poison."

"You said the cigar was from a box bought by Mafia members. Can't they be traced to Ralph's mob partners?"

"Here's the kicker." Terry's voice was so weak I had to strain to hear her. "He had no mob partners. All his bragging about Mafia ties was just that—him trying to act like a big shot." She gave a puny snort. "I see that a lot—punks thinking it gives them status to let on they're in with the mob."

"So then who was financing his restaurants?"

"Oh, he was laundering money all right. It just wasn't from the Corleones. It came from run-of-the-mill marijuana growers up in northern California. It's a cash crop up there, you know."

I was silent a moment, uneasily digesting this information.

Terry went on, "I also don't like it that your workmen couldn't ID either of them—"

"What?" I cut in.

"They didn't tell you, huh?"

"You mean the construction guys from my house? The ones who saw Ralph and Caitlin there?"

"Yeah. But when they were shown photos, both guys claimed it wasn't them."

"So what are you saying? The Joneses might not be the murderers?" My voice rose an octave. "You mean there's some other homicidal maniac still running around out there?"

"I think we have to consider that potentiality," Terry whispered.

"Oh, my God!" I started to feel dizzy; I stared at a stuffed panda propped against the opposite wall and it blurred into a checkered blob. "I've brought Chloe back to our house! I've got to get her out!"

"Hold your horses." Terry paused, then croaked out, "As long as the media keeps sending the message that it was the Joneses, I don't think you'll be in danger. So long as you don't go shooting off that you think it isn't."

"I think you can trust me on that," I said haughtily. "I'll tell you one thing, though. I'll never be able to open a jar of Skippy's again without wondering if it's going to be my last meal until this case is definitely solved."

"With what we've got now," Terry said, "you gotta face the fact it might never be." On that encouraging note, her voice faded out.

✳

I rode the elevator down to the main floor. Passing the admitting desk, I suddenly stopped and asked what room Cheryl Wade was in. A husky woman in a peach-colored uniform clapped some computer keys, squinted and frowned. "There's no patient by that name."

"She was in a coma," I said. "Or actually what they called a persistent vegetative state. She was on a respirator."

"Then either she woke up, or life-support was discontinued." She tapped a few more keys, then made a box of her bronze-painted lips. "Yep, got it. Life support discontinued yesterday evening. Patient pronounced at eight-oh-six P.M."

A shock of pain walloped me; I realized that, in the back of my mind, I'd been harboring a belief in a miracle—that Cheryl would at some point in time sit up, call for a ratting comb and some glitter eye shadow, hoist up her mini, and sashay out.

But Alison had pulled the plug. To put it all behind her tidily in time for her wedding shower this coming Saturday.

"I'm terribly sorry," the admitting nurse was saying.

I wasn't listening. I was thinking about the shower invitation that had been waiting in my mail when I returned. A lavish satin-finished card featuring, no one would be shocked to hear, a gauzily romantic portrait of Alison. Nor would anyone gasp in surprise to receive the news that it was being held at the hot spot of the moment, the New Cubana Room. My first instinct now was to go home and rip it to shreds.

But then an idea came to me with a jolt. Suddenly I wanted very much to attend the shower. I had formulated a plan.

TWENTY THREE

The organizing principle behind the New Cubana Room was basically that of a speakeasy, which is to say that only the chosen few would know how to find it, and once having found it, be admitted to its smoky, star-strewn premises.

I was one of the chosen. On the Saturday following my visit to Terry, bearing a present wrapped in silver, I strode confidently into Rosellini's, an undistinguished Italian restaurant housed in the lobby of a Beverly Hills office tower. "New Cubana," I hissed to the hostess, rather in the way I imagined people used to hiss "Joe sent me" at a speakeasy door.

"Certainly," she murmured. "Come this way." I followed her past tables of diners, Japanese tourists unwinding after a hard morning's forage through Rodeo Drive, local matrons grabbing an early lunch of pasta puttanesca washed down with copious amounts of Pinot Grigio. At the back of the restaurant, tucked discreetly beside the kitchen, was a doll house–sized elevator. "Please . . ." The hostess gestured for me to enter. I squeezed into the small glass cage; she turned a key and I whooshed up four stories. The door opened onto the hallowed halls of the New Cubana Room.

I stepped out and gazed around. There was nothing particularly Cuban-looking about the place, unless you counted the bartender, who bore a vague resemblance to Ricky Ricardo. It looked more like the kind of mid-century Anglophile gentleman's club where, after major wars, the heads of the victorious countries would gather to figure out who would get the Punjab and who'd end up with Alsace-Lorraine. The furniture had clearly been designed for the alpha male: burgundy leather wing chairs that Wilt Chamberlain would have found a little roomy; moss-green velvet sofas of vast length and proportion; coffee tables that practically begged to have mud-caked riding boots propped up upon them. But this man's world was now incongruously frosted with bridal decorations, loops and garlands of pink satin bows, tumbles of sweetheart roses and bowers of orange blossoms, so that the final effect was that of the wedding of, say, the heavyweight champion of the world to Little Bo Peep.

I placed my present on a table already groaning under skyscrapers of shiny packages, then braved the crowd. About fifty women were mingling and nibbling hors d'ouevres, many of them famous, almost all of them with power credentials. I spotted Alison, stunning in an Evita-wannabe tango dress and dramatic picture hat, but she was too thickly surrounded by well-wishers for me to approach. I veered instead toward the event's designated hostess, Bobbie Lomato, who was doing meet-and-greet duty by the bar.

Bobbie Lomato's distinction was twofold: First was that she was one of the few women to have achieved superagent status; second, and possibly the more impressive, was that in this land of the buff and bulimic, she was fat. Unabashedly, obesely fat. She even accentuated her bulk by wearing bright horizontal stripes and loud patterns. The neopsychedelic muumuulike number she was currently modeling was not what you'd call slimming.

I went up to her, held out my hand. "Hi, I'm Lucy Freers," I said.

She took my hand rotely, her brow squinching in agitation. I could almost hear her thought processes: *If you've been invited, you must be Somebody, but if I've never heard of you, you've got to be Nobody.* It was exactly the kind of unsolvable conundrum Captain Kirk used to pose to evil alien computers to get them to self-destruct.

"I'm Kit Freers's wife," I added helpfully.

This was the charm: Her face wreathed in smiles. "Oh, yes, of course, darling Kit, *such* a major talent." She faltered suddenly, putting two and two together. "Oh, but . . . so you're the one . . . about Jeremy Lord and all that."

"I guess I am," I admitted.

Her eyes, like little dried currants in an unbaked loaf, peered at me through folds of fat. "You've made my life a perfect hell," she snapped.

I was getting extremely tired of being blamed for the demise of people I didn't happen to kill. "Look," I snapped back, "I'm sorry if Jeremy was your client—"

"Huh, that dirtbag was no client of mine," she cut in. "I couldn't care a rat's fart if he was dead or alive. But your meddling is what put VitalHerb out of operation, and that's a holy fuck of a problem for me."

This was a surprise. I'd have pegged Bobbie Lomato as a more likely fan of the duck à l'orange, the potato whipped with butter and cream, and the double hot fudge sundae than of Caitlin Jones's herbal regimens.

But Bobbie graciously elucidated. "Do you fucking realize how many of my clients depended on those products?"

"Didn't you hear?" I said. "They were loaded with what were basically amphetamines."

"Pah. Everything in those products was completely natural."

"So is deadly nightshade," I returned. "And botulism."

Bobby placed her hands on the jutting shelves of her hips. "What the crap does botulism have to do with it? You know, I'm surprised you even had the nerve to show up here. Alison was distraught about losing her VitalHerbs."

This was no surprise—I imagined she depended on all that speed to keep her from blowing back up into the Two-Ton Tessie of her youth.

"She needs to be in peak shape right now, and she has a particularly delicate metabolism," Bobbie went on. "Fortunately, I think I've tracked down another product that can regulate her again."

"So she's not distraught anymore?"

"No, she's not," Bobbie said coldly.

"Not even about her sister?"

The black currants glared at me malignly.

"I'd have thought she'd be pretty upset about having had to pull the plug on Cheryl," I persisted. "Especially since it's been less than a week."

"Acting on the advice of her physicians, Alison agreed to terminate life support," Bobbie proclaimed, as if issuing a statement to the press. "It was a wrenching and difficult decision, made after much long and painful soul-searching. You can't imagine how grief-stricken she is."

The grief-stricken Alison chose the unfortunate moment to let out a raucous peal of laughter.

"Naturally she's putting on a brave face for the sake of her guests," Bobbie said stiffly.

"Laughing on the outside, crying on the inside," I said.

Bobbie's eyes contracted to pinpricks, and her massive body did a sort of hula within its splashy tenting. I had the distinct feeling she was going to pick me up by my relatively scrawny shoulders and physically eject me from the proceedings.

Then the elevator opened and a fresh gust of guests blew in. Bobbie swung her bulk around and recharged her Gracious Hostess face. "Diane!" she cooed. "Susan! Winona!"

After this encounter, I needed a drink, and possibly two or three. As I hit the bar, Denise Schumer materialized beside me. "I recommend the champagne," she said, twirling a spritzing flute. "It's eighty-nine Taittinger."

"Excellent idea." I ordered a flute and took a sip of the heady beverage. "Fabulous."

"Bobbie was going to cheap out and go nonvintage, but I changed the order. Wait'll she sees the bill." Denise gave a snorting giggle. She looked different, I noticed. Pretty, even. Hair shiny clean and slightly pouffed, so that even the omnipresent hair band (this one blue velvet) was becoming. Her periwinkle A-line dress was well cut and actually flattered her pear-shaped figure. Even her earrings were tasteful, simple pearl studs.

"You look terrific," I told her.

"Yeah, right, Janie Junior League." Another snuffle-laugh. "Sometimes I like to revert just to keep everybody confused. Hey, what do you think about the decorations? They suck, don't they? It's all Alison, she wants all this traditional here-comes-the-bride shit. She's ordered this wedding dress you wouldn't believe, lace and trains and puffy sleeves and all in white." Snort, snigger. "Alison the virgin—doesn't it crack you up?"

I remembered Cheryl's point of view on the subject: *Alison would screw a doorknob if it would get her through another door.* I drained my champagne, ordered another. "It kind of gives me the creeps," I said. "Not that she's throwing herself a white wedding, but that it's so immediately after her sister died."

"Cheryl died?" Denise asked blandly.

"You didn't know? You were right, Alison went ahead and pulled the plug."

"Oh, Jeez, poor old Cheryl. Now I feel totally crummy." Denise gave herself a quick shake, as if to throw off the bad vibes. "We were sure barking up the wrong tree, weren't we? About Alison being the murderer, I mean. Except you suspected the Joneses all along, didn't you?"

"I thought they were possibilities," I said evasively.

"You're so observant, it's amazing. Hey, guess what we're doing after the cake?" she said abruptly. A scavenger hunt!"

"Like the Wild Bunch scavenger hunts?"

"Yeah, exactly, except we're turning the tables. The things on our lists are all gonna involve men, making them look like the assholes for a change. I made sure you're on my team—I hope you don't mind. A lot of these women are too snooty to talk to me."

The little jazz combo that had been riffing softly in a corner now struck up a more vigorous rendition of "Take the A Train," and the guests began to herd toward another door. "Looks like we're going in to lunch," Denise remarked. "I better see if Alison needs me."

She darted off. I finished off my second flute and, a bit floatily, followed the crowd into a smaller room with a domed ceiling and painted, paneled walls. Eight round tables were festively set with bisque-colored cloths and linen, Villeroy and Boch china, and polished Christofle plate.

I located my name at a table on the periphery and the other nine places quickly filled up. We were sufficiently high-powered, boasting one Grammy winner, one not quite A-list director, and Beryl Kushman, the only female head of a studio.

Suitably, our conversation focused entirely on the forthcoming marriage. During the first course of crusted monkfish in a blood-orange beurre blanc, the topic was How Long Would It Last? with the majority of the table pronouncing a split directly after the honeymoon, while the romantics among us gave them a run of three or four years—unless, as the husky-voiced set designer on my right pointed out, Alison should end up before that on location with some particularly sexy costar, the names Pitt, Cruise, and McConaughey submitted for our consideration.

With the serving of the main course (rosy slices of wild duck breast over rock salt and citron, with polenta dumplings), we switched to a dissection of the couple's prenup. The Grammy winner stated she knew for a fact that according to the contract, Alison would get possession of all her homes, while her fiancé got to keep the season tickets to the Bowl, the opera, and all sporting events. Also that Alison would get custody of any new dogs acquired during the marriage, but Jack would have visiting rights and the pick of any subsequent litters. The studio head put in that if they did get divorced, the good doctor was strictly forbidden to go blabbing about the marriage on Oprah or Geraldo or accept any contract for a kiss-and-tell book. "I heard," confided the B-list director, "that there's a clause stipulating that if either of them gains more than ten pounds, it's grounds for separation."

My ears pricked up at this. "Was that Alison's idea?" I asked.

"I heard it was his."

I grinned to myself. No wonder Alison was so distraught about losing her VitalHerb quick fix. It could have nipped marriage number two before it even had a chance to bud.

Further chit-chat was cut off by the arrival of the cake, four tiers that coruscated like metal in the filtered sunlight. This puzzled me until the set designer filled me in: "It's covered with lemon leaves dipped in real eighteen-carat gold leaf!" More champagne fizzed and flowed, and we drank toasts to the blushing bride, who in turn rose for a misty-eyed little speech, how very touched she was to have her "nearest and dearest friends" to share her happiness. We also drank to this.

A rumbling sound made us turn. Two waiters pushed in carts towering with presents. Alison let out a little cry of surprise, as if she had somehow failed to notice when they were stacked in the other room. Denise, who had trailed the carts, took up a position behind Alison's chair and began to hand the gifts to her one by one.

What do you give as a shower present to a woman who rakes in twelve million bucks a picture plus a percentage of the gross, who owns four fully stocked residences and more cars than Avis, receives designer duds gratis, and is marrying a dermatologist with a seven-figure-a-year practice doling out Retin A? You might reasonably suppose the answer to be some elegant token, such as one perfect red rose to symbolize their love. Or if a more expansive gesture were desired, perhaps a generous donation to the Fresh Air Fund in the name of the happy couple.

But on both counts, you'd be wrong: The correct response is that you cough up something lavish enough to present to the Queen of Babylon, a two-hundred-and-fifty-dollar piece of Lalique being about rock bottom, and the blue, blue sky being the limit.

Or at least so you would conclude watching Alison rip into her presents. A film of greed slicked her face as she tore through white wrapping paper and ivory tissue, squealing with almost sexual delight at each new acquisition. Denise read the name off each accompanying card, after which the rest of us applauded. It seemed a rule of thumb that the more costly the gift and the more famous the giver, the bigger the hand. My little antique Baccarat bud vase rated roughly a two on the Applause-O-Meter, while the Georgian silver tea service for twenty-four from Madonna (sent in absentia) brought down the house.

After twenty minutes, Alison had barely made a dent in the loot. And now was the time to put my plan into action. I got to my feet, cursing myself for guzzling all that Taittinger—everything had suddenly taken on a misty focus. "Ladies' room," I murmured to my tablemates and headed out to the main room, making a supreme effort not to weave.

I went to the bar and motioned to the Ricky Ricardo-ish bartender. "How do I get to the humidor room?" I asked.

He jerked a thumb toward a corridor on his left. "It's the glass door at the end. But you can't get in without a key." Despite his Cuban bandleader looks, his voice was pure San Fernando Valley.

"I've got one." I displayed the gleaming brass key in my hand. "My husband's a member here. I jus' wanna get some cigars." To my dismay, my voice sounded slurred.

The bartender was evidently accustomed to soused women in search of cigars. He nodded in a rather bored fashion and went back to taking inventory of his martini glasses.

I followed his directions down the corridor to a frosted glass door. The brass key fit smoothly into the lock; I entered a sweeping semicircular room, checkered floor to ceiling with blond-wood lockers, each about the size of a breadbox, with an engraved brass nameplate on the front. Library ladders ran on rollers to provide access to the upper tiers.

Though the room itself was locked, the lockers weren't. There were, I estimated roughly, about two hundred and fifty of them. The nameplates swam dizzyingly before my eyes. I leaned against the door for several moments, taking deep breaths, until my head cleared. Then I began my search.

It didn't take long to locate Ralph Jones's locker, smack at eye level, wedged between Hulk Hogan and Danny DeVito. I pulled it open and peered inside.

It was empty. As I'd expected—the cops would naturally have searched it under their warrant. And it wasn't really Ralph's locker I was interested in anyway.

I continued scanning the nameplates until I hit Lane Reisman, two tiers above the floor. With rather more expectation, I opened it. It was filled with bundles of stogies, all with the identifying bands removed. Very clever, Lane, I thought. Taking no chances on being caught red-handed with a stash of contraband Cubans. He was really a chicken at heart.

I quickly rummaged through the bundles. They all appeared to be of an identical make, thinner and paler than the one Skye Castaneda had discovered in my Cherokee.

"Close but no cigar," I giggled tipsily and reshut the door.

I quickly located the next name on my list, Morton Levritz, gazillionaire housing mogul. His locker was one tier from the top, prestigiously abutting Whoopi Goldberg's. I rolled one of the library ladders into place and unsteadily climbed it.

The Levritz locker contained several boxes, all still sealed. And all from the Dominican Republic. Old Morty was evidently a law-abiding citizen. Not knowing if I was relieved or disappointed, I snapped shut the door, then started to ease myself down the ladder.

Footsteps sounded, coming rapidly toward the humidor room. I had a vision of Ralph Jones, his choir boy–killer face twisted with glee, bursting into the room and yodeling, "Vengeance is mine!" At the thought, I slipped my footing, rocketed down the remaining rungs, and landed glamorously on my behind.

The footsteps turned into one of the rest rooms across the hall. Ralph Jones, I reminded myself, was sipping piña coladas on the beach at Buenos Aires.

Sheepishly, I picked myself up and searched for the last name on my list: Alison Wade. It seemed to take forever to go over the rest of the wall. When I finally got to the end, I had not found her name on any of the brass plaques.

But she had definitely been on the membership roster. Why hadn't she been awarded a locker? I woozily puzzled over this a few moments.

Then suddenly I smacked my head with the flat of my palm, à la Denise Schumer. "Dummy!" I exclaimed and scuttled back to the center of the room. There it was, one tier above eye level, the name that should have caught my immediate attention: John H. Jampol. A.k.a. Dr. Jack Jampol, Alison's fiancé. She had no doubt given him the prized locker as an engagement present.

I yanked it open. There was one large cigar box nestled inside— an old-looking box, the wood with a greenish patina. The seal was broken. With trembling fingers, I flipped open the lid.

It took me several seconds to register what I was seeing: long, slender cigars rolled in rich brown wrappers.

With slightly faded pre-Castro Partagas bands.

Gasping, I let the box lid drop.

"Of course!" I exhaled. Alison, the rich and powerful, had scored the rare cigars. Alison, the greedy and self-absorbed, had laced a couple with poison and bullied her sister into passing them along to Jeremy. It all made perfect sense!

I rapidly shut the locker and hurried out of the humidor room. The shock of my discovery seemed to have greatly sobered me up. Nevertheless, I swerved into the ladies' room and patted cold water on my face until I felt ready to rejoin the party. Which must have been longer than I realized; when I got back to the main room, the festivities seemed to be over. Most of the women were gone, the remaining few cramming into the little elevator.

"I've been looking for you!" Fingers clamped around my arm. I glanced up into the mean little eyes of Bobbie Lomato. "The scavenger hunt's started, and you're on my team." Her tone clearly implied she had drawn the booby prize. She began propelling me toward the elevator.

"I've got to use the phone," I said.

"You can use the one in the car. Come on!" She hustled me into the elevator car and squeezed in herself, mashing me with her bulk. Back down we whooshed. Then, clutching my arm again, she steered me through the restaurant and onto the street.

A fleet of limos crowded the curb; the drivers stood beside them holding cards with numbers. "We're in three," Bobbie grunted and charged up to it.

She shoved me in the back, then appropriated the front seat beside the driver's. Denise and three other women were already in place: I recognized the star of a long-running sitcom, a business affairs executive who'd once sacked Kit from a Chevy Chase movie, and the set designer with the Lauren Bacall voice from my table—all rollicking in drunken hilarity. A bottle of champagne passed from hand to hand, foamy rivulets running down chins and dripping into cleavage. "One for the road!" shrieked the sitcom actress, thrusting the bottle at me. I made a token pass at my lips and sent it along to Denise, who upended it, giggling hysterically.

The driver took his seat and Bobbie gave him a Benedict Canyon address. "And step on it," she ordered.

"So where're we going?" I asked.

"Lane Reisman's place. He's on upper Benedict."

The business affairs exec waggled a Polaroid camera. "Our task is to get him full frontal nude."

This set off another round of raucous, screaming laughter.

"What if he's not there?" I said.

"He's there, okay," Denise whooped. "We just called his house. There's a party going on."

"I hear he's hung like a horse," growled the set designer.

"Hung like a hamster, you mean," Bobbie sneered, swiveling with some difficulty to face us. "He's got tiny little feet—that means tiny dick. And I hear he's a thirty-second wonder."

"*She* can tell us," declared Ms. Business Affairs, rolling her eyes in my direction.

"Me?" I blinked. "What makes you think that?"

Significant looks Ping-Pong'd around the car. Even Denise had a knowing glint in her eye.

"For Chrissake, it's common knowledge," Bobbie declared, "so you don't have to act wide-eyed innocent."

Common knowledge? Had there been some item in a gossip column, Liz Smith or the *Hollywood Reporter,* that I'd somehow missed: "Lucy Freers and Lane Reisman, two under the sheets . . ."?

"I really don't have a clue what you're talking about," I said briskly. "I do not sleep around." This came out somewhat more prissily than I'd intended. I added, "At least not since I've been married. And if I did, it sure as hell wouldn't be with a self-satisfied asshole like Lane Reisman. I happen to think he's totally and utterly repulsive."

A general round of smirks greeted this outburst. I could tell that my ranting had only made them more sure than ever that I'd had an affair with Lane, and that he'd dumped me and I was now Woman Scorned. I withdrew into a petulant silence. For the rest of the drive, I tuned out the chatter to brood on my new reputation as a Lane Reisman seductee. What if the rumor should get around The School? I'd have to put up with Significant Looks at least till the end of the semester. Or worse, what if it should get back to Kit? Who would he believe, me or the grapevine?

My fretting fest was interrupted by our arrival chez Reisman—an unremarkable two-story contempo with woebegone landscaping and a pitted driveway. We stared a moment, all having expected the Young Mogul to live in a more sumptuous pad.

"Is this the right address?" the business affairs exec inquired, no doubt totting up a quick appraisal in her head.

"Yeah, it's right, I've been here before," said the sitcom star. "He's just renting it temporarily. He got cleaned out in the divorce. Angie got to keep the Santa Monica house."

We all nodded. This made sense: Jettisoning your wife and kids to become the Grand Suzerain of the Wild Bunch had to be a strain on the wallet. We tumbled out of the car and filed up to the front door. A hard-rock selection boomed at high decibel from inside the house.

"Christ, he's having an orgy!" Bobbie hollered. Ignoring the bell, she pounded on the door. When that got no response, she tried the doorknob, found it unlocked, and shoved open the door. We all trooped in.

The entrance gave directly onto a large, open-plan space, done in the kind of furnishings that were the last word in sophistication circa 1978: heavy on the chrome and glass, with generous helpings of leather in the shade known in decorator circles as Palomino, though it had now soiled to a color that might be better described as Dry Gulch Mud. Two stringy young men were sprawled on the Berber carpeting, staring at a TV tuned to a football game. A haze of cigarette smoke haloed above their heads.

As we shuffled in, they goggled with startled alarm, as if we were not merely six women in wedding shower attire, but a pod of invading aliens—an impression Bobbie reinforced by hollering a take-me-to-your-leaderish "Where's Lane?"

"He's not here," one of the boys ventured.

"Bullshit, he's got to be here. Turn that music down!"

The other boy obligingly pointed a remote and clicked it off.

"I'll bet he's up in the bedroom doing something unspeakable," Bobbie declared. She turned to her platoon. "Let's look through the house. The clock's running, so everybody spread out."

"Hey, I don't think you should do that," one of the boys protested, stumbling to his feet.

Bobbie stared at him; one hit of the laser pinpricks and he crumpled. "Check it out if you want," he mumbled.

Following orders, we all spread out. I had no great wish to find Lane; in fact, the prospect of bumping into him was downright unpleasant. But I was dying to find a phone. I walked tentatively into a smaller room that led off from the main one and was awarded the sight of a cordless sitting on a desk. I lunged for it, pulled out the grocery receipt on which I'd jotted Terry Shoe's hospital number, and punched it up.

The *brrp, brrp, brrp* of a busy signal met my ear. It sounded almost exotic. In Hollywood, where most people would rather miss dinner than a call, there was always a means to leave a message, be it voice mail, answering machine, or a personal assistant; even the nannies had their own lines with call waiting.

I hung up, drummed my fingers a few moments, then tried again. This time the busy signal seemed like a slap. I slammed the phone down in its cradle, sat back, and looked petulantly around the room. It was a sort of cross between a home office and a Toys "R" Us: There was the rosewood desk with laptop and phone, but there were also both slot and pinball machines, an old Wurlitzer jukebox stocked with forty-fives, and several arcade video games. A punching bag was suspended from the ceiling, Lionel trains encircled the floor, heaps of CDs and laser disks moldered everywhere. The only printed matter appeared to be a copy of *Hustler* flung on a half-inflated blowup doll. Every good adolescent boy who died, I thought testily, probably went to a heaven that looked pretty much like this.

A chrome yellow pegboard was mounted on the opposite wall, a collage of snapshots fastened to it with colored pushpins. That Lane would sentimentally post photos of friends, families, or pets seemed definitely out of character. I got up to examine it more closely.

The snapshots were Polaroids, and the subjects appeared to be almost entirely women. Some were naked or dressed in scant underwear. Most of them were staring at the camera with expressions of surprise or disgust.

With a shock, I realized what I was looking at: These were the trophies from the famous Wild Bunch scavenger hunts!

Several familiar faces leaped out at me. Here was Pamela Pemmel, crouching behind Lane, whose jeans were dropped to his knees; she was gleefully planting a smooch on his naked buttocks.

And here was Cheryl Wade. I felt a stab of remorse as I looked at her, all gawky limbs and frantic hair. She was standing on a café table performing what appeared to be a strip tease. Her blouse lay dropped on the dirty dishes at her feet, and she'd begun to peel off her bra, one A-cup breast already bobbling bare. Fixed in the camera's flash, she looked startled and miserable.

I gasped as I came across Judie Lord Levritz. It was unclear where she was or what exactly she was doing, nor did it matter. The salient point was that one of these ace photographers had caught her without her wig. Her skull was bald, a tender-to-the-touch–looking pink dome patched here and there with light brown fuzz. She was glaring straight into the camera with an expression of unadulterated hatred.

A bubble of nausea rose in my throat. However low my opinion of the Wild Bunch and their arrested-in-the-eighth-grade antics had been before, it had just plummeted to new and heretofore uncharted depths.

I was about to turn away when one particularly riveting photo caught my eye. It featured a woman on all fours, stark naked except for a dog collar with a leash around her neck. The pink valentine of her rather substantial backside loomed hugely in the foreground. The foreshortened face looking back over one shoulder was somewhat blurry, but it was still unmistakably recognizable as Denise Schumer.

And standing beside her, fully dressed in black and holding the leash as if he were walking an Irish setter, was that wild and fun-loving guy, Jeremy Lord.

TWENTY·FOUR

"Pretty cute, huh?"

Denise's flat voice sounded right behind me. With a start, I whirled to face her.

"I was kind of wondering where that thing had ended up." She reached forward and snatched the picture off the pegboard, then ripped it tidily, first in two, then quarters, then into a near confetti. It struck me that for someone who'd been rollicking drunk as a skunk scarcely fifteen minutes ago, she now had an exceptional command of her motor facilities.

"So you were a scavenger-hunt target," I said; I attempted a non-judgmental it-could-happen-to-any-of-us tone, but somehow it came out sounding like an indictment.

"Obviously." Her round pale eyes fixed on me, as empty of expression as her voice. "Their task was to get me acting submissive. This was Jeremy's interpretation. We all know what a supercreative guy he was." She opened her hand and the shredded photo fluttered in a parti-colored snow to the floor.

I had a sudden and certain flash of realization. "You were in love with him, weren't you?"

She gave a barely perceptible shrug.

"And he played on that to get you to . . ." I hesitated, searching for the tactful way to put it ". . . to pose for this picture."

"It was out at his beach house. He made it all seem like fun and games, you know, sex fantasy stuff? And then suddenly Lane came bursting in with a camera. And the two of them, Jeremy in particular, started laughing like hyenas." She looked down at her shoe, where a piece of the Polaroid confetti had landed on the toe; she shook it off with the sort of fastidious revulsion with which I imagined Judie Levritz had divested herself of Jeremy's ashes.

"You shouldn't feel too bad," I said. "Look how many other women got tricked as well."

"None of the others are wearing dog collars," she stated, still in that flat, affectless voice. "And none of them have their assholes sticking right in the camera."

She had a point: In terms of conferring sheer degradation on its subject, her Polaroid nabbed the Blue Ribbon. "Look, Jeremy got his kicks out of humiliating women," I pursued. "Just the way some people get them from roller coasters or sky diving. Just ask Alison."

"She was never in love with him the way I was," Denise said with sudden fervor. "And she—"

"And she what?"

"Nothing." Denise turned abruptly. "Come on, we're leaving. Lane's not here, he went out with some bimbo a while ago. There's just a bunch of freeloaders here."

I followed her retreating back, completing her unfinished sentence: *Alison never hated him as much as I did.*

It was a far glummer group reassembled at Lane's door, the champagne high deflated to a low-key crabbiness. When we had piled back into the car, Bobbie rang up the club, then announced grumpily to us that it was no use chasing down Lane. "Beryl Kushman's team has already won. They got Burt Reynolds without his toupee."

There were complaints of "too easy" and "no fair"; then we all lapsed into a grumpy silence. Denise was up front with the driver, so I had no further contact with her, which was just as well—I needed time to process the jumble of new thoughts crowding into my mind.

We pulled back up to the Italian restaurant and I retrieved my car from the valet—or rather Kit's Beemer, which I was using until I replaced my stolen Cherokee. Since Kit had taken his cell phone with him, I decided to wait to call Terry until I got home. But I was no longer certain about handing her Alison as the new number-one suspect; there was now the Denise factor to consider.

I headed into a pink and aquamarine sunset, mulling over the Schumer-Lord liaison. From all I knew about Jeremy, I could pretty much reconstruct the scenario. He undoubtedly noticed that Alison's step-and-schlep, Denise, was carrying a torch for him, which probably meant nothing more than providing a quick laugh to share with his pals. Until he draws her name as a scavenger hunt target. Then he calls her, probably dishes up some line about wanting to talk about Alison, how he was concerned she still had hard feelings for him and perhaps Denise could act as a go-between.

So Denise more than willingly trips out to the beach house. He's got a good wine open, a vintage claret or Montrachet, and while plying her with drink, he comes on like *Father Knows Best,* wheedling into her trust. Then he turns up the heat, laying on the flattery as thick and slippery as the La Brea tar pits. Tells her what a fine mind she has, what fascinating depths he has observed in her personality. He pronounces her worth ten, no, a hundred times a shallow, selfish peahen like Alison.

Then on with the seduction routine. Lingering kisses, expertly sensuous petting. Finally he murmurs that he's always had this fantasy . . . but that he'd only trust a *very* special person to act it out with. By now, if he'd asked Denise to dance naked at the Hollywood Bowl, she'd start stripping off her clothes and strapping on tap shoes. So out comes the dog collar and leash, and just when he's got her obediently playing Benji, in barges Lane with his trusty Polaroid.

And in an instant, Denise's all-consuming love turns to all-consuming hatred. All she wants from that moment on is to see Jeremy Lord dead.

So she steals a pre-Castro cigar from a box scored by Alison's fiancé and injects it with a lethal poison, then sends it on to the mocking director via Cheryl Wade.

Except that Cheryl had specifically said that the person who had used her was rich and powerful. Plus it would take a small fortune to procure a poison like ricinase—not to mention to have the wherewithal to plant bugs throughout my entire house.

Which seemed to point back to Alison.

I banged the steering wheel in frustration. Maybe I should just throw the whole thing into Terry Shoe's lap, let her sort it out. To take my mind off it, I switched on the radio, tuned to Public Broadcasting: a commentator with a mellow baritone was analyzing recent fluctuations in the price of beef, fascinating no doubt to commodities investors and barbecue chefs, but not particularly to me. I switched to the oldies station that was my favorite road music and that was just spinning out "Dedicated to the One I Love" by the Shirelles. I began to sing along, getting into stride on "dedica-ated. . . ."

Then suddenly almost choked on the words. The juxtaposition of the oldies girl group and the commentator on NPR had jolted my memory— the ad using the knock-off version of "Too Many Fish in the Sea" was followed by a mellow baritone, who took over as the pseudo-Marvelettes faded out with the following query: *With so many mutual funds to choose from these days, how can you know where to trust your money?*

And the capper: *With help from the experts at the Schumer Investment Group.*

In a daze, I turned off the radio. Was it possible that Denise Schumer, who seemed Born to Serve, who trembled like a Jell-O mold when Alison frowned and waggled an invisible tail whenever anyone smiled—who practically wore a KICK ME sign permanently pinned to her back—could actually be to the manner born?

And if so, would she qualify for Cheryl's description of someone with "tons and tons of money"? Someone who could get "anything done they wanted?"

I whipped off Sunset onto Amalfi and sped the remaining blocks home, screeched into the driveway, and threw myself out of the car. Since I'd just had all the locks changed, I fumbled for several frustrating moments with the unfamiliar keys; then I tossed the key chain on the kitchen counter and, recalling that the kitchen phone had been temporarily sacrificed to the new construction, raced for the one in the den.

But before trying Terry again, I hesitated. With Terry "That's-Nothing-But-Speculation" Shoe, it was advisable to provide as much in the way of actual fact as possible. I flipped through my address book and rang up another number.

"Pamela Pemmel's residence," warbled a voice several registers higher than Pamela's foghorn.

I asked to speak to her and received the less than startling news that she was on another line. "Tell her it's Lucy Freers," I said, "and that I've just come back from Alison Wade's shower."

Pamela snapped instantly at the bait. "Babycakes, I want every minutest detail! Start with everybody who was there. I should have been invited, I was *supposed* to be, but that bull dyke Lomato black-balled me—"

"Pam, listen," I cut in. "I swear I'll give you a complete blow-by-blow, but first I need to ask you something."

A wary split-second hesitation, then, "Well, natch, ask away."

"You know Alison's personal assistant, Denise Schumer? Does she have any connection to the Schumer Investment Group family?"

Pamela let out an amused burp. "Only if you call her grandpa being the founder a connection. What cave have you been living in, Lucy? Everybody knows that."

So my big revelation was actually a well-known fact. "How much is she worth?" I asked.

"God knows. There's a whole mess of cousins who all come in for a piece of the pie. But the pie is huge. Denise herself is probably in for twenty or thirty mil."

I took a strangled breath. "Twenty or thirty million? Then why is she running around buying Alison Wade's panties? With that kind of dough, she could set up her own production company and hire her own slaves."

"Oh, well, it's all tied up in trusts and what have you till she's thirty-nine or daddy drops dead, whichever comes first. It's not like she can just cut herself a check whenever she feels."

"But she must get a pretty hefty allowance."

"Beats me. All I know is—"

The line went dead.

"Pam?" I said. I hung up, clicked several times. No dial tone. I switched to the second line, but that was dead as well. Then I tried the fax phone; my skin prickled at the ominous sound of silence.

Get out of here fast! was my instant thought. Get to the car!

I bolted from the den and into the hall, running smack into Howard the seven-toed cat. For a moment my feet were tangled up in fur, the way Charlie Brown used to get stumbled up in Snoopy; then Howard disengaged himself and shot upstairs in a gray streak. I ran on to the kitchen, grabbed my keys from the counter, and would have raced out the garage door if it hadn't been blocked by the sturdy figure of Denise Schumer.

"Stay where you are, Lucy," she said. She was holding a gun, aimed roughly at my thorax. A gun I recognized, one that was pretty much the same shape, size, and color as a Swingline stapler.

Goddamn it! I thought. Over the course of the past few weeks I'd had guns pointed at me by butlers and cops, by height-challenged carjackers and now by an heiress-cum-personal-assistant to a movie star. *Twice* even with the same goddamned gun! It was starting to get on my nerves. "How did you get in?" I demanded sharply.

"The place in your new wing where some big window's supposed to go. It's only tacked up with tarp."

I cursed Harold Green and his butterfingers crew.

Denise tilted the pistol up to aim rather more classically right between my eyes. "Back up and stay away from the window," she ordered.

"No one can see in from the street through these windows," I said.

"I don't need any of your wisecracks! Move!"

I hadn't intended the remark to be witty, but it hardly seemed the optimum moment to point this out. I edged backward farther into the kitchen.

Denise advanced a few steps forward, keeping me covered. "I knew you'd figure it out," she said in a rather whiny voice. "I tried to stop you. I mean, for God's sake, what more could I do?"

"Absolutely nothing," I agreed. Humoring her seemed suddenly the only feasible option. Had she declared a wish to be recognized as Mary Queen of Scots, I was ready to address her as Your Majesty.

"I was going to get some guy to rough you up a little," she said. "I thought like maybe if you had a broken arm or ribs, you'd be scared enough to knock off. But then it got too late—you'd already gone too far." She gave a disgusted little shake of her head at the idea of Opportunity Lost.

"You've certainly scared me now," I said. "Believe me, now I'm really going to knock off."

"Like I said, now it's too late," she shouted. She waved the gun, motioning me farther back into the room. I complied until I was up against the shelves on which my novelty cookie-jar collection stood.

"You had Cheryl scared, too," I babbled. "Wild horses couldn't have made her tell on you. You didn't have to kill her."

"Tell on me?" Denise gave a contemptuous snort. "She didn't know it was me. She thought it was Alison. When I gave her the cigar, I told her Alison wanted me to send it to Jeremy, but she ought to give it to him instead. She thought it was a good idea."

"She probably thought it was a good career move. Buttering up the director."

"But I couldn't let her hang around and be questioned, could I?" Denise said plaintively. "I mean, even if she didn't know it was me, somebody else might've put two and two together."

"So poor Cheryl went to her death thinking her own sister was out to get her."

"Big lousy deal. Alison would've snuffed her in a second if she had any reason to. The night she pulled the plug on the respirator, she and that slimy doctor of hers went out to a party and whooped it up till two in the morning."

Dancing away her grief, no doubt.

The conversation was beginning to lag. I searched frantically for a way to revive it. "How did you poison Cheryl?" I asked. "With something chocolate?"

Denise shook her head. "Banana Yoplait. Practically two whole days went by before she even opened the goddamned refrigerator."

"Which you knew, I suppose, because you had her place bugged as well."

"Well, yeah, I had to keep tabs on what was going on," she said matter-of-factly.

"How did you do it? I mean, breaking into our houses and planting the bugs and all?"

"*I* didn't do it. I hired an ex narc. For eleven thousand bucks, he came with his own van full of the latest spy shit. He could crack any security system in about ten seconds flat."

I was uncomfortably reminded of Bender, Kit's ex-Navy SEAL, arriving in *his* own van with all the latest body-building shit. The city suddenly seemed to be lousy with vans motored by former government employees and crammed with state-of-the-art technology.

"I hope you had a good time listening to my private moments," I said coldly.

Her eyes widened with affront. "I didn't do that. I mean, if you started to have sex or something, I'd always turn off. What do you think I am, anyway?"

Cold-blooded killer, yes. Eavesdropper, no. I was thrilled to know she had standards.

My real concern, though, was to keep her talking. "The guy that carjacked me," I went on, "you hired him, too, didn't you? To give you time to get back to my house and doctor the candy?"

"Petey? Yeah, he came cheap. Five hundred bucks and a couple of grams of coke. That included him giving me the gun." She glanced down at the ugly gray weapon, a little too fondly for my comfort. "He ditched your car in the Beverly Center, so it's probably still in the parking structure."

Now I could see how it all came together. Little Petey ditched my Cherokee at the mall, where Denise was waiting, then chauffeured her to my house, waiting behind the wheel while she left me a deadly treat. The driver with the "little bit of beard" the construction workers had seen wasn't the goateed Ralph—it was Petey with his hipster's unshaven stubble.

And the woman with the "great ass"—it wasn't Caitlin's buns of steel the guys had admired, but Denise's rather more generous rump.

"Where did you get the poison?" I asked quickly. "The ricinase . . . you don't just pick up something like that from a street dealer."

"You kidding? It took me ages to make a connection. I finally got a guy who smuggled it down from some lab in Canada. I had to shell out a fortune."

"So you do have a fortune," I said.

"I don't have zilch," she snapped. "There's all this money that belongs to me, and I can't touch it till I'm practically senile." Then, evidently remembering I wasn't too many years away from the senile age of thirty-nine, she added, "no offense."

I shrugged a no-offense-taken. "So how *did* you get the money to hire ex-narcs and muggers and whatever?"

Her lips buckled in a self-congratulatory smirk. "I hocked some stuff of Alison's. Jewelry and some silver and stuff. She's got so much crap, it would take her a thousand years to figure out something was missing. And there are these swanky pawn shops in Beverly Hills that are totally discreet. With my name and all, they just assumed the stuff was my old family heirlooms and didn't even ask for receipts."

"So what are you going to do now?" I said wearily. "Shoot me dead in my own kitchen?"

She gave her lower lip a thoughtful chew, as if weighing the pros and cons of such a course of action. I was instantly sorry I had brought it up. "I never wanted to hurt you, Lucy," she said. "I mean, I really do like you. I think you're a great talent, I hold you in very high esteem."

"Then don't shoot me. Put down the gun, Denise." I tried for the sort of calm, commanding voice which, in a movie, would result in the desperate but conflicted perpetrator dropping the weapon and collapsing in the hero's arms.

Denise neither dropped the gun nor displayed any imminent sign of collapse; instead she exhaled audibly, in the manner of someone who had been exercising great, even superhuman, patience but was rapidly coming to the end of her rope. For the first time, I noticed she was clutching something in her non-gun-toting hand—something she now tossed on the kitchen table.

It was a Snickers bar.

"I'm afraid you're going to have to eat that," she said.

"You're joking," I blurted.

"No, I'm not." Her voice became whiny again. "I'm not joking one bit."

"I suppose it's loaded with ricinase. I'll take a couple of bites and go the way of Jeremy and Cheryl."

She gave a little shrug.

"For God's sake, Denise, they'll catch you."

"No they won't. They'll think it was part of what the Joneses had poisoned, and that you just found it now."

"They hell they will. In the first place, the cops stripped this house clean of anything even remotely edible. They even took away some ancient Raisinets they found buried in the couch in the den. And in the second place, I'd have to be mentally deficient or totally insane to eat any peanut candy I happened to find around here. And I don't think the cops consider me to be either."

Denise looked taken short by my logic. She made a motion as if to give her hair a reassuring rake with her headband, then, realizing her hands were full with guns and poisoned candy, settled for another lower-lip chew. "Well, okay," she said, "even if they suspect that's not what happened, they won't have anything else to go on. Maybe they'll think Ralph or Caitlin sneaked back into the country and made you do it. Whatever, they've still got nothing pointing to me."

"You don't know that for sure," I said.

"Shut up!" she barked. She suddenly pulled back a catch on the top of the gun; it made a kind of *shut-shut* noise that was anything but reassuring. "You better go ahead and take that Snickers, Lucy."

I let out a long, resigned sigh, then reached out as if to take the candy. But at the last moment, I snapped my arm back and grabbed one of the cookie jars; I briefly registered that it was one of my most prized, a rather cockeyed bust of George Washington wielding his cherry tree hatchet, as I hurled it at Denise.

And missed. The Father of Our Country splintered in ceramic shards on the wall behind her.

Denise gave an indignant squeal. She re-aimed the gun straight at me and pulled the trigger. There was an ear-splitting explosion, fol-lowed by the sound of more shattering crockery.

And time suddenly seemed to freeze. The next split second seemed to go on for minutes as my brain processed the following information: 1. Denise had actually fired at me, but, 2. I was alive and still standing, not splattered à la a Jeremy Lord character in a gory collage over the cookie jars, because, 3. the gun's recoil had caused Denise not only to miss, but to lose her balance and stumble back against my Irish pine breakfront and that, 4. while she was thus discombobulated, there was a window of opportunity opened for me to effect a getaway.

In the next split second, I seized the opportunity and bolted out of the kitchen. Time resumed its normal operating as I raced for the front door.

My plans altered as another report rang out behind me. A Hockney lithograph exploded inches in front of my nose. I did a running about-face and dodged into the den; then, without thinking, I ducked beneath the computer desk, shoving aside a Skydancer Barbie and a catnip mouse that were already *in situ*.

"Don't think you can get away, Lucy," Denise was hollering. "This is an automatic, and I've got two clips for it, so I've got lots and lots of bullets."

From her voice, it sounded like she was heading for the stairs. Yes, I mentally directed her, go on upstairs. I felt wild elation as I heard her footsteps light for the stairwell, wilder despair as they turned and made for the den. In desperation, I peered out from my grotto and spotted the TV remote on a chair seat. I darted out, grabbed it, then dove back underneath just as the Trigger-Happy Heiress appeared in the doorway. From my huddle, I could just glimpse her upper half. Apparently she had Learned by Doing, since she now clutched the gun in an impressively professional-looking two-handed grip.

"Okay, no more tricks," she muttered, though whether this was meant for me, herself, or whatever hyperactive demon was currently directing her private show was not entirely clear. She hovered for a moment on the threshold, as if waiting for a more personal invitation to enter, then puttered farther into the room. It would just be a matter of seconds before she spied me scrunched under the desk.

With my hand shaking so hard I could barely grasp it, I pointed the remote at the TV—Kit's brand new projection Magnavox; I pressed the power button and rapidly tapped up the volume. The TV blared on, featuring for our entertainment pleasure the video of old Betty Boops that I'd been watching the night before.

Startled by the volume, Denise whirled and fired three shots at the screen. Being a projection model, it didn't explode. The video kept cranking on: A trio of plump Max Fleischer ghosts strutted across the bullet holes singing, "Hi de hi de hi de ho . . ."

Strutting spooks seemed to rub Denise the wrong way: She let out an enraged *eep* and began blowing the room to bits. I squeezed myself into a ball, flinching with each new shot. *Bam!* a window blew out. *Bam, bam! Sayonara* old convertible couch. *Bam bam bam bam!* General destruction of B-movie posters, fax machine, standing cut-out of Rocky with Kit's head superimposed on it. Another barrage of *bams!* and as- sorted souvenirs and gadgets bit the dust.

Followed finally by a series of clicks and another *eep,* this one uttered out of sheer frustration, then a moment of silence. Scarcely breathing, I craned my neck to peep out. Denise, with her back partially turned to me, was digging into her shoulder bag for more ammo.

It's now or never, I ordered myself. Flexing all my muscles, I sprang out from under the desk, hurdled a shot-up cushion on the floor, and charged out the door.

"Hey!" yelped Denise.

Without looking back, I hit the stairs and galloped up them two at a time. There was a lag of some seconds as Denise reloaded, then I heard her start running in pursuit.

"Fucking shit bitch bugger bastard shit cunt!" she shrieked. An impressive display of copralalia that, had I not been so absorbed in scrambling for my life, I might actually have admired.

A bullet zinged past my head and ricocheted off the banister, giv- ing me an extra jolt of energy: I executed a Bolshoi Ballet–worthy grand jeté onto the upstairs landing. On an inspiration, I slammed the guest room door, then pattered on tiptoes down the carpeted hall to my own bedroom at the end of the hall. Denise had now begun mounting the stairs, her breathing raspy and labored: It was obvious that she rarely clocked overtime on a StairMaster.

I burst into my bedroom and took quick stock. Howard and Furball were crouched on the bed, eyeing me balefully; it was obvious they considered this annoying disruption of the peace all my fault. I had an instinct to shimmy under the bed, but checked myself: That would be among the first places Denise would look. Ditto for inside the painted Mexican wardrobe. For one wild moment, I considered making a leap out the window, taking my chances with a twenty-foot drop.

Several fresh gunshots reverberated from down the hall. Howard, Furball, and I all jumped, the cats selecting the under-the-bed option I had rejected, while I leaped into the nearest closet.

One of the things I loved most about our house was its fantastic closets. I had a sudden memory of the day we first looked at the house. The real estate agent, Marsha Moss-Golson, had flung open the closet doors with as much fanfare as if presenting the Hall of Mirrors to a palace-hunting Sun King. "Master bedroom's got oversized walk-ins, his and hers," she had announced. "Check out the space! Incredible, huh? You'll never lack for storage in *this* home."

I had ducked into "his"—and not even Marsha Moss-Golson could have predicted the closet needs of a man infected with the Hollywood Mogul Virus. In the course of a prolonged spending spree, Kit had packed it floor to ceiling with new acquisitions. It was almost pitch black—just a faint ray of light seeped from under the door—and I had to hack and stumble my way to the back of the closet like someone lost at night in a particularly luxuriant forest. I groped past racks crammed with jackets, suits, and pants, some with price tags still dangling, and waded through shoals of athletic shoes, Oxfords, cowboy boots, and Venetian suede loafers. I yelped as I stumbled into an upright object that revealed itself to be a golf bag and which in turn toppled a pair of skis. I froze in horror as it all crashed around me, certain it would bring Denise blazing upon me in full throttle.

With relief, I heard her still taking target practice in the hall. I continued scrounging my way through an underbrush of leather luggage, tennis rackets, and still boxed-up audio components till I reached the back of the closet, where I took refuge behind a thicket of long, hanging Burberrys.

I became aware that my elbow was stinging. I touched it gingerly and felt something wet. Oh my God, I've been hit! I thought frantically. I must have been grazed by one of the ricocheting bullets. I forced deep breaths to fight down my rising panic.

Eerily, from far below in the den, I could make out faint strains of the Betty Boop video still burbling away. I could even tell which cartoon was playing. It was "Cinderella," the one in which Rudy Vallee appeared as the prince. The animators, objecting to this casting choice, had drawn him wearing flesh-colored tights, making it appear that Prince Charming was wearing no pants. It was the bare-assed Rudy's megaphoned voice that was now crooning, "I'm like a Cin-derel-la. . . ."

Okay, think of Betty Boop, I told myself. She was forever being chased around by all manner of scary things, pitchforks with legs and pipe-organ dragons and scatter-boned skeletons who clattered when they ran, and she never ever lost her moxie.

Yeah, sure, was my next thought—but not even the skeletons, as far as I'd ever seen, had packed automatic pistols with two extra clips of ammunition.

"I'm gonna find you, bugger suck-face bitch!"

I gasped as if slugged in the stomach: Denise's voice sounded as if she was right next to me. Then I realized she *was* right next to me, on the other side of the wall, in Chloe's room. The chinchilla in its cage began to chatter and scold the intruder.

Please don't let her kill any of the animals, I prayed. If Chloe came home to find her menagerie slaughtered, she'd never forgive me.

How about coming home to find a slaughtered mom? It's a *potentiality that has to be considered,* I could hear Terry Shoe say. Particularly since Denise's footsteps were now heading out of Chloe's room and coming toward mine.

I listened with horror as they clomped methodically into the center of the room. There was a dreadful silence as, presumably, she took stock. It amazed me that she couldn't hear my heart, whose thumping, to my own ears, sounded like the bass of a boom box turned up to maximum.

"I know you're in here somewhere, Lucy!" she suddenly hollered, causing me to flinch. Chloe's pets seemed to have inspired her to fresh imagery, for she added, "You can't squirrel yourself away like a frigging little mole."

She fired another shot. Terror rose hot and sour in my mouth; I whimpered as I heard her fling open the Mexican armoire and fire twice more.

Chloe . . . a horrifying thought struck me. She had spent the day with Miri Pleischer; Miri's male nanny, Renny, was to take them to Universal City Walk, followed by an early burger and Coke at Johnny Rockets. I expected her back at around seven-thirty, which meant roughly in a half hour. What if she walked in while Denise was still on her rampage?

No matter what, I could not let that happen.

So what are ya gonna do, just stand there? Terry Shoe's voice taunted me. *Look for some kind of weapon. You can take her by surprise.*

Yeah, but what? My eyes had finally adjusted to the near-darkness sufficiently for me to be able to pick out shapes. I could make out a fly rod upright in the corner. Maybe I could hurl it like a javelin, catch her in the throat. Or bean her with one of the set of seven-pound chrome handweights beside my feet. . . .

Or use the shotgun propped in the opposite corner.

I caught my breath. It couldn't possibly be real. It had to be a hallucination, something I'd conjured up out of sheer desperation. I eased out from behind the coats and reached for it; at the touch of cold, solid metal, I nearly sobbed with joy. Kit must have bought it without telling me, either for security or out of some Great White Hunter fantasy. Whatever his motive, I didn't care; I was just passionately grateful to find it here.

I picked it up as noiselessly as possible. I had no idea if it was loaded; I'd have to stake everything on a bluff. Terror seemed to have melted the bones in my body. My fingers felt made of modeling clay—it was all I could do to mash the ones of my right hand over the trigger and fit the others around the barrel. My deboned legs wobbled as I turned toward the door. My wounded elbow felt on fire.

Then the butt of the gun knocked against something on a shelf, a small pail that tottered, then overturned. *Whop, whop, whop, whop,* the old tennis balls that had been in it ricocheted like popcorn around my feet. I let out an involuntary shriek.

And the closet door flew open.

I stared at Denise outlined in stark relief in the doorway. She fumbled for a light switch, found it, and flicked it on . . .

And gave a strangled cry at the sight of me and my shotgun.

I hoisted it to shoulder level: Annie Oakley Freers. For a moment, we just stood there pointing our respective weapons at each other, like the showdown in some Western—except that instead of tumbleweed, we were facing off over half the contents of the Sharper Image catalog.

"Stay right where you are, Denise," I finally quavered. "Don't even wiggle a little finger."

"Just what do you think you're doing?" she demanded.

The question disconcerted me: I had assumed it was pretty obvious. "This is a shotgun I've got," I said. "Which means I've got far greater range and accuracy than you do. So drop your gun, or I swear to God I'll blow your goddamned head off."

She giggled.

"I'm not joking!" I rasped.

"I happen to be very familiar with shotguns," she declared. "I've been shooting trap since I was like nine. My father held a world record in skeet, if you really want to know. And I hate to tell you this, Lucy, but your breech is open."

I had the weird idea she was telling me my fly was open, the kind of thing Chloe and her friends pulled on each other so they could taunt "Made you look, made you look!" My eyes actually flicked to the zipper fly of my trousers.

"On the gun," Denise said with exasperation.

My glance slid up to the side of the shotgun. To my horror, I saw a gaping metal chamber. I had no idea what it meant, only that it couldn't be good news.

"So how do you think you're going to shoot me with no bullets in the barrel?" she said, in a *nyah, nyah* tone of voice.

I lowered the shotgun desolately. Was this going to be my last sight on Earth—Denise Schumer, grinning like a goon, framed by racks of Kit's leather and snakeskin belts and Italian wide silk ties?

And then one of the belts started to move.

This time I was certain it was a hallucination. But no, it had definitely begun to undulate and slither. A goony grin of my own spread over my face.

"I hate to tell *you* this, Denise," I said, "but a deadly poisonous snake is about to wrap itself around your neck."

She produced a nasal snort. "That is so-o-o pathetic . . ." she began.

Then she twitched. Her eyes sidled to the right, then rocketed out of their sockets as she jerked her head sideways.

Ratty, the long-missing rat snake, was oozing rather lazily onto her shoulder.

She emitted a Tarzan-like yodel. Arms flailed, gun went flying from her hand, then she launched into a sort of combination Twist and Watusi, with Ratty still draped like a boa over her clavicle. "Get it off!" she whooped. "No, God, help, get it off, get it away!"

I grasped the barrel of the shotgun with both hands. Getting a firm grip, I swung out and whacked her with all my strength on the temple.

She crumpled in a dead weight onto rows of expensive footwear, and Ratty slithered off into some warm corner. I picked up the ugly little handgun, then stood looking down at her. It took all my restraint not to keep smashing her head till it split open like a rotten pumpkin.

While from the floor below, so faint I might have only imagined it, I could just make out a plucky "boop boop a doop . . . oop!"

TWENTY-FIVE

It had been three weeks since the shrieking EMS ambulance had whisked me, in tandem with the still-out-cold Denise, to the Santa Monica Medical Center, where a toothy ER radiologist cheerfully informed me that the bullet had chipped my funny bone, then shunted me off to a sleep-deprived resident who encased half my arm in a shiny white cast.

It had also been almost three weeks since I'd led the insurance adjuster on a tour of the devastation Pistol Packin' Denise had left behind, the adjuster biting the nub of his pen and puffing his cheeks like a deep-sea fish while repeating that he had no *precedent* for this kind of thing—as if nobody in the history of insurance had ever filed a claim after a homicidal maniac had shot up their house and home.

That same day, Kit had caught the Keystone Studios private Gulfstream jet at Aspen and arrived home for four days to "sort everything out." Four days in which tension crackled between us like a wet wire. We kept up a splendid face for Chloe; in public, we were so cozy, we would have made Ward and June Cleaver look like sparring partners. But what we didn't say to each other constantly hovered like comic-strip balloons over our heads. In Kit's, the message: "I told you something like this would happen, and I can only hope now it won't jeopardize my career," while in mine, writ large, was the statement: "How can you seem more upset that your Magnavox was shot than that I was?" When he finally went back to New Mexico, I was left feeling there were more things between us than ever that still needed to be Sorted Out.

It was scarcely three weeks since Alison Wade had become a fixture in the media, declaiming her shock and distress over the horrid revelations concerning her ex-husband, her baby sister, and her "obviously disturbed" personal assistant, always adding in the next choked-up breath that she—Alison the Pure—had never had the *slight*est inkling of any of this going on. "If only my poor baby sister had trusted me with her fears, I'm sure I could have protected her," she boo-hooed into every available mike. "She should have come to me."

Of course, I could have clued her in to the fact that, since her Poor Baby Sister had considered her to be a ruthless killer, the likelihood of such a scenario had been slim. But it was also nearly three weeks since I'd received a call from Richard Landrotti at Leading Lady, informing me that Alison was dumping the schizophrenia project—and needless to say, me with it—so the likelihood of my ever being able to share this info with Alison was equally slim.

A week ago, Denise Schumer's lawyers, the most hot-shot assemblage of legal eagles since the O.J. Dream Team, had entered an insanity plea on all fourteen counts of various degrees of murder and mayhem. The day after this news broke, I rendezvoused with Terry Shoe in an orange-and-green Mar Vista diner that seemed to be patronized exclusively by cops. She was still Vogue-ishly skinny, but the fact that she managed to nibble a high-calorie pastry suggested she was on the high road to recovery.

"How can they possibly prove insanity?" I asked, angrily stirring my cup of Morning Thunder. "Denise's motives were totally lucid. It was a classic crime of passion. Not only did Jeremy reject her in love, he turned her into the poster girl for the Wild Bunch humiliation show. That could drive anybody to murder. I mean, hell, after seeing those Polaroids, I'd have been tempted to slip him some strychnine myself."

"So maybe a jury would feel the same way and be moved to acquit," Terry said.

"Okay, maybe with Jeremy's murder. But with Cheryl and me, it was clear, calculated self-interest. She simply wanted to save her own ass. Nothing crazy about that."

Terry produced one of her eloquent faces, this one mingling disgust with a dollop of resignation. "Sure, not to you or me. But by the time this gang of lawyers is done, they'll have the whole world convinced she's cuckoo as a clambake. They'll claim that as a kid she was abused by everyone from her grandma's cousin to the upstairs maid. I hear they're already leaking a rumor that she heard voices. I think they're saying she thought they were emanating from the Supreme Court."

I sipped my tea, distracted by the notion of Ruth Bader Ginsberg and her cohorts telepathically slipping Denise orders to poison world-famous directors, as well as anyone else that happened to rub her the wrong way. "But even if she's found to be insane, she'll still go to prison, won't she?"

"Yeah, sure, right in there with Son of Sam." Terry broke off a minute piece of her bear claw and conveyed it to her mouth. "But with that family's influence," she went on, chewing gingerly, "in a year or two they'll get her quietly transferred to some posh mental home. She'll spend the next ten or fifteen years throwing pots and taking long, leisurely strolls over the lawns."

I gave a sudden laugh.

"Glad you see the humor in it."

"It's more like the irony. In a way, you could say that I created Denise."

"Yeah?" Terry licked sticky sugar from her fingers. "How do you figure that?"

"Well, you know how in my animations I often like to use inanimate objects as characters?"

"Sure, all those skyscrapers with faces. And that one where all the kitchen appliances start up a war."

"Okay, well, there was Denise, the ultimate doormat. Kind of an inanimate object, right? But when I kept refusing to get out of her way, the doormat suddenly popped up and transformed into this arm-waving, cursing, fire-spitting monster."

Terry focused amber eyes on me. "The monster came out the second she decided to off Jeremy. Or maybe the monster was there all the time, just lying there pretending to be a doormat."

But that would be crazy, I almost said.

Instead, I reached for a sesame bagel and smeared on an enormous slab of cream cheese, for which I seemed to have developed a remarkable craving. And with the glum intuition that, in the next few months, I'd become even more heartily fed up with the subject of Denise and her dirty deeds, I let the rest of our conversation drift to weightier topics: kids and schools and the relative nutritional content of muffins and bagels.

And it was just a little more than an hour ago that the leave-'em-laughing fertility expert, Dr. Kelshok, after getting off a good one about a rabbi sperm, a priest sperm, and a minister sperm swimming to the same egg, confirmed the fact that I was five and a half weeks pregnant. Kit's and my one Halloween night roll in the hay had struck paydirt—little Hepzibah or Thaddeus was actually on the way. Or possibly both of them: "With fertility procedures, we can never rule out the possibility of multiple births," Doc Kelshok chortled.

I'd left the clinic in a daze. And now I was finally back home, cradled in the familiar cacophony of hammering and drilling and sawing. Harold's contractor buddy had taken over the job, a colorless, monotone-voiced fellow with a begin-at-7:45-sharp work ethic; the work on the new wing was rapidly steaming to completion.

Despite the racket, I thought I might grab a nap before calling Kit and the rest of the family with the momentous news. I headed up to my bedroom, which had been pretty much restored to order, if you didn't count the odd bullet hole in wall or ceiling; I curled on the bed and closed my eyes. I remembered how I'd hoped that a new baby in the house—or possibly two or three—would yank Kit's attention back to the Things That Really Mattered. It seemed more likely, now that we were rich, that a bigger family would just propel him to pursue bigger and bigger houses filled with more and even shinier stuff.

There was an unpleasant oily sensation in my mouth, the first hint of morning sickness. It shot me back suddenly ten years to when I was pregnant with Chloe. In my third month, Kit had scored his first producing gig, on a no-budget horror flick. Everyone was working for free; even I was recruited to design props and improvise oozing sores and pustules on the actor-ghouls. The shooting schedule was a brisk eleven days and our begged and borrowed cameras rolled way into the night—after dark, we circled our cars like Conestoga wagons and used the headlights to light the sets. We were all positive we'd be famous some day. In the meantime there was all this fun.

And after the wrap, and the drunk-on-jug-wine wrap party, Kit and I had cuddled up in the back seat of our bumperless old Volvo and made love under the heaventree of desert stars.

So we've been rich before, I thought foggily, and drifted off to a deep sleep.